He's Found Me

ALSO BY ALESHA DYKEMA

If She's Found
Everything I Wanted
He's Found Me

HE'S FOUND ME

ALESHA DYKEMA

JOFFE BOOKS

Revised edition 2025
Joffe Books, London
www.joffebooks.com

First published as *Without You* by Brandywine House Publishing in USA in 2024

This paperback edition was first published in Great Britain in 2025

Cover art by Nick Castle

ISBN: 978-1-80573-059-0

For my friends and family in real life that will read this book to support me . . . please skip over the spicy scenes so we can continue to look each other in the eye. Thank you.

CHAPTER ONE

Scarlett — Now

Dan's breathing shifts beside me, changing from long, deep breaths to shorter ones. His alarm will go off in sixty seconds, give or take. He's always had a knack for waking up just before his alarm. The tune rings out, and I jump, even though I knew it was coming. I close my eyes, sighing. Being tense is exhausting.

The ascending chimes stop abruptly, and the bed groans as Dan rolls over to kiss my head before jumping out from beneath the warm blankets and disappearing into the attached bathroom. He always wakes up like he's already had two cups of coffee.

I don't like the way the bed feels when he's gone. The way the sheets cool without his body heat. The water turns on behind the bathroom door. It pelts against the ceramic tub. Dan hasn't stepped into the stream of water yet. I strain my ears and wait for the sound to change. A few seconds pass, and the noise goes dull, with his body now between the showerhead and the tub's surface.

The coffee maker gurgles to life downstairs. My cue to get up. I listen to the sounds of the morning, searching for one that is out of place. But there isn't one. There never is.

The floor is cold against my feet, and it sends chills across my skin. I grab my robe from the back of the door and go downstairs. I can hear the birds through the walls. They chirp loudly and consistently. I love summer mornings and especially the wildlife, but it reminds me how thin the walls are, and I wonder, not for the first time, if someone would be able to cut through them and get inside. Could I test it out without Dan noticing?

A small blue box on the kitchen counter distracts me from my thoughts of cutting through walls. Beside the box is a card with my name on it.

There was a time when I was a little girl that I actually enjoyed my birthday. My father made it a huge affair, no matter how broke we were. He'd wrap gifts in shiny red wrapping paper, make all of my favorite foods, and we'd sing the birthday song loudly all throughout the day.

But then, everything changed, and I learned to hate the day I was born and my very existence. And I'm not even being remotely dramatic.

I stare at the jewelry box. If it is a ring . . . *the* ring, surely, he wouldn't have left it down here for me to open it on my own. I glare at it as though, any second now, my X-ray vision will kick in, and I'll be able to see what's inside without touching it.

"Happy birthday, Scarlett." Dan wraps his arms around me and kisses my shoulder. I hadn't heard the water turn off or him coming down the stairs.

"Thank you. You didn't have to get me anything."

"Oh, hush. Open it."

He pours from the coffeepot as I wiggle the lid from the box, holding my breath and praying it's anything but a diamond ring. The lid comes off, and there sits a thin gold chain that holds a small round ruby at the center. It's delicate and simple, and I love it. "Thank you."

I wrap my arms around his neck, and he sets the coffee decanter down to squeeze me back. He smells like his musky bodywash, and I relax into the embrace, breathing him in and counting to ten before stepping away.

"What are your plans for the day?" he says.

"Brunch with Marin. I have a few errands in town to run either before or after. Then back home." I shrug because the day looks much like any other day.

"Are you all finished with client work?"

I nod. "Finished up with my last one yesterday. I officially have the week off."

He smiles and sips from his thermos. "Good. You deserve a break. I'm leaving work early today. I should be home around three, and our reservations are at six. Isaac and Crystal will meet us there. Don't forget to ask Marin if she's coming. Sound good?"

"Sounds perfect," I say. And it does. My muscles lose their tension with each new bit of information. There is nothing I hate more than surprises.

"Good. I'll see you later, babe." He kisses me on the lips, and then he's out the door, and I'm alone.

I take the cup of coffee Dan poured for me downstairs to my home gym in the basement. I have time for a quick workout, though every minute I'm alone makes me squirm. I turn on the stereo and crank the volume dial all the way to the right.

On the far wall, there is a line of screens. I can see myself in the dark reflection, and just like every time I'm down here, I feel the itch to turn them on. Pressing the power button would trigger the cameras inside and outside the house to turn on. I'd be able to see the perimeter of my house and every room inside it. But just like every time I get that itch, I ignore it. I made a decision a few years ago that the cameras were only feeding my paranoia. I stare at the black screens as I bring my heart rate up and begin a boxing workout.

When I'm exhausted and dripping with sweat, I head upstairs and begin getting ready for the day. A quick shower, and I'll be ready to go. The less time I have to spend alone, the better. It takes me fifteen minutes flat before I'm walking to my car.

The street is quiet. Most everyone has left for work, and those who remain home will start to filter out in a few hours. I reach for the car door handle but jump at the sound of hard footsteps behind me. I spin around and let out a breath when I see Tiff, my neighbor, jogging down the sidewalk. I smile and wave as she passes, then punch the side of my car with annoyance when she's further down the road.

Slamming the door behind me, I back out of the driveway and head into town. I love living in a small town. The way everyone knows everyone. I love the lack of anonymity. The way there is nowhere to hide. It's the perfect place to disappear.

And disappear, I have.

But for how long? The thought is always niggling in my mind.

I pull into the parking lot of the only grocery store for twenty miles. Rick, the cashier, waves to me as I make my way to the spices in aisle six. The melody of some eighties hair metal band blares through the speakers. I can hear him singing along as I drift further into the store.

Besides Rick and his metal music, my footsteps are the only sound I can make out. There were two other cars in the parking lot. Rick's red Taurus and a gray Ford Ranger. Terry, the bank manager, drives a Ranger, but he should be at work right now. My stomach churns, and I move to the next aisle as I rack my memory for another owner of the small pickup truck.

Tom has a Ranger, but it's blue. Is Billy's truck a Ranger? It's gray and small. But I think it's an S10.

I collide with a person, turning into the freezer section. My hand flies to the back of my waistband, and I take a quick step away.

"I am so sorry!" says the man. I don't recognize him, and I can't decide whether that's a relief or not. "I didn't see you." There is a twang to his words. Round vowels. Tennessee, if I had to guess.

"No worries," I say, my hand still on the steel hilt of my knife.

I take a step to the left, wanting to walk past him. He wears a blue plaid button-up tucked into khaki pants. His haircut is recent, and his face is clean-shaven. Hoover, Illinois, is on the nicer end of tiny towns no one has ever heard of, but he's too clean-cut to belong here.

"Can you tell me where to find the frozen vegetables?" he asks with a laugh.

"Next aisle over." I nod my head to the side. "Not from around here?" I add a Southern hospitality smile to the end of my question.

"No, ma'am. I'm on my way up from Clarksville. Headed to Chicago to visit some family."

"Tennessee?"

He nods, pride in his eyes like a typical Tennessean. "Yes, ma'am."

"Well, good luck in your travels." I take another step, but his voice stops me again.

"I don't mean to bother you. But does this town have a hotel or anything of the sort? The GPS on my phone has been acting all kinds of crazy today."

"Afraid not. Your best bet is to drive north for about another hour until you get to Hillside. They have a few there. But Chicago is only about an hour and a half away. You're nearly there."

He nods his head like he's tipping his hat. "I thought I could drive straight through, but I'm afraid if I drive much further, I'll fall asleep at the wheel. I appreciate your time."

There is one small bed-and-breakfast in town. One I stayed in when I first arrived here. But I don't like strangers hanging around, and I'd breathe much easier knowing this one was on his way out. The fact that he's looking for frozen vegetables while on the road is odd, and it means I need to keep an eye on him and make sure he continues his travels.

"Happy birthday, Miss Scarlett," Rick says. He slides the contents of my basket across the scanner as he proceeds to sing the birthday song.

I cover my face, heat spreading across my cheeks, but smile and laugh good-naturedly. "Thanks, Rick. Tell Tammy I said hello, will you?" I grab the plastic bag from his outstretched hand and hurry to my car.

I hope the Tennessee stranger trusts me and doesn't ask the friendly cashier about places to stay in town. I drive to the edge of the parking lot and tilt my rearview mirror at the doors of the grocery store. The man exits, and I watch him slide into his truck. He sits there a few more minutes. Is he using his phone to look up a place to stay?

Finally, the truck shifts into drive, and he's moving toward the main road. I follow him out and all the way to the highway. I release a breath and the tension in my shoulders when he takes the on-ramp and disappears, heading north. My phone vibrates, and I glance down at the screen to see a message from Marin.

Where are you??

Marin is waiting for me at a table in the back of the diner when I arrive. She's on her phone, a small smile on her lips as she taps on the screen. When I get closer, her head snaps up. She grins when she sees me, but she sets her phone on the table face down.

"Happy birthday, doll!"

"Thank you."

She slides one of two mimosas across the table.

"Are you coming to dinner tonight?" I ask before taking a sip of my drink.

Marin's eyes roll to the ceiling. "I guess so. You're lucky I love you because I loathe being the fifth wheel."

"That was a good one."

"Thanks. The negative words are my favorite."

Two months or so ago, Marin got into a little spat with Tina Davis at a town meeting. Afterward, Tina bad-mouthed Marin to anyone who would listen, calling Marin's vocabulary that of a second grader's. Since word got back to Marin, she's been learning new words and practicing using them. I told Marin she should just slash Tina's tires. Her response: "Oh, I did. But she had a point. Never let your pride make you blind to where you can improve."

Mae, the owner of the diner, comes and takes our food orders. Her eyes crinkle in the corners as she walks away. I know she will tell us that our meal is on the house for my birthday when she brings one of her desserts out like she has every year for the past six years. I hope it's her caramel fudge squares.

"Why don't you bring a date?" I say.

Marin shakes her head. "Nah. I'll be fine."

I narrow my eyes at her. She's not as worked up about being the only single friend at an event as she usually is. There's something she's not telling me.

"Who is he?" I ask.

Her eyes widen, and her mouth drops open like she doesn't have a clue what I'm talking about. But then, the corners of her mouth turn up before she breaks completely. "Shit. How do you always do that?"

I shrug. "You're easy to read. Spill."

"I met him online." She throws her hands up, two stop signs, as I glare at her. "I know! Don't lecture me! We've just been talking. Taking things very slow. I've done my research on him, and if we meet in person, it will be done in a public place. I promise."

I sigh loudly. "You stress me out."

"You're so risk-averse. Live a little."

"You take enough risks for the both of us," I say.

After our meal, Mae brings us strawberry shortcakes. They're divine, and I tell her I'll be back tomorrow (when she'll actually let me pay) to order a box of them.

"So do you think tonight is the night?" Marin asks, scraping her fork across her empty plate in search of crumbs.

"The night for what? I've already lost my virginity, Marin."

She rolls her eyes. "Dan proposing, moron."

"Let's hope not," I say.

She throws her crumpled napkin at me. "Why are you the way that you are?"

I shrug. "Ask my therapist."

"You don't have a therapist. Despite my best efforts."

I throw her napkin back at her. "I just don't want to get married. Dan knows that. He's not going to propose. We're happy with the way things are."

"You're annoying," she says, and I blow her a kiss.

"I'll see you tonight," Marin says, getting to her feet.

"Please don't be stupid with this new guy. The internet is dangerous. He could be anyone."

"Okay, mom. I promise to use internet safety. Stranger danger. Stop, drop, and roll."

I watch her walk to her car as I walk to mine. She is borderline reckless, and it makes me feel like I have to be extra cautious around her. Though, I'm self-aware enough to know that her recklessness is what draws me to her. I've always been drawn to chaos.

Something like dread niggles in my gut during my drive home. There was a time when I trusted my gut feelings. But I've learned they aren't always dependable. I've been looking over my shoulder for seven long years, and no fearful feeling has ever been substantiated. I push the paranoia down. I'm always more on edge today. That's all it is.

But then I see it. Panic strikes me like a bullet through my chest. I pull in a shaky breath and park my car in the driveway. My legs tremble as I climb out and walk to my front door. On the steps sits a red box wrapped with a red bow. I don't need to look inside to know who it's from.

He's found me.

CHAPTER TWO

Scarlett — Now

I swing my head around, scanning the street. Is he here? Is he watching me right now? Darlene is across the street, sitting in her yard with her kids. She waves when she sees me looking. "Happy birthday!" she shouts.

"Thank you," I say back, hoping it was loud enough for her to hear. Did she see him leave the box on my porch? Surely, a strange man leaving a box on my doorstep would raise someone's suspicions.

I'm doing what I always do. I'm being paranoid. It's my birthday. Someone has left me a gift on my doorstep. It's purely a coincidence that they chose a red box. Everyone knows it's my favorite color. That's all it is.

I pick up the box and carry it inside. All I have to do is open it and prove to myself it's a gift from a neighbor. It's the first time since I turned my cameras off that I truly regret it. I set the box on the kitchen counter gently, like it might explode. And what if it does? What if there's a bomb ticking down the last seconds of my life? What if it's a head?

No! Stop it!

I have to stop doing this to myself. I'll be the first one to admit that I'm always on the paranoid side. I have to be. But this day brings it out of me tenfold. I wonder if there will ever be a birthday where I'm not jumping at every sound and suspicious of every gift.

My phone vibrates, and I jump. "Ugh! Stop it, Scarlett!" I shout at myself and pull my phone from my back pocket. I half expect it to be him. But it isn't. It's Marin asking what I'm wearing tonight so we don't match. Then another text.

Never mind. You're wearing something red. Am I right?

My hands shake as I type, sending her a thumbs-up emoji. She knows me well. As well as I allow anyone to. I set my phone down and shake out my hands, forcing out a loud, calming breath. Every part of me wants to skip dinner tonight and shut myself inside with Dan for the entire week I have off work.

But Dan tries so hard to make my birthday special and enjoyable. And I love my birthday tradition of going to the Hoover Eatery with everyone I love. I can't let my paranoia ruin this for me or for Dan. He has not found me. If he had, I'd be dead already. But the red box is just so odd. Too similar to the ones in my past. To the ones that I hide.

I grab the box and shove it into my coat closet. I'm not doing this. Not right now. Out of sight, out of mind, right?

I grab my phone and turn on the alarm system. Just in case. A metallic click rings out as the house locks itself up tight. An alarm will blast loudly if a bird so much as gets too close to a window.

I need to shower, but I can't help thinking about every female in horror movies who dies in the shower. That is not the way I intend to go. I grab my 9 mm from my purse and slip my sandals from my feet. I'm just humoring myself. I know there isn't someone hiding in my house and waiting for me to be vulnerable. I'm being silly. But still, I move through the house, checking behind furniture, in closets, and under beds. When I'm absolutely sure I am the only one in the house, I grab the red box from the coat closet and go into the bathroom, locking the door behind me.

Above the toilet is a ceiling panel that lifts up when pushed. I built it when I bought the house. Inside, there is a line of similar red boxes. Three, to be exact. I slide the new box into the space and make it four. With that taken care of, I get into the shower.

I spend only a few minutes under the scalding hot water, never closing my eyes. When I'm clean, I turn the knob all the way to the right. I suck in harshly when the ice-cold water pelts my bare skin. Every one of my muscles seizes, and I have to force myself to relax and push air in and out of my lungs.

I count. 1 . . . 2 . . . 3 . . . all the way to 180.

When I step out of the shower, I feel better. More alert. Focused.

I've texted Dan twice. Any more than that and he'll suspect something is wrong, and I can't allow my anxiety to worry him. I peek through the curtain and search for faces hiding in bushes or peering around cars. There are other houses all around mine. There is nowhere good for him to hide. It's why I chose to stay here. Well, that and Dan.

My phone buzzes in my hand, and I sigh with relief when I see Dan's name on my screen.

"Hey, you. I'm on my way home now. Everything okay?"

"Yeah. Yes, of course. I just wanted to hear your voice." I laugh. I'm being strange. "Drive safe. I'll see you soon."

"I love you."

My heart constricts. "I love you too."

We hang up, and I force my feet to stay planted. I will not pace my house in a fit of anxiousness. The idea of fleeing enters my mind, and I push it away just as quickly as it appeared. I love my life here. I love Dan and my friends. I have everything I thought I never could. I deserve none of it. But it doesn't make me any more willing to let it all go. Especially over my own paranoia.

I hear a vehicle out front and snatch the curtain aside. Dan. Thank God. His presence will calm me down. Ground me. He climbs out of his truck but reaches back in, fiddling with something. He pulls out a large bouquet of red black-eyed Susans, my favorite flower, and I smile.

I jog to the front door and open it, ushering him inside. He smells like butter and smoke when he takes me into his arms. "How was work?" I ask into his shoulder as I push the door shut behind him.

"It was good. We had a nice lunch rush." He lets go of me and pulls the bouquet of flowers between us. "These are for you."

I take them with a wide grin on my face. "Thank you. I love them. And you." I lift onto my toes and kiss him. "Will you get me a vase from the cabinet and fill it with water?"

"Sure thing," he says, and I follow him into the kitchen to prepare the flowers. I grab the kitchen scissors and begin cutting the stems when another rogue thought finds its way into my mind: Would Dan get in the car and leave with me if I asked him to? No. I don't think he would. Not because he doesn't love me, but because he isn't the type to not ask any questions. He'd want to know why. And if he knew why, he wouldn't *understand*. His whole life is here. His family and friends. His lifelong dream of owning and running his own restaurant. He wouldn't love me if he knew everything I've been keeping from him. He would never forgive me.

"I'm going to run through the shower. We'll head to the restaurant in about an hour. Sound good?"

I nod with a tight smile, hoping he doesn't see the panic rising inside me once again. He hesitates, eyebrows pulling together. I try a more convincing smile and pucker my lips as a request for a kiss. He leans in and presses his lips to mine. "Hurry. I want to make sure we get my favorite table," I say, shooing him away.

I have never been a decisive person. I have always leaned on those around me. Seeking out strong personalities to hide behind so I never had to completely stand on my own. Running away to start a new life was the biggest and most independent decision I ever made. Those first months on my own were excruciating. I felt like a jellyfish washed ashore.

But I did what I had to do. And despite all odds, I survived. I survived my father before *him*, and now I finally have a life that doesn't hurt. A person who doesn't make me question my desire to be alive in the world they provide.

Footsteps overhead tell me Dan is out of the shower. The dresser drawer opens, then closes, and then he's on the stairs.

"The bathroom is all yours," he says. I watch him move through the kitchen, grabbing a glass and filling it with water from the tap. The day we met, I was so broken. He'd made me laugh two minutes into a conversation, and even though I was in no place to be in a relationship, I couldn't walk away. Always weak.

What would my life look like now if I'd just walked away six years ago? I don't even want to imagine. My chest is tight with the idea of never having met the people in my life today. Not having Dan or Marin, especially.

I go upstairs and begin getting ready for my birthday dinner, a day I hated for so long until Dan made it a celebration. There is nothing good about my coming into the world. Like I've said, I was born from evil. My existence is the consequence of the worst humanity has to offer, and that darkness embedded itself under my skin as it formed in my mother's womb.

So . . . I've never been much for birthdays.

And now that is only half of what makes the day a hard one.

I will spend the evening with the people I've come to love. I'll drink and eat and try to laugh with my friends. At the end of the night, I'll say goodbye. I'll hug them and tell them I love them. And in the morning, all this pent-up anxiety will ease up, and I will go back to my normal level of paranoia.

I link my fingers through Dan's on the drive to dinner, and he pulls my hand to his lips. I have to keep reminding myself to be present because every time I let my mind wander, it goes right back to the red box on my doorstep. The box now hidden inside my ceiling. I'll open it tonight, after dinner with my friends.

"You seem even sadder than you usually are today," Dan says. The sound of his voice breaks the silent atmosphere of the truck cab.

I squeeze his hand. "No. I'm not sad. You know I don't like my birthday."

He nods. "I know. But it feels like more than that."

"It's not. I'm okay. I promise." I can't swallow past the lie that sits like a rock in my chest. How many lies have I told him over the years? He doesn't deserve any of them, but it doesn't change the fact that I can never tell him the truth.

Dan helps me out of the truck. My long red dress scrapes the gravel as we walk, and I take comfort in the feel of steel against my leg. My gun sits comfortably in my thigh holster. I always carry a gun. Usually a knife as well. I like to know I can protect myself. We get the table in the back corner, a round one that I move around until I'm facing the door, another habit I've acquired in the last decade or so.

Marin is the first to arrive. She's wearing a navy-blue dress that dips low, exposing the flesh between her breasts. She has a runway model's figure and is able to pull it off without looking cheap. Marin isn't big on hugs, but I pull her into me and hold on, despite her initial stiffness. I'm feeling more sentimental than usual.

Isaac and Crystal show up ten minutes late. Crystal is frazzled, and Isaac breezes in, greeting everyone and taking a seat. He is notoriously late for everything, and Crystal is a stickler for time.

"Relax," I say into her hair when I hug her. "We all just sat down. You're fine."

She blows out a breath through bared teeth that is meant to be a smile. "I will figure out how to make him on time to things if it's the last thing I do."

I laugh and reach over to half hug Isaac. The stiff fabric of his button-up scrapes against my cheek, and I can feel his muscles tense and then release as he stretches to embrace me. "I'm going to start slipping Valium into her water," he jokes.

"Is your mom watching the girls?" I ask Crystal.

"Well, Isaac's mom sure isn't watching them," she says, which earns her a look from her husband.

"All right, assholes. Sit down and stop hugging. I'm hungry." Marin grabs her menu and flips it open.

I grab my own menu and peruse the options, though I already know what I'll get. We come here for my birthday every year, and each year, I make my way down the entrée options. This year will be shrimp and crab fettuccine. Skimming down the list, I read the descriptions of the meals I plan to have in the future. Fried shrimp. Lemon pepper chicken. Rosemary-and-Parmesan-crusted filet.

The hair on the back of my arms rises, and I look at the door. There is no one there, but I can't shake the feeling like ice on the back of my neck. Am I being watched? Or am I giving myself this feeling because I *think* I'm being watched?

I scan the restaurant, searching the other tables for a face that doesn't belong. I wouldn't be able to see anyone through the windows. It's too dark out. But they'd be able to see me.

"Hey, Earth to Scarlett. Did you hear me?" Marin snaps her fingers in the air, and I shake my thoughts away.

"Sorry, no. What did you say?"

"I said my date is going to join us after dinner if that's okay."

"What? Really? Is this the first time you're meeting him?"

She makes a face. Guilt. But not real guilt. The kind you pretend to feel when you're about to reveal something.

"I know I told you we hadn't met yet, but that's only because I wasn't sure if he was going to make it to town on time. We met in person a few months ago and have been seeing each other every few weeks. I want you guys to meet him. He wanted to let us have your birthday dinner with just friends but said he'd join us after we eat for drinks."

"I can't believe you lied to me." I swat her arm but smile because I'm genuinely happy for her. She deserves someone to love. And I'm happy I'm getting to meet him. I look forward to doing the best friend bit and being able to make sure he's a decent guy who will take care of her. Not that Marin ever needed much caring for.

The evening passes much too quickly. Marin gets up to have a cigarette, and I lean my head onto Dan's shoulder. Dinner has been perfect. Exactly what I needed on a day that has caused me so much unnecessary stress.

Katie, the waitress, clears the table of our dinner plates, and we all order a fresh round of drinks. I get Marin her usual martini. Katie starts back toward the bar when Marin reenters the room. "Oh, Katie! Add a Manhattan to that."

My nose crinkles automatically. I never cared for the drink. And now I only associate it with him.

And it's as if the thought itself summons him into existence. He stands in the doorway, right behind Marin. I blink, and my mouth drops open. I beg reality to come back into focus and for his figure to dissolve before my eyes.

"Everyone, I want you to meet my boyfriend, Evan. Evan, this is everyone."

CHAPTER THREE

Scarlett — Then

I throw up on the sidewalk leading up to the giant blue house. The woman . . . Susan? Sarah? . . . The social worker . . . pats my back and attempts to pull my mass of brown hair away from my face.

"It's going to be okay, Scarlett."

I stand and move away from her hand, glaring at my feet.

She sighs. Quietly, but I still hear it. "Miss Pamela is waiting for us inside. Come on."

I yank the handle of my backpack dramatically, flinging it onto my shoulder with such force that it knocks me off balance. I correct my step and follow her up the wide stairs to the blue house.

A large woman stands in the foyer. She's as wide as she is tall. Not fat. Just . . . large. Her face reminds me of my best friend's dog, Sammy. He's a Saint Bernard, and Miss Pamela's cheeks sag in the same way. She smiles, and her eyes light up. She looks kind, and it makes me feel bad for thinking she looks like a dog.

"You must be Scarlett. I'm Miss Pamela. Let me take this for you." She pulls the backpack from my shoulder, and I let her. "Come on through here, and we'll get you all squared away."

We follow her down a hallway and into a room. An office. Miss Pamela turns to the side and wiggles behind her desk. The social worker and I take the two chairs on the other side. The room is small. Too small for three people to be in here at once. Every wall except the one with the door on it is a bookshelf. I focus on the spines of the encyclopedias next to me.

Miss Pamela sits down with an exhausted sigh like it's tough carrying around her whole body. "I got your file here." I drag my eyes from the books and look at her. She points to a tan file folder on her desk. "What I don't know from those papers, I'll learn from you while you're here. We got a lot of rules here, and typically, the kind of kids that come here don't much like rules, but you'll follow them. Understand?" She drops her chin, staring into my eyes.

I stay quiet.

She nods. "Most of my kids have to learn their lessons the hard way. That's okay if you need to. Not my first rodeo. But it'll be easier on you if you just follow the rules."

"Which are what?" I ask. It's the first time I've spoken in days, and my voice sounds hoarse. I can feel the social worker looking at me. Miss Pamela grabs a hard candy from a bowl and pops it into her mouth. She offers the bowl to me, but I shake my head.

"No leaving the property without consent and supervision. In the house by seven and in your room by ten. Stay in your room until six the next morning unless you have to go to the bathroom. No fighting. That's physically or verbally. No weapons of any kind. Any reading, watching, or listening material must be approved. And any and all communication outside the house will be monitored. Treat me with respect and I will return it. Disrespect me and there will be consequences."

Tears build up in my eyes, but I don't say anything. They might as well have put me in jail. The foster home was bad, but this is a prison for kids.

"Cry if you need to, but this is no place for self-pity. You didn't wind up here by being a good kid. You'll learn to face the consequences of your actions here. You'll be okay," she says. "We'll take a little tour, and then I'll show you to your room. You're eleven, right? There are plenty of kids your age here. Try to make friends. This can be a really good experience if you let it be."

I don't roll my eyes, but I want to. No part of any of this is a good experience. I follow the giant woman throughout the house. Calling it a house isn't exactly right. It's a house, but it's massive. It feels more like a hotel or a school. And I guess it's both. A kind of boarding school for bad, broken, and unwanted children.

You can tell the place is old. The dark wood floors are scuffed up, and the staircase is big, the same wood color as the floor, and the railings are a cool design. The walls are painted a greenish blue. Those are kind of scuffed up too.

We go to the dining hall first. The biggest dining room I've ever seen. Six long tables fill the room. Two rows of three. Kids sit in different groups at a few of the tables. Most of them look my age. A few are older. They all look at me when we enter the room.

"This is where you'll eat. You can hang out here during the day too."

Miss Pamela doesn't introduce me, and I'm glad for that. She turns and walks further into the house. A kid sprints past us, and she snatches the back of his shirt. "What did I tell you about running in these hallways, Todd? This is a house, not a barn." She lets him go, and we keep walking like nothing happened.

The bathrooms are big shared spaces like in a school. Rows of stalls and sinks. "The showers are on the west end of the house. I'll show you them later, but they're private with doors that lock. I have keys to every room, so don't get any stupid ideas."

What kinds of stupid ideas is she talking about? What kind of trouble could I get up to in a locked shower?

"As you may have noticed, this is a co-ed home." She raises her eyebrows at me, and then I get the point she's making. My face burns, and I curl my lip. Gross.

Miss Pamela laughs. "Too early for boys, huh? That's good. The hormones start earlier and earlier these days."

I stare at the floor.

When the tour is over, she leads me to a long hallway of doors. It looks straight out of a scary movie, and I know I'll have nightmares. My room has the number four painted on the door. It's my favorite number. Inside, there are two beds. Neither of them has sheets or blankets on them. There are two desks and two dressers, but other than that, the room is empty.

"I try to let the newcomers have an empty room. Sometimes we get more kids and we have to double up, but right now, we have the space that only a few share rooms."

Another relief. I don't think I'd be able to sleep in a weird room with a stranger.

"Scarlett, why don't you start unpacking. Choose whichever side you like. I'm going to talk to Lauren just out in the hall."

Lauren. That's her name. I wasn't even close. I turn and unzip my backpack. All I have left is in this bag. It's all they let me bring from the house, and I was lucky to be able to grab it from the foster home after what I did.

I can hear the women whispering in the hall. They're louder than they think they are. And the old house lets sound carry easily. I stop pulling things from my bag when I hear my dad's name.

"Luther Wright . . . Chicago serial killer."

". . . in her file. She knew . . ."

"Violent tendencies? . . ."

My chest feels tight. I'm tired of people talking about me. I'm even more tired of people talking about my dad. I drop a book on the ground. The loud smack causes them to stop whispering, and Miss Pamela peeks through the door.

She spots the book on the floor. "I'll have to make sure that's approved reading material, Scarlett."

After I unpack, the social worker leaves, and Miss Pamela shows me where to get clean bedding each week. She tells me to head to the kitchen to grab dinner and meet some of the other kids in the dining hall.

I walk to the kitchen and tear at the skin next to my nails tucked into my hoodie pocket. I'm not hungry. My stomach rolls with each step that brings me closer to the loud voices down the hall. Against the far wall of the kitchen is a bunch of big silver upside-down bowls.

I look around, not sure what to do when a girl walks in behind me. She goes to the bowls and lifts one up. She grabs something and leaves the room. She looks at me as she passes but doesn't say anything. I copy her motions and grab the food beneath the bowl. A hamburger. At the end of the table is a stack of blue-and-white paper plates. I take one and go to the dining hall.

The girl I just saw sits at a table with two other girls. They stop talking when I walk past them. I think I might throw up again, but I take long breaths through my nose and sit at an empty table. There are two boys at the table next to mine, but they don't pay attention to me.

I'm not hungry, but I take a bite of my hamburger anyway because I don't know what else to do with my hands, and I don't want to look weird just sitting here. One of the girls whispers to the others, and they all look over at me, then break into a fit of laughter.

My stomach drops, and I really do think I'll be sick. Why did I have to be so stupid and get kicked out of the Millers' house? I don't want to be here. I don't want to live here. I'm so stupid. So dumb.

"What's your name?"

I jump and turn to see the two boys from the other table have moved to sit next to me. The one with light brown hair is looking at me. He must've been the one that asked the question.

"Scarlett." My heart is beating so hard that I can't hear my own voice over it pounding in my ears.

"I'm Evan," says the boy. "This is Darcel. Did you get here today?"

I nod. I'm happy to have a distraction from the girls at the other table, but I can't help feeling like maybe I'm still being laughed at. What if they're only pretending to be nice just to play a trick on me?

"Don't worry about them." Evan nods toward the girls who are watching and making ugly faces like they smell something gross. Evan stands up, and my body tenses. He's going to leave, and I'll be alone again. "Izzy peed the bed every day for two weeks when she first got here," he says loudly. My eyes go huge, and I stare up at him. "And Megan and Hattie can't even read, so they really shouldn't be laughing at anyone."

The three girls glare at Evan, and he stares back with a small smile like he's daring them to say something. The girl with curly blonde hair — Izzy, I think — looks like she might cry, and then she stomps out of the room.

Darcel laughs and fist-bumps Evan.

"We're going outside to play Frisbee. Do you want to come?"

I nod and stand up, following them out the front door.

* * *

Nights are the hardest. I've learned to cry quietly, and it helps not having to share a room. But it's when I miss my dad the most. I know he's a bad man. But he wasn't a bad dad, and people don't like to think about that. About a man like him raising a little girl.

He told me to be brave when they took him away. I'm trying my best, but I'm not a brave person. My alarm clock beeps, and I smack the top of it to shut it up. How many days in a row can you stay awake before you go crazy? Maybe that's what happened to Daddy. He was always up at night.

I shuffle to the bathrooms with my toothbrush in hand and have to squint in the bright lights. There are a few bottles of toothpaste on the sink, and I grab one, smearing a blob onto the pink bristles. My eyes look tired. Dark circles make them look sunken. I wish I could sleep.

Izzy comes up behind me, and before I can react, she grabs me by the hair, and I'm suddenly looking at the ceiling. Her face appears inches from mine. She hasn't brushed her teeth yet.

"If you tell Miss Pamela, I'll suffocate you in your sleep." She stands up and clears her throat. A thick wad of spit rockets from her mouth and lands on my cheek. My stomach instantly tugs, and I scramble onto my hands and knees, crawling for a toilet as my stomach explodes out of my mouth.

I grab for toilet paper to wipe it off, cringing and panicking. I need to wipe it off! More footsteps outside tell me more of the girls have come into the bathroom, and I'm thankful for all the practice of crying quietly.

When I'm out of tears, I wait another ten minutes so hopefully my eyes aren't red when I come out. Most of the girls have come and gone. A toilet flushes a few stalls down, and I wait until I hear the sound of paper towels being thrown into the trash can before I leave the stall. My toothbrush lies on the floor. I snatch it and run it under the water, turning it as hot as it will go.

Everyone is already eating by the time I make it to the dining hall. There is an empty seat next to Evan and Darcel, and I cross the room, keeping my head down as I make my way to them.

"What happened?" Evan says the second my butt hits the chair.

I avoid looking at him. "What are you talking about? Nothing happened." I poke at my French toast with my fork.

"You're not a good liar. I'll teach you how to if you want. But tell me what happened."

He doesn't react as I tell him the story of Izzy pulling my hair and spitting on my face. When my story is over, he simply says, "I'll take care of it." Then he takes a bite of his French toast. Evan looks about my age, but he seems older just now. Scarier.

After breakfast, Darcel has therapy, and Evan asks if I want to walk outside with him. I tell him I do, even though I don't really want to. I wish there was another girl I could talk to and hang out with, but all the girls are friends with Izzy, who hates me. And I don't want to be alone, so I walk with Evan.

"You haven't been sleeping," says Evan. He looks like he's studying my dark eye circles for a test.

"No," I admit.

"So how did you end up here?" he asks, shifting subjects without warning and leading me across the big yard.

"The police took my dad away." I don't want to tell him why they took him away. I don't want anyone else thinking badly of my dad. Or me.

"They don't put kids here when their parents are gone. That's foster care or something like that. Why did they put you *here*?"

I chew my lip. I don't want to tell him that either.

CHAPTER FOUR

Evan — Now

I anticipated feeling victorious in this moment. Smug. I wanted to see the fear and disbelief on her face, but now all I want to do is hold her. Kiss the lips she's painted red. This moment has been planned for months, and a lot of work went into it. I wonder if she even appreciates that.

Finding her was hard enough. Finding a way into her life, especially when she chose to integrate herself into such a small community . . . that was nearly impossible. But here I am. Having drinks with her and her new friends.

Marin loops her arm through mine, and I have the urge to chop it off. Instead, I put on my most charming smile and extend my hand to the first man.

"Nice to meet you."

"You too. I'm Isaac. This is my wife, Crystal."

I reach over and shake the woman's hand. I never used to shake women's hands until Scarlett pointed out that most men don't introduce themselves to the women in a group, only the men. It bothered her. So now I make sure to do it because I am many things but never a chauvinist.

I move to the man who has been sleeping with my wife. I show incredible restraint by not breaking his hand or jabbing my knife through his eye socket.

"Dan," he says. *Dan.* It's a dumb name.

I hold my breath, and for the first time in seven years, Scarlett and I meet eyes. I hold my hand out. Will she take it? Play along? What choice does she have?

She reaches out, and I want to weep when her hand touches mine. Seven years. It's a lifetime to be away from your soul mate. I want to scoop her into my arms, spin her around, and kiss her lips. I want to press my thumbs against her beautiful, slender neck until she tells me why she abandoned me.

I let go of her hand and notice a small tattoo on her wrist. I can't quite make out what it is, but instead of staring, I take my place next to Marin. Marin hasn't told her much about us. At least that's what she's told me, and I'm almost certain she isn't lying. She isn't a good liar. Most people aren't.

Scarlett will be putting together the information she had with what she knows now. She'll be trying to fill in the blanks. Her face fell when she first saw me, but she recovered quickly. Everyone's eyes were on me, so no one saw. Now she smiles, feigning excitement at meeting her best friend's new boyfriend.

Does she even appreciate what I've gone through to make this happen? How many painfully dull conversations I've had to have with this miserable woman? She's loud, obnoxious, and abrasive, and if I didn't need her, I would have carved out her heart ten minutes into that first date.

"Evan," Dan says. "Tell us about yourself. Marin's kept you under pretty tight wraps."

"I have been known to be very enigmatic," Marin says.

Scarlett laughs and rolls her eyes. "No. No, you have not been known for that. You're the most open-book person I know."

I give Marin an adoring smile for her attempt at "big words." Does it make Scarlett jealous? Does it elicit the kind of murderous rage that seeing her with *Dan* does in me?

"I'm in pharmaceuticals," I say. "Never in one place for very long, which always made it hard to date. Meeting Marin changed a lot for me."

I sneak a glance at Scarlett, still smiling politely. I put my arm around the back of Marin's chair and watch Scarlett's lips twitch, but she doesn't break. I finally get a better look at her tattoo and see that it is a small bird. A phoenix, I think. Is that how she sees herself? A bird risen from its own ashes?

"So you travel a lot? That must be fun. Exciting," Isaac says. His wife eyes him.

Oooh, fun.

I'm tempted to start an argument between the couple. It's obvious he feels chained down. Maybe he thinks he settled. Maybe his wife knows that he did.

"It's a lot of fun. New people and places. Lots of different experiences. It's a good time," Evan says and Isaac leans forward.

"But it's only fun for so long. I think eventually, it's in our nature to want to settle down." I'm not here to play games with boring small-town couples. I kiss Marin on the head, risking looking like a bitch to the men of the group but wanting to push Scarlett. I want to see proof that she still loves me.

Her eyes shine, going glassy. But is it jealousy? Anger? Fear? I can't be sure.

CHAPTER FIVE

Scarlett — Now

He's watching for my reaction. But I learned how to hide my hand from the best. His game has changed everything. Because he's involved himself with Marin. He has sat down with my friends and my boyfriend, introducing himself to everyone I love. I can't attempt to run again, knowing he has formed ties with my best friend, and he knows it.

My brain struggles to keep track of my varying thoughts. The gift on my porch that I tried so hard to convince myself wasn't from him. I hate myself for not opening it now. It had to have been from him. Just how long has he known where I am? What else does he know? Has he slept with Marin? Does that bother me? How did he get that new scar across the back of his hand? Does he think I look different?

I need to find a way to speak with him alone. But everyone here only knows him as Marin's boyfriend and a stranger to me, so that won't be easy. Is he staying at Marin's? How long is he "in town" for?

I put my glass to my lips and pretend to swallow. As badly as I want alcohol right now, I can't afford to dull my senses.

"Does your being in town mean my brunch with Marin is going to get canceled tomorrow?" I ask, winking at Marin.

Marin frowns dramatically. "No, I'll be there. Evan is only in town for the night. Back on the road after drinks."

"Might want to switch to water. Darryl parks at the grocery store at night looking for drinkers heading home at night," says Crystal.

Evan grins. "I won't be having more than this." He raises his glass and takes a drink. I catch his glance at me, and butterflies take flight in my stomach. I try not to overthink the underlying cause of them.

"Good thing you're heading out. Marin seems thrilled about our brunch tomorrow. It'd be a shame if you got in the way." I bump my shoulder into Marin's and laugh, hoping I sound genuine and relaxed.

"You're all Marin talks about. Don't let her facade fool you."

Code: Marin has told me all about you.

I don't like his other insinuations. Like he knows Marin better than I do. I know her facades and her complexities. Her insecurities and her goals. It takes effort not to sneer at him.

"Aw, well, I love her too." I smile over at her. "She's my best friend. And I'd be failing at best friend duties if I didn't give you the obligatory speech of how I'll kill you if you hurt her." I laugh but hope he sees the warning in my eyes.

"Okay, enough of the sappy shit. I love you to pieces, Scarlett. Now, let's talk about something else before I puke," Marin says.

I have to force myself to look elsewhere as the group chats. He is like a physical pull, and it takes all my concentration not to stare at him. It is so strange to see him after all this time. Every familiar curve of his face. I know exactly what his lips feel like pressed against every part of my body. They're slightly thinner than Dan's, but they fit his sculpted face well.

I watch him lean into Marin as she talks, making her feel like the only woman in the room. I can feel my face flush, and

I hope that he can't see it. Marin is basking in his attention. She is smitten with him, and it breaks my heart. She doesn't deserve to be used like this. But heartbreak is the least of the danger she is in, and she doesn't even know it. And she doesn't know it's all my fault.

The evening is winding down. Crystal moves her purse strap from the back of the chair to her shoulder, and I know everyone is about to leave. Evan and Marin came here separately, so they shouldn't leave together. But I have to make sure. I can't let her leave with him.

"It was great meeting you all. And again, happy birthday, Scarlett," Evan says as he gets to his feet.

"When will we see you around here again?" I ask.

Evan grins. "My next few months are a bit unpredictable. A lot hinges on this one client of mine, and until I know their plans, I can't really say. I'm slated for a pretty sleepless night preparing for that meeting."

"If you need a spot to sober up or just to sleep before hitting the road, there's an empty dead-end road off Cutler I've used a time or two," I say.

Marin gives me a look. "Yeah. Or I live five minutes away."

I laugh awkwardly and shake my head. "Yeah. Of course."

"Well, good luck. Nice meeting you." I turn to Marin. "You drove here, didn't you? I think I left my lipstick in your car last time I let you drive me home. I can't find it anywhere."

"If you weren't such a fucking lush, these things wouldn't happen." She bumps her hip into mine. "I'm just going to say bye to Evan, and I'll meet you at my car. I'll unlock it so you can start looking."

"I'll just wait for you," I say quickly.

She eyes me but walks out into the parking lot with Evan. I follow, pulling Dan along with me. I need to keep everyone in sight. Isaac and Crystal wave goodbye as they walk to their car. My eyes stay on Marin.

It has cooled off significantly. Goose bumps spread down my arms and legs, and it makes me shiver. The moon illuminates the paved lot, casting dark shadows beside cars. Too many places to hide. Marin and Evan stop a few feet away from a black Audi, and she wraps her arms around Evan's neck.

"Can you start the truck?" I ask Dan. "I'll just be a second."

"Yeah, sure." He leans in and kisses me. I barely return it, embarrassed to kiss someone else in front of Evan and afraid it will set him off.

Marin's back is to me, and when her head dips down, his eyes meet mine over the top of her blonde hair. I wish looks could kill because we'd both be dead, and these people I love would be safe.

Marin lifts onto her toes and kisses Evan on the lips. Red-hot fire burns in my chest, but I keep my face neutral. Bored. "Marin, hurry. I'm cold," I whine.

"Dude! You're being a cock block," she says over her shoulder.

"A parking lot full of people is not the place to receive cock, Marin."

"Speak for yourself. I'm coming."

She starts toward her car. I take a second longer to follow. To make sure Evan understood my message of where to meet. And my warning to leave my friends alone.

"See you soon, Scarlett," Evan says. I'm the only one close enough to hear it, and another shiver works its way through me.

CHAPTER SIX

Scarlett — Then

Just like every night since I left my house, it's only minutes after I lie down for the night that the first tears begin to tickle the bridge of my nose as they slide onto my pillow. I roll onto my other side but jump, swallowing my tears, when I hear the doorknob to my room wiggle. It has to be Izzy and her friends about to beat me up.

Evan sticking up for me on my first day only made things worse. They call me names, push me in the hallway, and Izzy even spit on my breakfast sandwich this morning.

The door opens, and I grip the blankets in my fist.

"It's me. Don't be afraid," Evan says from a crack in the door. "Can I come in?"

I nod, but I don't think he can see me because he doesn't come in. "Yeah," I whisper.

Evan slides into my room and quietly shuts the door.

"What are you doing here? Won't we get in trouble?" You're not supposed to leave your room except to go to the bathroom. And boys are not allowed in girls' rooms. And the same the other way around.

"Miss Pamela won't know. She likes to scare kids into thinking she can keep track of more than she can." He walks to my desk, looking over the few things I have. I watch him in the light of the moon shining through my window, which doesn't open and doesn't break. "I wanted to make sure you slept tonight."

"How are you gonna do that?" I ask, propped up on my elbows.

He jerks his head to the side. "Scoot over."

My face heats up, and he must notice the look on my face.

"It's okay. I'll keep you safe."

I scoot against the wall, and Evan climbs under the blankets next to me. His fingers touch the top of my hand, and my heart starts freaking out. Am I breathing loudly? He covers my hand with his, and I try to match my breath to his so I don't seem as nervous as I am.

There used to be nights I couldn't sleep at home. I'd tiptoe from my room to my dad's. Sometimes he was there. Sometimes he wasn't. Either way, I'd crawl into his bed and fall asleep on the right side because he always slept on the left. His sheets smelled like cigarette smoke and laundry detergent, and it always calmed me so I'd fall right to sleep. He wasn't always there when I fell asleep, but he was there every time I woke up, lying on his back with his mouth half-open and his hair wild and funny-looking.

I wake up to the sound of my alarm clock. It takes a few seconds to remember that Evan was in my room last night. He isn't here now. When did he leave? Then I realize I actually slept. I feel better than I have in weeks.

The hall is empty when I step out of my room. I forgot to put my socks on, and the wood floors are cold under my feet. I want to find Evan and thank him for staying with me until I fell asleep last night. I start down the hall but freeze when a horrible scream breaks the quietness of the house. Other doors in the hall open, and people step out, looking around for the noise. The screaming happens again. Down the hall.

Miss Pamela runs into the hall — well, as close to running as she can get. She opens the door where the screaming is coming from. Number twelve. I don't know anyone else's room numbers yet. Miss Pamela makes a noise, and it makes me want to go back into my room. It's like a cry mixed with a yell, and I know that whatever is in the room must be really bad.

CHAPTER SEVEN

Evan — Now

I drive to the abandoned road Scarlett mentioned. It wasn't exactly a smooth message delivery, but I suppose it did the job. The engine of my Audi purrs quietly in the dead of night. It's so silent here. The only sound is that of crickets and the occasional owl. I miss the noise of the city. It even smells different out here. It reminds me of the cabin. A place I always enjoyed myself, but I was always eager to get back home. I could never live here.

Scarlett appears in the glow of my headlights like an apparition. And she still feels like one. Seeing her after all these years has felt like some strange fever dream. If I'm being honest, the whole of the last seven years has felt like a nightmare.

Scarlett stands about fifty feet away on the side of the road. She crosses her arms, making it apparent she isn't coming any closer. She's making me get out and come to her. Smart girl. I get out of my car and walk toward my wife. I'm almost nervous to be alone with her after all this time.

She's so beautiful. Aging well, as I knew she would. My hand twitches, the desire to touch her face so strong it hurts to resist it. Her jaw is set, eyes narrowed. She's ready for a fight, but so am I.

"Hello, Scarlett. I've missed you."

CHAPTER EIGHT

Scarlett — Now

"How long have you known where I am?"

"A few months," he answers simply.

"How long have you been involved with Marin?"

He shrugs. "A few weeks shy of a few months." He grins mischievously. "Does that make you jealous, darling? It wouldn't exactly be fair for you to be angry with me. You've been quite the adulterer."

I hope the darkness covers my reddening cheeks. "I want you to leave. And to leave Marin alone." I choose to avoid his question and accusation.

He laughs, confidence shining in his eyes. "That isn't going to happen, love, and you know it."

I grit my teeth and open my mouth but shut it before I can make more trouble for myself. *Composure.* I can't let him see my fear or frustration. He obviously isn't going to leave after simply being told that I want him to. Not after looking for me all these years. "What do you want?" I ask.

"You know what I want."

"I don't," I assure him. Does he want me back? Or does he want me dead?

He looks off to the side. Chews his cheek. He looks uncomfortable. Unsure of himself. But I don't know if I can believe the emotions he's showing me. Finally, he says, "I want you to come home."

I shouldn't be surprised, but I am. Evan's attachment to me was just as strong as mine to him. Maybe I'm more surprised that he seems to be letting down his guard and setting aside his pride to tell me he still wants to be with me. Despite everything. "I don't want to come home with you. I *am* home."

He flinches. It hurts to say those words to someone I once loved more than anyone or anything. It hurts more to watch him being told them.

"I'm not leaving without you, Scarlett." It sounds less like a problem and more like a threat.

"You can't force me to be with you."

"I don't know if I believe that," he says. "But at the very least, you owe me an explanation."

I owe him nothing. Because he broke his promise to me first. Lied straight to my face, betrayed my trust, and left me no choice. I walked out on my marriage. I broke those vows, and I accept that. But so did he.

Despite all that, he's not going to accept me not answering, and I can't tell him the truth. Not the whole truth, anyway. So I tell him only a sliver of it. "I wanted a new life. I wanted to start over."

He shakes his head, bewilderment seeping through his facade. I stand up taller. *I am the one in control.*

"Without me?" The pain in his voice tears at my resolve.

"Yes. Without you," I say gently. As gently as words like that can be said. In a flash, I remember the day we got married. Spontaneously and full of joy with all the optimism for our future together. I never could have imagined this moment between us happening back then.

"Why?" His voice is a whisper, and I can feel myself softening to him. Wanting to comfort him because I cannot stand to hear him in pain.

But this is what he does, I remind myself. He's manipulating me. He knows that showing vulnerability and pain will hurt me. He knows me, and he's doing it on purpose. I can't let him take advantage of me. I am not the same girl he knew.

"You know why. Or maybe you don't. Maybe you're so cocky that getting caught in your lie never even occurred to you. But you are not as cunning as you think you are, Evan."

His expression shifts right before my eyes. His drawn eyebrows and downturned lips slide into a grin, and a shiver runs down my spine at the sudden and seamless shift.

"Clever girl. I wish you'd bothered to talk to me instead of running away. How many times have I told you that we can't deny who we are? What we are. And you can't just walk away and wash your hands of me and our life together. Not to mention, you shouldn't betray the person who knows all your dark and dirty secrets. Not smart for a girl so clever." He tsks at me.

Fire burns in my chest at the implied threat. At the way he keeps calling me "girl" like if he can just make me feel foolish and silly, I'll see things his way once again. "Are you threatening to turn me in? You'd only be giving yourself up."

He shakes his head. Still so confident he's in control. Sure he has the upper hand. "Think about it. *Really* think about it. It would be easy to have you take the fall for it all."

"You wouldn't do that to me," I say, though I'm not at all sure it's true.

"Oh, I would. What does it matter to me? If you don't want to come home, you can rot just like your dear old daddy."

I will never allow that to happen. I would sooner end my life than spend it in prison. And I don't doubt for a second that he has something on me. I once thought that Evan loved me unconditionally. We have seen the very depths of hell in each other, and still, he loved me. But it was always conditional, and I was naive to think otherwise. As much as I hate to admit it, it doesn't matter what Evan has done. It doesn't matter that I want a life without him and that I am scared to death of him. I love him. I always have, even as I ran as fast as I could in the opposite direction.

Hate and love are so thin a line.

"Is your love for me so selfish?" I ask because I have to know the truth. If when it really comes down to it, he would destroy me rather than let me go.

"Don't. Don't do that."

"Do what?"

"Don't try to appeal to my love for you or try to diminish it. I love you more than life itself, and living without you is not an option. So you see, *I* have no choice. But you do."

"It doesn't feel like I do."

"You do. And it's this: come home with me. Leave these people and come home and spend your life with me like you swore to do fourteen years ago. Or don't. And pay the consequences of that choice."

"And what exactly are the consequences? Let's stop being vague."

"I destroy your life here. Piece by piece until you have nothing left. And then I will turn you into the police and let you rot in prison, knowing you are responsible for all these people's deaths."

Bile rises in my throat, but I swallow it down.

He takes a step toward me and lowers his head. "So think it over carefully. You have three days to decide. When you get back home to our apartment in Chicago, your friends and this town will be safe. If you're still here in three days, I'll understand your answer. And then all bets are off."

"Does that mean you're leaving and going back to Chicago until I make my decision?"

His brows pull together. "What fun would that be?"

And with that, I know what I have to do. I can't take any chances with the lives of the people I care about. "I'll come home," I say just as he turns to go back to his car. He pauses. I hold my breath.

"I don't believe you."

He still isn't looking at me, and I don't respond until he does. When he finally faces me again, I can see the uncertainty on his face. He doesn't believe me. But he wants to. "I don't want anyone to get hurt because of me," I say. I could tell him I've missed him. That being away from him all this time has been so much harder than I ever thought it would be. It wouldn't necessarily be a lie. But that isn't what I say because I can't tell him exactly what I know he wants to hear. He'll know I'm lying.

"Is that the only reason?"

"Would you believe me if it wasn't? The reasons I left are complicated. But I didn't leave because I didn't love you anymore."

"So you still love me."

"Of course I do." My voice goes soft with the honesty of my words. Evan is a part of me. And like an infected limb, I had to cut him off to survive. But his absence has been felt in every moment of the past years. I felt it like the ache of a phantom limb. Missing him dearly but knowing he'd kill me if I kept him around.

And now, he is back.

I'd be lying if I said there wasn't part of me that felt like a mad scientist just told me he could return my arm to me. Evan takes a step closer to me, and I don't back up. I can smell his cologne. It's the same as the one he used when we were together, and I wonder if he really uses the same one or if wearing it was just one of the details in his plan of revealing himself to me tonight.

Our eyes lock, and I dare to close the remaining distance between us. His hand lifts, and I nearly flinch, but I don't. I let him cup my face, and I shiver when his thumb strokes my cheekbone. My chin tilts up. I almost forgot how tall he is. The cinnamon gum he loves brings back all sorts of memories I've done my best to keep locked away. He leans in, and his eyes flutter shut. Just before our lips touch, he goes stiff.

His eyes open. "What—"

I step backward, the needle still in my hand.

CHAPTER NINE

Scarlett — Then

Izzy is dead. The police carried her body out in a black bag while Miss Pamela stood outside the room, crying into her hands. There are red stains on the bottom of her yellow dress, and it smears onto the floor every time she paces, but she hasn't noticed it yet. I want to tell her to go get cleaned up. Wipe up the floor for her. Look inside the room and see how much of Izzy drained onto the floor before they took her away.

Evan leans against his doorframe. He looks concerned. Sad. Maybe even a little afraid. He looks over at me, and when our eyes meet, he smiles. There is something in his face. Something that says *you're welcome.* But then he looks back at Izzy's door, and all the sad emotions cover his face again. How does he do that? Switch back and forth so easily? My dad always said my face was louder than my voice. I could never hide what I was feeling.

And right now, I feel happy. Relieved that Izzy is gone, and I can brush my teeth without looking over my shoulder. To celebrate, I do just that. I take my toothbrush to the bathroom and scrub my teeth, a toothpaste grin reflecting back at me. No one else is in the bathroom. Probably still upset over Izzy, but I can't get myself to feel even a little bad for her. She was mean and a bully, and she got what she deserved.

When all the excitement of the morning has faded, all the kids slowly gather in the dining hall. No one has seen Miss Pamela since the police left. Luckily, she made breakfast before Izzy was found, so I follow Evan into the kitchen, and we fill our plates. Megan and Hattie stand near the door to the dining hall. Megan's eyes are red and swollen. She shared a room with Izzy and found her this morning. They spot me and Evan and hurry away.

"They won't bother you again," Evan says as we sit across from each other. He watches me for a second, looking almost nervous, but not quite. Curious.

"Thank you," I say and watch the corner of his lips pull up. I know I should be upset with Evan. He did a terrible thing. But is it so terrible when it happens to someone like Izzy?

"How did you do it?" I whisper, looking at my hands.

Evan is quiet, and for a second, I think he won't tell me. Then he whispers back. "A knife."

Miss Pamela enters the room as we finish our breakfast. Her face is splotchy. Black makeup runs beneath her eyes, and her few eyelashes clump together. "Isabella Yanez was killed in her room sometime last night," says Miss Pamela. Some of the kids gasp. Some start crying. Miss Pamela looks around the room like she's looking for the killer. "We will have stricter rules going forward until we figure out what happened. The police will be here to talk to you all, and you'll have to stay in here while they search your rooms. If you know something, you better tell the officers. Do you understand?"

My heart beats out of control. If they find out what Evan did, they'll take him away. And then I'll be alone again. Even with Izzy gone, I don't think her friends will suddenly start to like me. I can't let Evan get caught.

One by one, the police pull kids from the room. They're gone for a few minutes before they're brought back. Some kids act tough, like it doesn't bother them that a kid was killed down the hall. But everyone here is here because they're bad, so I guess that makes sense. A few cry, though. Hattie, the third girl in Izzy's trio, cries a lot. Megan still hasn't come back. I bet she went crazy.

A man with a mustache and a suit calls my name from the dining room door. I look at Evan. I can't breathe, and now I think I might cry too.

"Relax," Evan whispers.

But how am I supposed to relax when the police are about to ask me about Izzy and I have to lie? The man leads me to Miss Pamela's office, and I sit in the chair he points to.

He asks me questions about last night. About Izzy. If we were friends. I tell him the truth because there is no point in lying about that. Someone else will tell him Izzy hated me. And I have no reason to lie about what I did last night. I only have to lie about not knowing what *Evan* did last night.

And I do. I tell him I don't know who would hurt Izzy but that she was always hurting other kids. I tell him that she bullied me and that I was afraid of her, but I'd never hurt someone. Though Miss Pamela probably let him read all our files, so he must know I'm lying. I'm messing this whole thing up. They're going to know I'm lying and that I'm hiding something. What if they think that I did it?

To my surprise, he leads me back to the dining hall after a few more questions. I wonder if he'll come back with handcuffs. He tells me to go sit down and calls Darcel, Evan's friend, out. Evan isn't in the room. He must be with the other guy . . . the other detective. Will they find something that gives Evan away? What did Evan do with the knife? That's what they're searching our rooms for, right?

I let out a breath when Evan comes back into the dining room. He walks slowly toward me. I want him to hurry so he can tell me what happened. When he finally sits down, he doesn't say anything.

"Well?" I say.

"Well, what?"

I roll my eyes. "What happened?"

Before he can say anything, a shout from the hall gets everyone's attention. Someone is yelling. A boy. He's cursing and angry. Everyone inside the dining room is silent, listening to the commotion.

"Who is that?" I whisper.

"Darcel," Evan says. "I think they just found the bloody knife taped to the back of his dresser."

My mouth drops open. Darcel is his friend. His best friend. Why would he make it look like he did it? But there are too many people too close to us to ask any more questions.

When we're released from the dining room, Evan and I walk around to the back of the home. "I hope you'll feel safer now Izzy is gone."

I nod. "She was the worst of them. I think the others will leave me alone now."

"They will if they're smart," says Evan. He stops at the tree we sit under on nice days. "And I hope you can see that I'm your friend too."

"I know that." I sit in the grass and begin plucking blades of it and laying them across my leg. "Why did you make it look like Darcel did it? Isn't he your friend?"

"He is. But the police would keep looking into it if they didn't find anyone to blame it on. And I didn't want to risk going into anyone else's room. It was just easier to blame it on Darcel. His meds make him sleep hard, so I was able to wipe off my fingerprints and put the knife in his hand while he slept."

I don't know what to say. I never would have thought of all that, and it makes me want to know more about how he got here. I've never asked.

Evan sits down next to me. "If you want to talk about stuff. You can tell me," he says, changing the subject.

I shrug. "Like what?" I can feel him looking at me, but I stay focused on the blades of grass.

"I don't know. Whatever you want. You can talk about home. About why you were sent here."

"I don't want you to think I'm a bad person," I say.

He laughs, but not in a mean way. "I would never think you're a bad person. Remember where you are. Everyone here has done bad stuff."

My stomach growls. Despite having breakfast, I'm still hungry. Evan must hear the noise because he leans to the side and pulls out a rolled-up bag of sunflower seeds. I take them and pop a few into my mouth.

I know Evan is my friend. He's been the only person nice to me since I got here. Except for Miss Pamela. And Darcel. Though, I don't think I'll be seeing him again.

"You don't have to tell me why you were sent here if you don't want to. Just tell me about you. Your life."

I shrug. "I lived with my dad." Mentioning him makes my heart hurt. I miss him. And I'm still so mad at him. All he had to do was be good, and he couldn't do it. He couldn't stop hurting people, even if it meant he'd be taken away from me one day.

Evan reaches over and squeezes my hand. "What happened to him?"

"The police took him away." I rip out a handful of grass with my free hand.

"Why?"

Do I tell him the truth? He probably already knows. I hear the other kids whispering about me when they think I can't hear. Or maybe they know that I can. Evan has to have heard the rumors. He only wants me to say if they're true or not.

"He killed a lot of people. My dad is Luther Wright."

Evan looks up at me with big eyes. "The Chicago Harvester?"

I nod. I hate when people call him that.

CHAPTER TEN

Scarlett — Now

Evan collapses to the ground, and I move quickly to grab his head before it hits the cement. His eyes are still open. He can still blink. Breathe. But that's about it. He looks at me accusingly. "Don't look at me like that," I say. "You left me no choice."

I set his head down and stand up, looking around to make sure there is no one around. "Okay. Stay put. I'll be right back." I jog back to my car and pull up beside Evan. My heart is hammering and not at all from the physical exertion, though getting him into the trunk of my car is going to be no easy task.

I had always hoped Evan wouldn't find me. That he would give up eventually and go about his life without me. But I never counted on that happening. Nerve agents are not easy to come by. But in the world we live in today, nothing is impossible to get your hands on. And ever since I was able to acquire it, I've never left the house without it.

I grab Evan under his arms and drag him to the back of my car. He is tall and muscular and extremely heavy, especially as dead weight. But I manage. I struggle to get his top half onto the edge of the trunk. Sweat rolls down my back as I use all my strength to heave him upward. I just manage to get enough of his body in that he doesn't fall out when I let go. I have to use my shoulder to lift him from between his legs in order to get his bottom half in. "Sorry," I groan.

He finally rolls all the way into the trunk, and I lean against the car, trying to catch my breath. "We have to get going. I've been gone way too long." I shut the trunk and run to Evan's car. The keys are still in the ignition. I ease it into the woods, trying to be careful. There is a high-pitched screech, and I cringe, knowing the trees are scratching up the paint job. I'm not sure why I care, but I feel bad.

When I am far enough into the woods that I know the car won't be seen in the daylight, I get out and lock it. I'm careful not to fall or twist an ankle on my way back to my car. This moment feels so surreal. It has played out in my head a million times. Always slightly different scenarios and sometimes with different outcomes. Outcomes where it all works out in my favor and some when it doesn't. I tried to prepare for both. But so far, everything is going right. Injecting him was the scariest part. The part with the biggest chance for something to go wrong. And now, it is done.

I almost forget to stop at the store to grab the medicine I said I was going out to get. Last second, I remember and yank the wheel to the left, nearly missing the turn. I hear a dull movement in the back. "Sorry!" I shout.

I move quickly, parking the car and running inside the twenty-four-hour convenience store. The cashier is a woman I know in passing but have only spoken to a few times. She has worked the overnight shift here for as long as I have been here, so our paths don't cross often. With my decoy medicine procured, I hop back into my car and pull onto the road.

My fingers strum on the steering wheel the whole drive home. Dan will be awake and waiting for me, so Evan will have to stay in the trunk for a while. The nerve agent will last about eight hours, so I have some time.

Getting the dosage right was no easy task. I couldn't trust the estimations that were given to me by the seller. This was always going to be a life-or-death matter and no place for a guess. Educated or not. And it's not like I could test it on anyone. Anyone other than myself, that is.

And that is exactly what I did. Long before Dan moved in, I spent nights in my basement testing an experimental nerve agent on myself. Using a timer on my phone, I'd start it just before injecting myself. I recorded the dosage and the time it took to wear off. It was terrifying the first few times. I had resigned myself to die the very first time, even though I used only half the recommended dose for my weight.

The sensation of being alert but unable to move was absolutely horrifying. The hours stretched on for what felt like forever, and I thought maybe it would never wear off. I'd be stuck in my basement and slowly starve to death. But eventually, I regained movement in my fingers and toes. Then, it spread until I could move completely, though it felt like each limb had ten pounds of sand in it.

The living room lights are still on when I park in the driveway. "I'll be back in a while to get you," I say loudly so Evan can hear me through the back seat. I put his car keys in my glove box and lock it. Step one of my plan has gone perfectly.

CHAPTER ELEVEN

Scarlett — Now

The porch light flicks on, and I look up to see Dan in the doorway. My nerves kick up all of a sudden, and I have to take a breath to fight back the unexpected wave of nausea. I open the car door and walk inside.

"You okay?" he asks and squeezes my shoulder when I get to the doorway. "Sit down. I'll get you water and pour the medicine."

I accept his offer and let him believe that my stomach-ache is what is bothering me and not the fact that my husband is in the trunk of my car just outside. He brings me a glass of water and a small plastic cup full of pink liquid. I swallow it and take a sip of water. "Thank you."

He extends his hand, and I take it, letting him pull me to my feet. And then, in one swift motion, he sweeps me into his arms and carries me toward the stairs. I can't help but smile.

His warmth and the cool of the sheets make me shiver when he pulls me into him. I close my eyes and try not to cry again. His thumb slides back and forth on my bare shoulder. His breaths are long and even, and I try to match mine to his. Try to push thoughts of Evan and his ultimatum out of my mind.

Dan's thumb goes still and his limbs limp. His arm twitches. I wish I could fall asleep with him. Escape the fear that is embedded in my bones and the thoughts that fly by like cars on a busy highway. My plan is working, and that is great. But anything could still happen. Any number of things could go wrong. And then what?

Maybe I should have actually left with Evan. It would mean safety for the people I care about. So long as Evan kept his word. It would also mean I stay alive and out of prison.

And I'd be with Evan again.

The desire scares me. That there is part of me that still craves him. That it would almost be a relief to have the decision forced on me to absolve any guilt I would feel for leaving Dan and Marin and my home.

Disgust so thick I nearly choke on it rises from my chest. What is wrong with me? I have to remember why I left. Not because I couldn't handle what Evan and I were doing, though I wish that was why. I left for reasons he can never know about. For the secret I have to keep safe no matter what.

Maybe a better plan would have been to shoot him and be done with it all. I still could. I should. Thoughts of Evan are consuming me, and I am desperate to push them away.

I roll over, facing Dan, and kiss his chest. His parted lips. He stirs as I trace my fingertips down his stomach. His hand grips my hip. He kisses me back, eyes still closed. My hand brushes the fabric of his boxer briefs. He kisses me harder, and I suck his bottom lip between my teeth, biting down gently and pulling it out just a little bit.

He groans and rolls onto his back, pulling me on top of him. I circle my hips and feel him grow hard beneath me. I peel my top off and watch as his hands slide up to cup my breasts. With hooded eyes, he tugs on my shorts. I lift up so he can pull them down, then slide his briefs down afterward.

My heart pounds loudly when we're done. His chest is damp with sweat beneath my cheek, and we both breathe hard from the exertion. Dan runs his fingers along my head, pulling the stray hairs away from my face.

"You're so beautiful. You know that?" he says, his voice already drowsy.

"You deserve someone better." I say it so quietly that when he doesn't respond, I think he hasn't heard me. But then he kisses my head and sighs.

"I wish you could see yourself through everyone else's eyes."

I don't wish that. Not at all. To see just how well I've been able to fool the people I love, to see how large the difference is between the person they see and who I really am . . . it would be too much.

But there is nothing I can do about who I really am. My blood was poisoned from conception, and I will hate my father for bringing me into existence for as long as I live. And not for the first time, I wonder why he did. Why did he want a child? Did he want to train me to be like him? No. I don't think he did. He tried to hide a lot of it from me. Though sometimes I think his crazy slipped out unintentionally.

Dan has fallen asleep next to me, and it is finally time to open the mysterious red box. Evan will need another dose of the nerve agent in a few hours, and I'll need to move him from my trunk while Dan and the rest of the neighborhood are asleep. But curiosity wins over, so I decide a few minutes of indulgence won't hurt. I slip from the bed and creep to the bathroom. Once I have the door closed and locked, I climb onto the sink and remove the box from the ceiling panel.

The ribbon is meticulously tied across the top of the box. I grab scissors from a drawer and snip it.

My heart pounds so hard I can feel it in my head. The room is blurry. I grip the counter and close my eyes. Deep breath in. Deep breath out. Repeat.

I open my eyes, hold my breath, and slowly lift the lid off the box.

I exhale in a sob.

A framed collage of pictures sits beneath a neatly written note.

Happy Anniversary, my love.

I'm much younger in the pictures. Back when I wore more eyeliner and had streaks of red in my hair. The man in the photos is young too. He has a confident smile. Short, brown hair. He looks at younger me lovingly in one picture. His eyes are closed, mid-laugh, in another. I let my finger trace his frozen image beneath the glass. Evan. My beautiful, terrible husband.

With shaking hands, I put the box back and go down to the basement. This house hides many secrets. I push against a wall behind a box of resistance bands to open the concealed room I built myself. Dan doesn't go into the basement. I made sure to have the circuit box relocated upstairs so there is never a reason for him to come down here, even when I am not home. The box of nerve agents sits inside a drawer against the wall to my left. I grab one and take it out to my car.

Evan lies motionless, his eyes still open. I quickly inject him in the neck and shut the trunk. Once I get him downstairs, I can run an IV so he doesn't get dehydrated or starve. Now I know the effects of the drugs won't be wearing off anytime soon, I return to the basement to get the equipment I need to move him.

The basement has a walk-out exit in the backyard that is always locked up tight. That is how I will get him downstairs. I unlock the door and push the big utility basket on wheels onto the back walkway. I've seen them used in high school gyms in the movies and bought mine at a flea market many years ago.

The wheels rattle and squeak against the concrete as I push it around the house and to my car. Why did I not think to grease the wheels? I look around for signs of life. Lit-up windows in neighboring houses. Or worse, in my house. But everything remains dark.

There is a blanket on the bottom of the cart, and I pull it out and drape it over the edge, then use my foot to engage the brakes on the wheels when I get it positioned against the trunk. Taking one more look around, I take a deep breath and hold it. Another big moment for something to go wrong.

I pop the trunk and avoid looking at Evan's accusing eyes. He has no right to be upset with me after everything he's done. And I'm being ridiculous for feeling any kind of guilt. I am protecting myself and the people I love from a monster.

I grip his clothes and pull him toward me and the basket. When I get him right against the ledge of the trunk, I begin trying to roll him over it, bottom half first so he doesn't just plop in all at once and potentially break my cart. It's much easier than getting him inside my trunk, and within minutes and with minimal sweat, he is folded into the cart. I put the blanket over him and close the trunk as quietly as I can before pushing him toward the back door.

The cart is much harder to push with Evan inside, and the wheels squeak even louder. The sound echoes in the silence. I stop halfway back and suck in a breath when I see my neighbor's back porch light flick on. *Shit. What do I do? What do I do?*

Lionel peaks his head around the back corner of his house, squinting his eyes to see into the darkness. The brightness of his lights illuminates him completely, and I can see he is in his pajamas and a blue robe. His scalp reflects the light through his thin and mostly missing hair.

"Scarlett? Is that you?"

This is it. I messed up. I made one small mistake by not greasing the fucking cart's wheels, and now it is all over. I'll go to prison, and Evan will look like the victim. He'll be free to hurt everyone I love. "Hi, Lionel," I say, trying to keep my voice down to avoid waking anyone else.

"What on earth are you doing? It's two o'clock in the morning."

"I know. I'm so sorry. I didn't mean to wake you."

He just needs to go back to bed. Just let me keep going without asking questions. Please. But of course, he doesn't. Because Lionel is a kindhearted man who would do anything for his neighbors. He steps through his side gate and walks over. "What in the world are you doing?" he asks, eyeing the cart. Thankfully, the blanket covers Evan completely, and he cannot move or speak.

"It's a gift for Dan," I say quickly. "That's why I'm trying to get it inside while he's asleep. It's a surprise."

Lionel smiles and narrows his eyes conspiratorially. "Let me help you push it inside," he says. "It looks heavy, and those wheels could really use some WD-40."

"Oh, you don't have to do that. It's two in the morning. Go back to bed. I'm so sorry I woke you."

"No, no." He grabs the edge of the cart and pushes. I stumble to grab on and keep step with him.

"Uh — thank you."

Lionel helps me push the cart all the way to the back of the house and through my basement door. "Right here where you want it?"

"Yes, thank you. Right here is perfect."

"You need help getting it out of there or putting it together?"

"No. No, I got it. I just wanted to get it inside. I'm heading back to bed now." I am light-headed with apprehension. All he would have to do is lift the corner of the blanket out of curiosity. I imagine what his face would look like as he took in Evan's motionless body. As his brain tried to connect what he was seeing with any kind of logic. What would he say? Would he run, sensing he was in danger?

"Well, let me know how the surprise goes. I'll keep my mouth shut so I don't ruin it," he says. And then he walks out into the yard. I watch him cross the lawn and close his side gate behind him before going back inside. When his light turns off and the night is returned to darkness, I finally allow myself to breathe freely.

I shut and lock the basement door and pull the blanket off the cart. "That was close," I say to Evan, who cannot respond.

I push him into the hidden room, more comfortable with the noise because the basement is thoroughly soundproofed. Another DIY project done with the help of videos on the internet. I don't have the energy or strength to move Evan into the recliner I have set up for him. For a second, I consider leaving him in the cart until morning. But guilt has me working to tip the cart on its side to get him out.

It feels like hours have passed before I finally have him in the chair and hooked up to a saline drip. I turn for the door before I think of what I nearly forgot. What was nearly another mistake. "Where is your cell phone, Evan?"

I dig through his pockets but come up completely empty. That means it must have either fallen out in my trunk or on the road when I loaded him up, or he left it in his car. I sigh and lock up the hidden room before going upstairs.

Morning comes, and I have not slept. I stare at the ceiling, running through last night's events. Where is Evan's cell phone? Marin will no doubt be expecting to hear from him. What happens next? Should I turn the house cameras on now?

"What's wrong?"

I jump. I didn't realize Dan was awake. I'm distracted and not paying attention the way I normally do. I roll my head to look at him. The corners of his mouth are pulled down. Concern is etched in the lines of his forehead.

"Would you run away with me?"

He laughs softly. "We're not teenagers forbidden to see each other. We don't have to run away."

"What if I wanted to leave? Start over in a new town far away from here? Would you come with me?"

The lines on his forehead deepen. "I couldn't leave my family. My friends. My business. I love it here. I thought you did too. What's going on, babe?"

His sensibility is something I've always loved about him, but I hate it now. I wish he was more spontaneous, romantic, whimsical.

I sigh. He is not those things, and I have loved him for six years because he is who he is, though it really doesn't work in my favor right now. At some point, and soon, I will have to decide what to do with Evan. He can't stay this way forever. I will run out of the drug that keeps him immobile eventually, and I can't get even close to that point without making a decision.

"Hey," he says and kisses my forehead. "I don't know what's going on up there. But everything is okay. I love you. And we have a great life here. Together."

"I know." I nod. And I do know. I love my life here. It's so much more than I ever hoped for or deserved to have, and it makes me physically ill to think of leaving. Of never seeing Dan again. Can I really go through with killing Evan? I really don't know if I can. Even if it means I will get to keep my life here.

"I wish you'd talk to me," Dan says.

I stare at a spot on his chest. If I meet his eyes, I just might tell him everything, and that would only make matters worse.

"I'm okay," I say instead. "Promise."

Another lie.

CHAPTER TWELVE

Scarlett — Then

Every day, Evan asks me questions about my dad. He asks me questions about me too. Those are my favorite. He asks me things I've never thought about, and I feel like I'm getting to know me at the same time as he is. He asks me what my happiest memory is: going to the zoo with my dad every summer. He asks me what my worst one was: the police breaking into our house in the middle of the night. Them dragging him away and him yelling to me. Telling me to be brave. He asks what I want more than anything in the world: that my dad never hurt anyone. Evan frowns when I answer, but he doesn't say anything. But one day, when we're sitting under our tree in the backyard, he asks me about my mother.

I asked my dad about her only once. He told me I have her eyes. And then he showed them to me, bobbing around in a glass jar. I didn't ask him about her again. And I didn't like looking at my eyes in the mirror after that either.

"You don't know anything about her?" asks Evan. "Not her name or how they met or anything?"

I shake my head.

"I bet they say something about her in your file. They'd have your birth certificate at least."

I flick a piece of fallen tree bark. I want to know who she was. More than I want to show. But I can't explain why. Only this feeling that I want to know the other half of me. Maybe there is part of me that isn't him. I love my dad. But I know he's bad. I know there is the part of him in me that makes me want to be bad sometimes too. But maybe there is part of me that wants to be good.

I hadn't noticed Evan watching me. I feel my cheeks get warm. He hasn't been able to sleep in my room for the last few weeks since he killed Izzy. Miss Pamela has been watching him closer, like she knows what he did but can't prove it.

But now, I wake up to a note beneath my door every morning. Evan writes me nice things to make me smile. It's a pleasant way to start my day. I started writing him notes too. I slip them under his door while he's in mandatory therapy. It's become our thing, and I like it a lot, but I'd prefer him to be able to sleep in my room again.

"I'll break into the office tonight and find your file," he says.

"Miss Pamela will catch you."

He shakes his head. "She's been watching less. I overheard her on the phone yesterday. Two more kids will be here this afternoon. She's distracted. Once they get here, I'll be able to sneak to your room at night again."

"Really?" I ask. Too excited. I let my face fall back to normal. "If you want to, I mean."

"I want to."

"So, tonight. I'll sneak into the office and see if they say anything about your mom in your file."

I nod, chewing my lip. If he reads my file, he'll see what I did to get here. I still haven't told him. But I really want to know about my mom. I stop chewing my lip and smile. "Okay. Thank you, Evan."

I toss and turn the whole night. Straining my ears for any sound at all and praying that Evan won't get caught. I've been doing that lately. Praying. There's a church service in the dining hall every week, and Miss Pamela said I should try it. She doesn't make us go, but I like going. Evan says it's silly. Like worshiping Santa Claus. I didn't tell him that I still believed in Santa Claus. I've had my suspicions, but Dad was always so convincing.

The next day, I run from my room the moment my alarm goes off. I stand awkwardly outside Evan's bedroom door, not sure if I should knock or not. The door swings open and Evan smiles at me in greeting like he knew I'd be standing here.

"Good morning," he says.

"Good morning." My fingers go to my mouth, and I chew at the skin next to my nail. Evan reaches over and gently tugs my arm down.

"Don't do that. It's a dead giveaway that you're nervous and uncomfortable."

"I *am* nervous and uncomfortable," I counter.

"No one else needs to know that."

I'm not sure why it matters, but I let my arms hang at my side.

"I read your file. I'll tell you about it outside after breakfast so we aren't overheard."

I follow him to the kitchen, barely able to taste my food. I need to know. I need to know her name.

Evan eats painfully slowly. I lift my hand up, ready to start biting my nail, when I remember what Evan said and put it back down beside me. *No one needs to know that.*

When he finally finishes eating, we walk outside. It's getting colder. Grayer. I dread the winter when we won't be able to sit outside for hours. I don't know how we'll pass the time.

"Her name was Eloise Chambers."

Goose bumps spread across my arms. *Eloise Chambers.* It's a pretty name. Did she name me? Or did Dad? I know Dad killed her. Or at least, he wanted me to think he did, but I don't know why he'd lie about it. How long did she know me before she died? How long had she held me? Days? Hours? Months?

I finally look at Evan. He seems uncomfortable. "You know more than that, don't you?" Did he read about what happened at my foster home? Does he know?

He looks me in the eyes. In my mother's eyes. "It's not good. And it's okay if you'd rather not know. But I'll tell you if you want me to."

I think about it for a second and decide I need to know. I know plenty of bad things I wish I didn't. How bad can it be? I need to know everything I can about her. "Tell me."

He nods. Takes a breath. My stomach tightens. "Your dad kidnapped her. Well, she wasn't a kid, but he took her. He raped her and held her captive until she gave birth to you. Then he killed her."

I try to swallow, but it gets stuck. I cough. What did I expect? A love story? Of course this is how I came to be. The fact that I was created from kidnap and rape makes any good part of my mother that might be in me feel unimportant.

Evan reaches over and laces his fingers between mine.

"I'm sorry," he whispers. He lets me cry into his shoulder, and it feels nice to have someone hold me again. He doesn't ask about the other stuff in my file. What I did to get sent to this place. Maybe he only read the papers about my parents. Maybe he still doesn't know.

CHAPTER THIRTEEN

Evan — Now

This has to be one of my top five worst moments in life. Number one would obviously be the day Scarlett disappeared. Those days and weeks of not knowing if she was okay. Believing she'd been in some horrible accident. That was the worst. Then there was the day Lottie was fired. And the day the police took me away from my home as my mother turned her head, not even able to look at me. Those all rank somewhere in there too.

But this . . . this is un-fucking-real. My nose itches. And it's all I can think about. My hand won't budge. Won't even flinch. I can feel a bit of drool seeping from the corner of my mouth, and if I could scream, I would. How did I let this happen? Where the fuck did she get whatever she shot into my neck? I'm a pharmaceutical rep, and nothing I'm aware of would do this.

The door opens behind me. At least, I think that's what the sound is because I can't turn my head to look. But then Scarlett is in front of me, and the suspense is over. I want to say something sarcastic, though nothing comes to mind because what does it matter?

She wipes the corner of my mouth with her thumb, and I want to remind her of the times she's done that during sex. The thought makes me grin. Internally, at least.

"I have to find your phone today. It's time you and Marin ended your relationship," she says. I want to laugh and tell her *good luck*. She won't find my phone. It's not something I just leave lying around. I am more than a little nervous about not being reachable to my job. I've worked for the same company since I was eighteen years old, and they've been good to me. Holding a steady job is important for someone like me. Serial killers aren't often known to be the reliable and steady type. Not never, but not often.

Scarlett kneels in front of me. I can smell her shampoo. I hate that I can't reach out and touch her. Throttle her. Being so completely out of control is not something I'm used to. And actually, it's my worst fucking nightmare. I'm used to having power. Control is my comfort zone, and it makes me wonder if that is exactly why Scarlett has chosen this specific form of hell for me.

I can move my eyes, at least. God, what if I wasn't even able to blink? My wife is just inside my range of vision, though it kind of hurts to move my eyes that far to the left. She's screwing around with something, and then I hear a drawer shut. She's back in front of me with nothing in her hands. What was she doing?

"I'm going to look for your phone, and I'll be back in just a bit to give you another dose."

And then she is gone, and I am once again left alone. I couldn't see when she brought me inside, but I could hear. Hear the moronic neighbor unknowingly partaking in kidnapping and unlawful restraint. And I could hear that I'm inside Scarlett's house. The question is how the hell do I get out and regain my position of being a few steps ahead of her? I didn't work this hard for this long to be outwitted.

My stomach growls. I didn't eat much before going to meet Scarlett at her birthday dinner. Nerves. And now there's an IV in my arm that will keep me from dying but does nothing to staunch my hunger pains. I want a burger and fries.

Okay, focus. I have to figure out how to get out of this. But the more I think, the more hopeless the situation feels. What does she plan to do with me, anyway? She can't keep me down here like a fucking pet forever. Or can she? Exactly how much of this paralysis drug does she have?

It becomes apparent pretty quickly that I will only be getting out of here if Scarlett makes a mistake. This shit has to wear off eventually.

CHAPTER FOURTEEN

Scarlett — Now

I really hope Evan's phone is inside his car and not lying in the middle of the road. The road is a dead end that no one really goes down, but it's not impossible. The last thing I need is for someone else to find it or for it to be run over and smashed beyond repair. I need to be able to text Marin. And Evan's work. If he goes dark, the chances of him being reported missing are much higher. And I definitely don't need that.

I pull onto the empty road and park my car. At first glance, I don't see anything on the road. But just in case, I walk the length of it and scan the concrete carefully. But it isn't here. It has to be in his car.

I take off into the woods, imagining all the missed texts and calls he's receiving. All the people worried about him not responding. Evan was rarely without his phone back then. He had to be responsive to his employer. The only time he turned it off was for our trips to the cabin. And those times were prearranged pretty far in advance.

I get to his car and mash the unlock button on his key remote. Inside, I paw through his center console. He keeps his car very clean, which makes it easier to realize his phone is not there. I feel between the seats, get out, and look beneath them too. I go around to the passenger side and do the same. I come up empty.

Where the hell is his phone?

The sun is already warm, and I'm starting to sweat. That, combined with the woods around me, is making me itchy. I'll need another shower when I get home. But first, I have to figure out how to get his phone. He didn't pull it out at dinner last night. But he must have it close. As a last shot in the dark, I pop his trunk to search there.

There is a duffel bag, and a spark of hope ignites in my chest. But after a thorough search, I still can't find it. The bag is an overnight bag with a change of clothes, a toothbrush, and deodorant. I shut the trunk and walk back to the road, defeated.

My heart stops when I see the sheriff's car parked next to mine. Darryl sits inside his car, trying to look into my windows. He stops when he sees me emerge from the woods and rolls his window down. "Scarlett," he says. "I saw your car parked and stopped to say hi, but you were nowhere to be found."

I smile broadly. "Hi, Darryl. I was just out for a run." I am in athletic clothing, so it's plausible.

"In the woods?"

I nod. "Off-trail training."

He nods, a smile lifting his features as he pretends to have a clue what I'm talking about. Everyone knows me to be a bit of a fitness fanatic, and Darryl isn't the suspicious type. Which probably is not the quality you want to lack as a sheriff. "Well, you be careful out there. It would be easy to twist an ankle."

"Absolutely." I hold up my cell phone. "That's why I always have this handy in case I need to call for help." This seems to make him feel better.

"Good, good! Smart thinking. Well, I'll be on my way. Good luck with your trail training."

"Off-trail."

"Hmm? Oh. Yeah, yeah. Off-trail training." He nods goodbye and rolls his window up. I walk to my car and wave as he turns around and drives away. My whole body sags in relief when his car disappears around the corner. I am encountering far too many close calls.

On the way back home, I think about a possible plan. I have to find his phone. And to do that, I can think of no other way than to talk to Evan. Under the effect of the drug I'm giving him, that is not possible.

But slowly, somewhat of a plan begins to form. I just need Dan to be out of the house for a while.

CHAPTER FIFTEEN

Scarlett — Now

The house is nice and cool when I go inside, and I sigh with relief. Today is going to be excruciatingly hot. I love the summer and its warmth, but I enjoy having central air on days like today too. The basement is cool as well. There are a few vents that heat or cool the basement since it is also my gym year-round. Evan should be comfortable.

I push the hidden door open, and for some illogical reason, I brace myself like he's going to be waiting for me with a knife. But of course, he isn't. I can see the top of his head peeking over the back of the recliner. I toss his car keys in the drawer next to my stock of nerve agents before dragging a stool to sit in front of Evan.

His eyes are tinged with red and look heavy from sleep. "I'm glad you were able to get a little rest." His eyes roll. It's the only way he is able to communicate. "I couldn't find your phone. But I have a feeling you knew that would be the case. I need to know where it is, Evan. So, I'm going to chain you up and skip your next injection. That way, we can talk, and hopefully, you come to some sense and tell me where to find it."

This plan makes me unbelievably nervous. But I can't see any other way. I can't let his work report him missing. Not yet. Not before I've figured out what to do with him long-term. I stand and get the chains and cuffs from the cabinets on the other side of the room. "I'm going to get Dan out of the house so we can be alone for our conversation," I say as I secure the restraints.

Back upstairs, I text Theresa, Dan's sister. She and her son, Sam, are often home alone because her husband is a truck driver and often on the road. I ask her if she'd be up for a visit this evening, and she texts back almost immediately with an all-caps "YES!"

I text Dan next and tell him of our plans. I'll go with him, but a half hour or so into our visit, I will feign a work emergency. I work freelance and have finished up with all my client work to have time off for my birthday, but I will tell Dan a repeat client of mine asked for a quick favor. I'll tell him it will only take an hour and leave him at his sister's. I'll drive so he can't come back until I come and get him.

I think it is as good a plan as I'm going to be able to put together with the time I have. The hours pass slowly, especially with nothing to fill my time. I work out, shower, eat lunch. I text Marin, who is trying not to appear anxious that Evan hasn't responded to her texts or called when he got to his hotel like he said he would. I reassure her that he is just busy or something happened to his phone.

But I also try to work in that maybe he is not as good of a guy as she thought he was. I weave that in very lightly. Marin does not like negative input on her relationships, even though she usually needs to hear it. I am usually more likely to let her be angry with me for saying what she doesn't want to hear, but I cannot manage an argument with Marin on top of everything else I'm dealing with right now. And so I tread carefully.

I keep considering whether or not I should turn the house cameras on. The whole point of them was to watch for Evan, but now he is chained and drugged in my basement, so what would be the point? When it's finally time for Dan to come home, I wait for him in my car. I have the engine running for the air and play solitaire on my phone until he pulls his truck beside me. He opens the passenger door and climbs in. "No time for a shower?"

"You can shower later. I figure we'll be outside at least for a little while, and you'll get all sweaty anyway."

"Good point."

Sam is playing in the sprinkler on the front lawn when we get there. He squeals and jumps up and down when he sees our car, and I can't help but smile. He loves his Uncle Dan and freaks out every time he sees him, even though he sees him at least twice a week.

Theresa has a pitcher of lemonade and a cooler of ice on the porch, and we help ourselves to a glass, taking a seat on the steps beside her. Sam grabs Dan's hand the moment he sits down and drags him toward the sprinkler. "No, no, no! I'm not getting wet, bud!" But Sam decides that he most definitely is, and Dan cannot say no to his nephew. Theresa and I laugh as Dan screeches when the cold water sprays his back.

"He really needs to learn to say no," Theresa says.

"He never will." I laugh.

We're quiet while we watch them run around. I have always gotten along with Dan's family, but Theresa is probably the closest to not agreeing with our relationship. She doesn't like that I don't want to get married or have children. It's something she wants for her younger brother, and I understand that. But it isn't up to her, and Dan has told her as much. She keeps her dissent to herself these days, and we get along well enough.

Still, I can feel the unsaid words. How good a dad Dan would make. It's true. He would make a great father, and I've had more than one conversation with him about how he deserves to be with someone who can give him a family. But Dan insists that all he wants is me. Whatever that looks like.

I grab my phone from my back pocket and put my plan into motion. "Oh, shoot," I say. Theresa looks at me, waiting for more. "One of my clients needs a favor."

"I thought you were done with work for now?" she says.

"I am. This isn't a planned project. Just an emergency favor she's asking for. She's one of my best clients, so I really don't want to turn her away."

She shrugs. "You're on vacation."

I smile like I always do when we come to an impasse, and I walk over to the edge of the lawn. "Babe? I have a work emergency I need to take care of."

He shakes the water from his hair and jogs toward me. "Work emergency?"

I repeat my story and tell him it will only take about an hour. "Stay and visit. I'll get it done really quick and come back."

"Actually, can you wait just a few minutes, Scarlett?" Theresa says. "I really need Dan's help moving a few boxes into the attic. I'd wait for Brent, but the boxes are blocking the hallway, and it's been a pain in the ass. Can you stay out here and keep an eye on Sam? It'll only take a minute. Five at the most."

"I'm sopping wet," Dan says. "I don't want to track water through the house."

"You have clothes here." She starts walking toward the house. "Hurry up."

"Theresa, can we do this when I come back? I really need to get this done." My whole body is tense. I need to go. I need to get this done with Evan.

"It will take five minutes. I swear."

I sigh as Dan kisses my cheek and says, "I'll hurry." Anxiety fires through my veins. Sam is old enough to be told to come inside while they do this. But there is no arguing with Theresa, so I sit back on the front steps and watch Sam leap through the sprinkler.

Minutes tick by, and I keep looking at my phone, watching the number on the clock tick higher and higher. Five minutes come and go. When eight minutes have passed, I peek my head through the front door and call out to them. "I really need to get going."

"Almost done. You're on vacation. This lady is lucky you're helping her at all. She can wait," Theresa says.

I shut the door before I say something I might regret. Another five minutes pass. Then another. I'm about to tell them I'm leaving and that Sam can come inside when they finally emerge from the house.

I immediately run to my car and call over my shoulder, "I'll be back in an hour." Theresa will likely keep him busy with household tasks Brent doesn't have the time to do. I push my foot down on the gas pedal, eager to get back.

Not being home while Evan has not had a recent dose of nerve agent makes me more than a little nervous. He is chained up, but that doesn't do much to ease my anxiety. I need to get him talking quickly so I can give him another injection before it's time to go back and get Dan.

I take the basement steps quickly, almost losing my footing before catching myself with the railing. The falling sensation has lightning-like splinters shooting up my fingers and toes, and I force myself to slow down and take a breath.

It has been a long time since I've dealt with such high-stress situations. All my stress for the past six years has been in preparation for this. And in paranoia and anticipation that every day could be the day Evan finds me.

But that stress is nothing compared to the feeling when I get downstairs and see that the door to the hidden room is open. I did not leave it that way. Fear consumes me as I walk into the room, searching with my eyes and ears for anything amiss. Evan's head does not peek over the top of the recliner the way it did earlier today. I walk closer to see what I already know. Evan is gone.

CHAPTER SIXTEEN

Evan — Now

I still can't feel my face, and my hands are bleeding, but I'm free, and it feels incredible. Getting through Scarlett's neighborhood on foot without looking suspicious is a problem. It's early evening, and the only thing working in my favor is that it is so incredibly humid outside that most people have retreated to their air-conditioned houses. Still, a strange bleeding man carrying a box of needles is going to catch anyone's attention who might be looking.

I damn well made sure to take all the injectable needles and drugs I could find in that basement. I'm assuming that was her entire stock. Unless she's hiding a stock of illegal nerve agents upstairs in her kitchen cabinet next to the peanut butter.

Once I was able to move again, I managed to pry the handcuffs off. Scarlett's empathy has always been her biggest weakness. She left the cuffs too loose, probably sure I wouldn't be able to move anytime soon. Once the effects of the drug started to fade, it all wore off fairly quickly. I went from being able to move my fingers and toes to having control over my body in about an hour. Though it's hard to tell how long it was without a clock.

I turn off Scarlett's block and head east. She conveniently left my car keys next to her drugs. As I make my way to the last place I saw my Audi, I try to come up with a reasonable explanation for my current state if I'm stopped by someone.

I'm actually pleasantly surprised by Scarlett and all she's done to prepare for me. I haven't been far from her mind. I know that now. I'm impressed with her little hidden room in her basement. I tried my hardest to get through the door leading to the rest of her house. I wanted to have a peek around, but the door wouldn't budge. The one leading out to the backyard was the only way I was able to get out.

I thought about waiting for her to come back and surprising her. Overpowering her and turning the tables. But in the end, I decided it would be more fun to continue with my plan. I don't want to get to the end of things too soon.

Somehow, miraculously, I get to the abandoned dead-end road without incident. And my car isn't there. Of course it isn't. I'm about to kick a rock in annoyance when I see tire tracks near the treeline. I follow them for what seems like an eternity. The shiny, black tail-end pokes out of some thick trees, and I almost faint. There is no chance the paint isn't scratched.

First things first, I need to get my phone. I unlock my car and slide into the driver's seat. The hard plastic housing below the steering wheel pops open with a button hidden behind the wheel. My phone is there, plugged into the charger I wired into the compartment. One missed call from Marin and three missed texts. Two missed calls from work and a not-so-nice email from my boss.

I step outside the car with my phone to my ear. Work first. I make up some excuse of dropping my phone and having to get a new one. My boss isn't happy. He isn't the understanding type. But since this is a rare occurrence for me, his lecture is short. When we hang up, I shoot off a few emails to reschedule the appointment I missed while being drugged and held captive in my wife's basement.

Next up is Marin. She answers on the fourth ring, likely making me wait on purpose. But the fact that she answered at all means I'm probably okay. I tell her I lost my phone and just found it now. She clearly doesn't believe me, but I tell her I'll show her the missed calls and threatening email from my boss. This convinces her. Then I tell her I'll be in town in twenty minutes if she doesn't hate me. She laughs and invites me over, and it's all too easy.

Secretly dating Marin for the last few months has been damn near an Olympic sport. She mostly insisted on meeting out of town so she'd come over to whatever hotel I pretended to be staying at for work. The few times she allowed me over to her house, I could only come in the middle of the night and park in the garage. Then she'd banish me before the sun rose like we were sneaky, horny teenagers afraid to get busted by our parents.

Scarlett was smart to pick this place to hide in. It took me far too long to find her because I searched every major city first. Even big cities in other countries. I've always known her to be smart, but she's been even more clever than I thought her capable. The little trap I fell right into is proof of that.

A shower sounds otherworldly right now. Inevitably, having to share one and then fuck Marin does not. But it's the price I have to pay. Now that I've "met" her friends, I need to know more about them. Particularly my wife. I feel a new sense of purpose now that my plan is back in motion.

Marin skips out of the house when I park at the curb. Any residual anger for me is clearly gone. When we first met, she always tried to play cool. She'd wait for me to text her first, not answer my call and pretend she'd been busy. Just a few months later and she's like a high school girl with her first boyfriend.

I roll down the window, wanting the car door as a barrier, if only for a minute longer. I make sure to keep my bloody hands out of view. "Do you still want me to park in your garage, or am I allowed to be seen from the street now?"

She laughs. I resist the urge to mock her immaturely. "You can park on the street if you'd like. Now that my friends know about you, I don't have to keep you a secret."

I smile and roll up the window in her face. Keep me a secret. She really is a fucking high schooler. When I step out of my car, she wraps her arms around my waist, and I do my job. My fingers wrap around the base of her head, not her neck, and I kiss her as though I like her. She doesn't ask to see my phone and the proof I promised when I called her.

I lead us both inside because I need to wash the blood and sweat away.

"Mind if I use your shower? I came straight here and haven't had a chance." I have my sweater draped over my hands. I need to see how bad they look once the blood is gone.

"I don't mind at all," she says.

Three days. That is all I have left to endure in this town. I decided to show Scarlett how kind and understanding I still am by resetting the time clock on the ultimatum I gave her. But then it's all over, and all of this will come to a head. And in the meantime, I get to have a little fun at the expense of these trite people my wife has chosen over me.

The hot water is incredible. I quickly wash the blood down the drain and am happy to see my hands don't look as mangled as I thought they would. I'm still not sure what to say caused it. Just like I knew she would, Marin steps into the shower behind me just after I've rinsed the soap from my body.

God, this is exhausting. Her fingers trail my back, my waist, and when I turn around, my cock. She grips me hard. A little too hard, but that's all right because we always get a little rough. It's the only way I can get off with her.

I spin her around and push her into the shower wall, lifting her leg onto the ledge. I make no attempt at foreplay. She whimpers when I push into her. I wrap her damp hair around one fist, yanking her head back as I thrust harder and harder. I use my free hand to grip her waist right where her back arches, and I push into it, making her arch more.

It takes too long to finish, but I'm thankful to get it done in the shower, where I can immediately rinse off without seeming rude. I let her wash up first, like a gentleman, and then sigh with relief when she steps out of the shower and then the bathroom and I can have a moment of peace.

She's waiting in bed when I dry off and leave the comfort of the warm steam in the bathroom. I steel myself for round two, but Marin is mercifully asleep when I lower myself onto the mattress. I need a good night's sleep. There is much to do tomorrow.

* * *

I smell a freshly lit fire when I wake in the morning. I drag myself out of bed and into the living room. Instead of our usual glass of wine, she's poured mugs of coffee. We haven't spent many mornings together, and it feels off. I take a seat, grabbing a cup on my way to the sofa. "Little warm out for a fire, no?"

She shrugs. "It's not warm in here. And I thought it'd set the mood better."

It's not warm in here because the air-conditioning is on, but I'm not going to reason with her. "No work today?" I ask and take a sip of my coffee, burning my tongue. I bite my cheek and set the mug down on the coffee table before the urge to sling the scalding hot liquid at her face wins out. Not even a fucking heads-up that the coffee is nuclear?

"I called in and told them I'd be in this afternoon. Headache." She smiles like she's so clever.

"Nice. You have plans with Scarlett today, don't you?"

She nods. "Brunch. Usually, I use my lunch break, but I'm just going to meet her before I go in today."

"Won't your boss find out you went to brunch with a friend before coming into work when you claimed to have a headache?"

She shrugs. "What are they going to do? Fire me?"

She says it like it is not a legitimate possibility, and it's yet another reason I hate these small hick towns. Of course you should be fired for blowing off work. But she's probably right. Who would they replace her with?

"How guileful of you," I say.

"Oh, I like that one! I'm going to write that down to use it later."

"It means showing cunning intelligence."

She laughs. "Thank you. I didn't know the exact definition, but I have a basic idea of what it means." She taps the side of her head. "Context clues and all."

"Right. Well, anyway. It'll be nice to have the morning together." I smile, and she climbs into the armchair across from me. I take another sip from my coffee — too sweet — and try not to sneer as she stares at me with stars in her eyes.

"It was good to finally meet all your friends. They seem nice."

"Yeah, it's nice to have it over with. I was nervous and hated keeping things from Scarlett."

"You guys are really close, huh? I force myself to sound casual. I've had to keep my questions about Scarlett to a minimum to avoid raising any suspicions or just coming off like a creep.

"Mm-hmm," she says, sipping from her own coffee.

"You said she moved here a while back, right? You guys didn't grow up together or anything?"

"Yeah, that's right. Six years ago. Been inseparable ever since."

I nod. Sip. She's been here six years. But she's been gone from me for seven. Where was she that missing year? "That's nice. I imagine moving to a place so small where everyone knows everyone already wasn't easy. But it looks like she fit right in."

"She did. It's almost like she's always been here. Like she belongs here."

"Mmm." Don't snap her neck. Not yet.

"I met her through Dan. His mom is the hairstylist in town. She was constantly trying to get us together, me and Dan, but we've never been into each other like that. I've known him since we were born, pretty much. Dan came into the salon to tell his mom about the amazing girl he'd just met at the diner while I was getting highlights. He was all torn up because she was supposed to be just passing through. But I guess she decided to stay."

"You never asked why she decided to stay? Or where she was going? Or coming from?"

She lifts an eyebrow and laughs. "Well, she stayed for Dan. I thought that part was obvious. And her family all passed away." She looks off like she's remembering something. "She was so sad back then. You could tell she was lonely."

That's enough. I'm not going to sit here and let some small-town bimbo tell me about my wife like she knows her better. She doesn't know Scarlett the way I do. I drop my mug onto the ground to put an end to the conversation and jump up. "Oh, no. I'm so sorry. I'll grab a towel."

I walk to the hall closet, taking deep breaths. Scarlett had everything she's ever needed and walked away like it meant nothing. She can play the victim all she wants, but I know the truth. And if she isn't careful, everyone else will too.

And suddenly, I have an idea. I toss a towel onto the spilled coffee and help Marin clean it up. "You know, I was thinking, I only got to chat with your friends for a few minutes. I'd love some more time to get to know them."

"I'd love that too." She smiles up at me, and I play the adoring boyfriend.

"What do you think about a little barbecue? We can have it here and invite everyone over."

Marin finally notices my cut-up hands and stops cleaning. "Woah, what happened to your hands?"

"My car overheated last night. I scratched them up under the hood, trying to get it working again. What do you think about the barbecue?" I know nothing about cars and really hope she doesn't get hung up on my explanation.

"That would be so nice. When are you thinking?"

Thank God. "This evening. After you get home. I know it's last minute, but I can start preparing while you're at work." I make a decision to also get rid of Scarlett's paralysis drug while Marin is at work. I don't need her getting her hands on it, and I don't know enough about it to use it for myself. I'd end up accidentally killing her, and that isn't what I want. At least, not that way.

"I think it's a great idea. I'll tell Scarlett at brunch and text everyone else."

Good girl.

CHAPTER SEVENTEEN

Scarlett — Then

Darcel never came back to Miss Pamela's. I liked him, but if it means Evan is safe and still with me, then it's worth it. I've been here for six months now, and I finally get to go into town. Miss Pamela came into the dining hall this morning and announced we'd be taking a trip into town for a movie. We each got to pick from the list of movies that will be showing this afternoon, and I haven't been this excited for something in a long time.

Evan and I choose *Cheaper by the Dozen*. It's one I'd been wanting to see before my life exploded. We take a bus to the theater, and I stare out the window the whole drive. There was a snowstorm a few days ago, and everything looks like it's wearing a fluffy white blanket. I've always loved winter, though now we can't hang out outside as much, and that part I don't like.

When we arrive, we all walk single file into the theater. I thought Miss Pamela would have rented out the theater to have it closed to other people, but that isn't the case. A handful of people stand in the popcorn line.

"All right, now, everyone listen up," Miss Pamela says. There are a few kids still talking, and she claps her hands loudly. "Shut up, you little cretins!" A few of us laugh, including me, and she continues. "I will stand at the ticket counter, and you are all to line up single file to get your ticket. I'll give you each ten dollars to spend at the snack counter. Go into the theater on your ticket and stay there until the credits. I will be staying by the door, so no funny business."

I stand in line next to Evan. His arm presses into my back, and it makes butterflies dance in my belly. Sometimes I think he knows how he makes my heart go crazy and he does it on purpose. I make it to the front of the line and tell Miss Pamela the movie I've chosen. She tells the ticket guy and hands me a ticket and a ten-dollar bill.

I wait for Evan in the popcorn line.

"Don't buy anything. Save the money. Come on." He takes my hand and leads me to the theater.

"I wanted popcorn," I complain, though the feel of his hand warm against mine takes the edge out of my protest.

"I have something better planned." He looks back, a smile on his lips that makes my heart stop. His face glows in the light of the door, the dark theater behind him. When did I start feeling all weird around a *boy*? But Evan isn't just a boy.

We sit near the back of the theater. The red seats look so fancy, and I really wish I had popcorn to make the experience whole. As the movie starts, Evan leans over and whispers into my ear, "We're going to sneak out that bottom door."

I shake my head, but I don't know if he can see me in the dark. "We can't do that."

"Don't be a goody-goody. Darcel and I did it last time we came here, and we didn't get caught."

I don't respond. I don't want to sneak out. I don't want to get in trouble, and I want to see the movie.

"Trust me," he says, and his fingers lace with mine once again. I nod.

"I'm going to walk down and slip through that door." He points to the illuminated exit sign on the other side of the theater from where we came in. "Watch me. And then in two minutes, do it exactly like I did."

He stands before I can say anything, and I watch him disappear through the door. My heart pounds against my rib cage, and I think I might throw up. Has it been two minutes yet? I get to my feet, and my knee bangs against the chair in front of me. I suck air through my teeth and feel light-headed. I'm going to get caught. I'm not smooth and sneaky like Evan. I can't do this.

But I keep moving. Only because I know Evan is waiting for me behind that door, and he pulls me toward him like a magnet. I pull the door. It doesn't move, and I almost cry. Then it begins to open. The other way. *Push.* Evan's face peeks through the opening in the door, and he reaches through and grabs my hand, pulling me to him.

We run from the theater, hands clasped between us. My heart is still hammering, but I can't fight the smile on my lips, so big and wide it hurts. The excitement is overwhelming, and I think maybe this is what my dad felt when he did bad things. I am wild and powerful and free. I can't be stopped.

Evan slows down to a walk once we're a block down from the theater. We are both breathing hard and looking around like we might still get caught, though he's smiling too.

"Now what?" I ask between breaths.

"Let's get food at that place." He nods toward a little restaurant, and I follow him.

We order hot chocolates and nachos to share. It makes missing out on popcorn worth it. Evan chews on a nacho chip, and I reach over to grab one for myself. I plop a jalapeno on top before biting into it. That's how my dad always ate them. It burns my mouth, but I keep eating them that way. I can feel Evan looking at me. I glance up and see that I was right.

"We still never talked much about the stuff in your file," he says.

He always says what he means to say right away. I don't like it because it doesn't give me a chance to think about what I want to say back. So I shrug and take a drink of my hot chocolate to buy myself some time.

“I’m over it,” I say, though I’ve thought of nothing else since the day he told me about my mother. Evan never pushed me to talk about it. Until now, apparently.

“It’s okay if you’re not, though. I know it wasn’t what you wanted to hear.”

I don’t want to talk about it. I put another nacho chip in my mouth and keep my eyes on the plastic basket.

“You can’t help who you are, Scarlett. You shouldn’t feel bad about something you can’t control.”

It sounds like something the therapist would say. He sounds so much older than me, and I wonder if he’s just repeating something that’s been said to him.

“I hate that there is so much bad in me,” I say.

Evan nods like he understands. “It’s not our fault. It’s just who we are. A lion doesn’t feel bad about being a lion. It just does what lions do.”

I know he means that we are lions, but I don’t understand what he’s trying to say by comparing us. What is it that lions do and don’t feel bad about that is supposed to make me feel better about who my dad is and what he’s done?

We pay for our food and hot chocolates with our movie theater money, and then Evan leads me back into the cold.

“You have to get better at lying,” he says as we walk down the sidewalk.

“I don’t like to lie.” I don’t know why saying that feels like I’m tattling on myself.

“It’s not about what you like,” he says, his voice soft. “It’s about survival and doing what you need to do.”

I’m quiet for a few steps, thinking about what he said. “Teach me,” I say finally.

“You have to believe what you’re saying. Pretend what you’re saying is the truth. In your own head. If you believe it, the person you’re lying to will too.”

“How can I believe a lie when I know it’s a lie?” It seems impossible.

"Just practice. Like when we get back to the theater and Miss Pamela asks you about the movie. You have to make believe you saw it. Talk to her like that really happened."

I remember playing dolls with a girl from my class. How we pretended to be rival singers in a pop band. How upset I got when her doll won the competition. I didn't talk to her after that. It seemed silly after a while, but the competition felt real. The sting of losing felt real. And I think that is probably what he means. Make-believe like when you're playing dolls.

I don't tell Evan about the dolls because he might think it's childish. But I tell him I think I understand. Then, Evan sticks his hand out across my body, stopping me in my tracks. I follow his eyes down the snowy alleyway. I don't see what he's looking at right away until something moves, drawing my eyes.

A person huddled under a coat, sleeping against the brick wall of a building.

"He must be cold," I say.

"That's exactly what I was thinking."

I follow him closer to the man, wondering if Evan means to give him the remainder of our theater money. Or maybe his coat. He reaches down and picks up a bottle. Clear liquid sloshes around. Evan unscrews the bottle and puts his nose to the rim. He pours the liquid around the man and on him, drenching his thin coat.

My eyebrows knit together, and I shout a whisper at him. "What are you doing?"

"Warming him up."

He pulls a yellow lighter from his pants pocket. How did he get a lighter? How hasn't he got caught carrying it around?

He nudges me forward. I take a step, still unsure what Evan's intentions are.

We run as the man's screams echo down the alley. The bile rises in my throat, and I have to stop to spit out the nachos from earlier. Evan yanks on my arm, and I wipe my mouth on my coat sleeve as we run back to the theater.

We sneak back in the way we left. No one noticed. I stare at the movie screen as the last half hour of the movie plays, and I try to push down the awful feeling of what just happened. Evan grabs my hand again. I'm mad at him. But I can't turn away the comfort he's offering. I squeeze his hand as tears fall from my eyes. I wish we'd just stayed and watched the movie.

The credits roll onto the screen, and as the lights brighten, Evan turns in his seat to face me. He runs his thumb across my cheek, wiping the tears. I expect him to say something, but he just stands, and I numbly follow him into the lobby. Miss Pamela waits by the front door as our group slowly makes their way to her.

I can hear Evan's voice in my head from earlier, telling me to make believe. So I pretend in my head that we had gotten the popcorn. Extra butter. We watched the movie, and Evan held my hand. We laughed, and at the end, I cried because their family made me miss mine.

CHAPTER EIGHTEEN

Scarlett — Now

Trying to remain calm in the face of Evan having gone missing and taking my nerve agents with him is nearly impossible. His keys are also gone. The question is, has he gone far? One text to Marin tells me he has not. I do everything I can to get Marin to come over, but nothing works. The thought of her sleeping next to him makes my stomach turn and I tell myself it's only because I fear for her safety.

I get not a minute of sleep and text her first thing in the morning, begging her to meet me for lunch a little earlier than we'd planned. I need to know what kind of mental state Evan is in. Whether she is safe, for now.

Before I leave to meet Marin, I finally turn the cameras back on. Hindsight is twenty-twenty, but I can't believe how stupid I was to not turn them on sooner.

At lunch, Marin assures me everything is okay with her and Evan. She tells me his story of losing his phone, and I fight the urge to roll my eyes. And then I get another surprise. An invite to a barbecue at her house.

Marin has never once hosted a cookout in all the years I have known her. I know immediately it was Evan's idea. I wish I had a way to contact him. To ask where we stand now that I have tried and failed to stop him. I await the time for the cookout anxiously.

* * *

Dan and I are early because every minute my best friend spends with Evan has me on pins and needles. He had given me three days, now down to two, but Evan is every bit of the liar I am. I don't know when he's going to stop playing nice and hurt someone I love. He'll get tired of his own game eventually, and the second that happens, Marin is dead. And that's only if my stunt hasn't already signed her death warrant.

Dan and I walk up the driveway hand in hand. The contact makes me nervous. Is Evan watching us right now? Am I antagonizing him with Dan? I don't see Evan's car. I don't think it'd be in the garage, but I can't be sure.

I tap on Marin's front door twice and twist the handle without waiting for an answer. "Whoa, you're just going to walk in?" Dan pulls back on my hand.

"It's fine. She's probably busy cooking in the kitchen and setting up. We're here early to help, remember?"

He's hesitant but follows behind me. The kitchen is through the entryway and to the left. Sure enough, Marin is simultaneously stirring something on the stove and another bowl on the counter with headphones in, bopping her head and her hips. I can't help but smile.

I run over and take the spoon from her right hand, taking over stirring what looks like taco salad. She jumps, and her face brightens when she sees me. With her newly free hand, she takes the headphones from her ears.

"Hi! Thank you! Oh my God, I'm going to burn my house down."

"Not with this world-famous chef I brought with me." I nod toward Dan, and he laughs.

"I brought chicken and ribs. The ribs are done; we just want to keep them warm. Do you have the grill set up out back? I can start the chicken whenever you want."

"You are the best. Have I ever told you that?"

"I don't think you have, actually."

"Well, you are. The grill is out back, but it isn't set up."

"No worries. I got it."

Dan walks to the back with his stacks of marinated meat.

"Where is Evan?" I try my best to be casual.

"He's at the store, grabbing paper plates and plastic silverware."

I set the large bowl of taco salad aside on the kitchen island to make space for the next dish. I spot a hardcover pushed to the top of the counter. It's bookmarked toward the end, and I pull it closer to read the title. "*Husband Theft and Black-Market Babies: A Memoir*," I read aloud and look over at Marin with an amused grin. "Sounds wholesome."

"You have to read it when I'm done. Batshit crazy."

"Don't you ever read happy stories?" I ask.

She shakes her head. "No way. I get bored if there isn't at least one good murder."

Her comment makes my stomach turn. If only she knew she was currently taking part in her very own "batshit crazy" story. I need to change the subject. "This feels like a very last-minute shindig," I say, laughing to hide my discomfort.

"Well, that would be because it is. It was Evan's idea. He wanted to be able to get to know you all a little more since he was only at dinner for like an hour." She stops stirring and looks at me, her grin like a girl in love. "Isn't that sweet?"

"That he wants to know your friends? I'd say you can afford to raise the bar just a bit." Her face falls, and I immediately want to slap myself. "God, I'm sorry, Mar. That came out super bitchy. I didn't mean it like that."

She laughs but isn't amused. "No, it's fine. I just thought it was a nice gesture."

Turning back to the stove, she resumes stirring. Shame burns my cheeks. I know who Evan is, but she doesn't. To Marin, he is the first nice guy she's met in years, and her best friend is being passive-aggressive.

I wrap my arms around her shoulders and squeeze her. "I love you. I'm sorry. You just usually date jerks, and after that last one, I just don't want to see you get hurt again. Not just any old chum deserves to be with my best friend."

She wiggles free, and I catch a glimpse of a grin. "Okay, okay. Just try to put a lid on your jealous girlfriend vibes."

"Will do."

It's believable enough because it's the truth. If he were anyone else, I'd still be on guard. Marin acts tough, but she stopped eating for days when her last relationship ended and she found out he was cheating on her. How would she feel to find out her new boyfriend is actually my husband and only with her to mess with me? And even more, that her boyfriend is a murderer, and she is in danger of becoming his next victim?

I hear the front door open and brace myself.

I feel him before I see him. Like the atoms in the atmosphere shift in his presence, and somehow, I can sense it. He pauses, only for a split second, and our eyes meet. He sets plastic bags full of disposable cutlery on the counter, rounding the island to kiss Marin on the cheek. She doesn't see his eyes still glued to me.

"Hi, baby. How's everything coming? Hello, Scarlett. Thanks for coming so last minute."

"Wouldn't miss it," I say.

Marin turns the burner off and smiles at him. "Good. Dan is out back making the chicken if you want to see if he needs a hand?"

"Of course," he says, and only because I know him the way I do, I notice his jaw clenching. He doesn't like to be told what to do.

He walks past me, and his shoulder brushes mine. I grit my teeth, not wanting to feel what the contact stirs up. And then he's out the back door, alone with Dan. I need a reason to go outside. But it will seem strange when Marin needs help inside.

"I'm going to use the bathroom. Be right back." I stride to the other side of the house. The bathroom is near her bedroom, where there is a window to the backyard. They stand side by side, facing me but with heads bent down toward the grill. They'd look like your average Midwestern men, bonding over grilling, if I didn't know better.

I wish I knew what he was saying. At what point do I stop playing along with his game? I don't know how to put an end to it without catastrophe. Because Evan isn't the only one with terrible secrets. His skeletons are mine too. And if they come out, he won't be the only one in prison. I'll lose everyone I love, and I'll end up just like my father. And I can't allow that to happen.

I slip the small camera from my purse that I brought from home. My moral lines are admittedly screwed, but spying on my friends isn't something I'm comfortable with. However, desperate times and all that. The camera fits right on top of the doorframe. Marin will never notice it. Hopefully, neither will Evan.

I sneak into the bathroom and flush the toilet before flipping the faucet on. Marin is mixing the noodles she's been cooking on the stove into a bowl with Italian dressing. "Can you chop those cucumbers and tomatoes?"

"Sure," I say. "I think you're supposed to chill those noodles first, though."

"Are you?"

I pause to think for a second. "Actually, I'm not sure," I say with a laugh. "Want me to ask Dan?"

"Absolutely not. I don't have time for that. They'll chill in the freezer until everyone else gets here."

"Let's not tell Dan, just in case. He'll have a stroke."

"I'll tell him right after he finishes a big serving of my freezer-chilled pasta salad." We both cackle at the image. Dan is a food snob, though he denies it. It's why he owns his own restaurant. Or maybe it's the other way around.

After adding the chopped vegetables to her large bowl, she puts Saran Wrap over the top and sticks it in the freezer. "Need me to take anything outside?" I ask.

She bites her lips between her teeth, circling the room. "Yes . . . can you take the plates and silverware out? There's a table set up, but you'll have to put the tablecloth down first."

"Got it." I grab the bags Evan brought in and hurry outside.

They both look up when I exit the house. It's disorienting. Having both their eyes on me at once. Like two different dimensions colliding into one. "Hey, babe," Dan says at the same time as Evan says, "Hello, Scarlett."

"Uh, hi," I say to both of them. I hold up the bags and start toward the table. "Setup duty." The tablecloth is a plastic one still in its wrapping. I tear it open. "What are you guys chatting about? Chicken-grilling techniques?"

"Butchering, actually," Evan says.

I swallow.

"I was telling Evan how we get our meat for the restaurant from Gilbert's farm in town."

Still unsure why that led to a conversation about butchering, I nod like it makes total sense. It's not like we butcher the animals ourselves. Bobby Gilbert delivers the meat fresh every week. So I know he's just trying to mess with my head.

Crystal and Isaac arrive with their two girls in tow, along with a few others. I watch Evan carefully as he works his way through the guests. Every time he shakes someone's hand, I feel him permeate my new life a little bit more. I hate him for this. For tainting the one good thing I've ever been able to keep.

I sit in a lawn chair across the yard, trying to keep my eyes on Evan while simultaneously fiddling with my phone. It isn't the most social behavior, but the app I need just finished installing, and now I have to attempt to guess Marin's username and password. It takes me three tries and I'm in and viewing all of Marin's health data from her athletic watch she wears night and day. So besides when she's in the shower, I'll know that her heart is still beating.

Evan moves over to the grill and begins moving things around with a set of tongs. Dan and Isaac walk over, and they all begin chatting. Crystal sits down beside me and launches into a story of her youngest at the park the other day, but I can't hear the words anymore. I glance between them and Crystal, trying my best to appear like I'm paying attention.

And then I watch, as if in slow motion, as Evan glances at me before moving the metal tongs in his hand to press against Dan's arm. I can see them glowing red from here.

Dan shouts. "Shit!"

"Oh, God. I'm so sorry, man. I wasn't paying attention. Are you okay? Let me get you an ice pack or something." Evan scrambles like it was a sincere accident. But while everyone's attention is on Dan, Evan's eyes meet mine, and I'm met with the familiar smirk he wears when he inflicts pain on someone. Then his mouth moves, and I read his lips. *Still three days.*

I follow Dan inside, where he runs his elbow under cold water for a few minutes. "I'm fine, guys. Really. It's not bad," Dan says. But I look at the burn and already see a blister forming.

"We should get some antibiotic cream and a bandage on it, at least," I say. I look over my shoulder to Marin, who makes a face.

"I have ibuprofen. Will that help?"

I turn back to Dan. "Let's head home and get it taken care of."

"Nah, we don't have to leave. I'll let it air out, and we can take care of it later. It's really not that bad."

I'm torn between wanting to get Dan away from Evan and wanting to stay to keep an eye on him. The burn isn't terrible. But what if we stay and Evan takes another crack at trying to hurt him? What if it's far worse next time? What if we leave and he targets Marin next? Or Crystal, Isaac, or their girls?

And then there are his words: still three days. Is he saying I still have three days? He is letting me know that not only is his game still on, but the timer has been reset. I'm not sure what to think about that.

Everyone is looking at me like I'm overreacting to Dan's burn, and to them, I guess I am. It's infuriating, and I want to throw something at Evan's face for putting me in this position. Something like a knife.

CHAPTER NINETEEN

Scarlett — Then

Tomorrow is Evan's birthday. I've been thinking about it for days, and I still haven't come up with an idea for a present. He's in classes most of the day and therapy right after, so I have the day to figure it out. But after a few hours of brainstorming in the dining hall, I still have nothing.

Someone sits beside me. I look over to see Miss Pamela. "What is it?" she says.

I shrug. She doesn't like Evan much. I don't think she'll want to help with his birthday present.

"Bull. What's wrong?"

I sigh and give in to her. "It's Evan's birthday tomorrow, and I don't have a gift for him."

She nods slowly and looks up like she's thinking. "I need to make a trip into town. Come with me and find something."

"Really?"

"Yep." She stands up. "Come on. Go get ready. I'm not waiting on you."

I grin and run to my room. We get a small monthly allowance here, but most people spend it the minute they get it on extra clothes, games, books, or whatever. I never know what to buy, so I have a few months' worth saved. I grab it from my desk drawer and run to meet Miss Pamela at the front door.

We don't get to go into town often. Most of everything comes to us. School. Therapy. Church. Even clothes we can buy. They come in a big truck and set up in the dining hall, and we're allowed to shop with clothing tokens or our allowance. So being able to leave the house today is a treat I wasn't expecting.

Miss Pamela drives us to a Target. I follow her as she shops for the things she came for before she finally looks at me. "Do you have any ideas of what you'd like to get him?"

I chew on my lip and think. Evan is hard to buy for. I know he likes to read. But the books I think he'd actually like probably wouldn't be approved by Miss Pamela. He likes baseball. "What could I get him for baseball?" I ask.

"Hmm . . . He doesn't have a Cubs hat. I think he'd like that."

I nod, smiling. I think he would too. He only has one baseball cap, and it's a plain black one. He loves the Cubs, and we don't get that kind of stuff here to buy for ourselves. It's perfect.

When we get back to the house, Miss Pamela goes in first to make sure the coast is clear. She waves me in, and I giggle, feeling like a secret spy. She tells me to go hide it in my room, and I do. I look around and decide I will wrap it with notebook paper and tape. I've just gathered my supplies when someone knocks on my door.

I open it to find Miss Pamela holding a stack of red boxes. She comes in and sets them on my bed. "I had these lying around. You can find one that fits the hat."

"Thank you," I say. "Do you want the others back?"

She shakes her head. "Keep them. Maybe you can find something to do with them because I have no use for 'em. They're just crowding my closet."

I thank her again, and she leaves. I find the perfect-sized box to put the hat in and step back to take a look at it. I'm proud of my gift, and I can't wait to see his face when he opens it. He's going to freak out.

There are three more boxes, and Evan is in therapy for another forty-five minutes. I sit on the edge of my bed, kicking my feet while I think of how to use them. It only takes a second to come up with an idea. I climb down off my bed and onto my knees, shoving the mattress up.

There's lots of paper under there. On one side, there are letters from my dad. I've never read them. Never even opened them. On the other side are letters I wrote to my dad. They're folded up and shoved into the corner. I don't plan to send them ever. Sometimes it just helps me to feel like I can talk to him. Tell him things, like I used to. My therapist said it was a good idea and told me to keep doing it. So I have.

I scoop the letters I wrote out and put them into one of the boxes before scooting it beneath my bed. I decide to leave my dad's letters beneath my mattress. I don't know why, but I don't want to touch them. I will have to think of what to do with the other two boxes.

Evan and I spend the evening playing Phase 10 in the dining hall. I have to try hard to hide my excitement over his gift so I don't ruin the surprise. Evan can tell all my feelings so well, but I think I'm getting better at hiding them. When he doesn't ask what I'm hiding by bedtime, I feel even more excited about being able to trick him.

The next morning, I swing my bedroom door open before Evan is able to knock. I'm grinning and bouncing on my toes, and it makes him smile. "You're happy today."

"Happy birthday!" I jump into him and hug him, only feeling embarrassed once our arms are around each other. I pull away. "I got you something."

"Really?"

I lead him to my desk and hand him the red box. "Open it!"

He does, and his face doesn't disappoint. He is just as happy as I thought he'd be, and it makes me giddy all over again.

"This is awesome. Thank you. How did you get this?"

"It's a secret," I say.

He laughs and puts it on. It looks nice on him, and I tell him so. His eyes catch on something behind me. "Is this another surprise?" he asks, moving past me. He has his hand on the other red box under my bed by the time I realize what he's talking about.

"No!" I shout. "That's nothing." I move around him and push it back under the bed. His face is a big question mark. "Let's go eat," I say. "I'm starving."

CHAPTER TWENTY

Evan — Now

The barbecue could have gone better, if I'm being honest. I didn't get as much time with Scarlett as I wanted. But I did get to have a nice little chat with ol' Dan. He's so open with his life, telling me all about his family who live nearby, his pride and joy that is his very own restaurant, and his lovely *girlfriend.* He told me how she's on the cautious side, always has been.

He doesn't know that I'm the reason she has always been careful and afraid. I like knowing that she's spent all these years looking over her shoulder for me.

But then I grew bored of Dan and couldn't help having a little fun at his expense. Scarlett overreacted. It's not like I was going to kill him right there in front of everyone. She used to be that way when we were younger. Dramatic and wearing every fear plainly on her face. I taught her better. Seems she's let all those good lessons go to waste.

"Can you grab this for me?" Marin calls from the back door. I pretend not to hear her over the running water where I'm rinsing off dishes from the barbecue. "Evan?" she calls louder. I sigh and turn off the tap.

"What was that? Are you calling me?"

"Yes. Help, please." She sounds strained, and something hits the ground, which prompts her to curse. I run over and grab the dishes from her arms.

"Sorry, love. I couldn't hear you over the sink."

She smiles. "That's okay. Thanks for helping me." I nod at her and carry the remaining bowls and plates to the counter. It's late now. The sun went down while Marin napped. She claimed to be drained from the work of setting up and socializing. I guess I could have started cleaning up while she slept, but I didn't think it should be all on me.

"I need to text Dan and make sure he's okay," she says, collapsing onto the couch, even though the cleanup isn't complete.

"I'm sure he's fine, Marin. I apologized a dozen times. I feel horrible, but it really was just a small burn."

"I know." She reaches out and squeezes my arm. "It would just be rude not to check in."

She hardly seems to care about being polite in almost any other circumstance, and her insisting she needs to be polite to check on *Dan's* little burn irks me. I don't know what everyone sees in this guy.

I walk toward the bathroom, calling over my shoulder, "The dishwasher should be ready to be loaded."

I nearly miss it. The camera sitting atop the doorframe that leads to Marin's bedroom. Oh, Scarlett. You'll have to do better than that. I pass beneath it and try not to pay it any attention. Should I take it down? Or should we have a bit of fun?

I vote fun. It's the perfect way to relieve some of the irritation I'm feeling.

The breakers to the house are in the garage. When I come back into the living area, Marin's back is turned to me, and she's stuffing half a dozen glass bowls into the dishwasher. I slink across the room and quietly pull open the garage door. The breaker for the main power is clearly labeled. I switch it off and have to fight back a laugh when Marin shrieks.

"Evan? The power went out. Where are you?"

I roll my eyes. I can *see* that the power went out, but thank you for the confirmation. I keep quiet, stepping back into the house. It's pitch-black, and it's the only time I've found this tiny town beneficial. You'd never have this kind of darkness in a house in the city. I hear her bump into something, and she calls out for me again.

Does Scarlett's camera have audio? I hope so.

I grab a quarter from Marin's change bowl on the counter and whip it across the room. I'm not aiming for her, but I wouldn't be mad if it hit her either. It doesn't. It smacks against the counter, making a loud noise that makes Marin shriek again.

"Evan! Where are you? Was that you?" She hits her foot on something and swears.

I *kind* of want to throw a knife and see what happens. I don't really need Marin anymore. Not really. I've made contact with Scarlett. Unsettled her. She has two more days to make a decision. I can go home and wait.

But not having Marin to use later might prove to be a bad decision. And it would piss Scarlett off before I really need to. *Ugh!*

"Marin? Hold on, let me check the breakers. Are they in the garage?"

"Yes!"

"Okay, stay where you are so you don't get hurt."

I flip the power back on and feel like a sullen child. That could have been far more fun.

CHAPTER TWENTY-ONE

Scarlett — Then

Evan lies next to me, brushing my hair from my face. It sticks to my cheek, wet with tears. "It's going to be okay. I'll visit and get busy setting up a life for us outside of here."

"A year, Evan. It's a whole year." My lip trembles, and I bring my hands up to cover my face.

I feel his lips against my head. Then he pushes my hands aside, and our lips connect. I don't feel like kissing right now, but the response is automatic. My heart races, and I arch into him. Our bodies fit like puzzle pieces.

The door swings open. "Time to go, Mr. Brewer."

Evan pops up, looking embarrassed, though I know he isn't. "Yes, Miss Pamela." He nods at her, a charming smile, and looks back at me. He wants me to see him out. I get up and wipe the remaining tears from my face. Miss Pamela squeezes my shoulder and offers a small, comforting smile.

She lets me follow Evan to the front door. He stands in the open doorway, looking at the house over my shoulder. "It's going to be weird living somewhere else," he says.

The lump in my throat swells.

"You have all the tools you need to succeed," Miss Pamela says from behind me, and Evan nods. And he does. He was accepted into a schooling program when he was just sixteen. He took courses in pharmaceuticals, and now, at only eighteen, he has a job lined up with a company in Chicago, and Miss Pamela helped him get an apartment there too. It's only thirty minutes from us, but it might as well be on the other side of the country.

I leap into Evan, and he catches me like he knew it was about to happen. I hide my face in the crook of his neck and focus on the smell of him. On the pressure of his arms against me.

Evan kisses me, and even though it's against Miss Pamela's rules and she's standing right there, she doesn't say anything. Then, he turns and walks to the road, where a car is waiting to take him to his new home. When the car pulls away, I can't control my sobs.

"I know it's scary," Miss Pamela says. "But Evan will be okay."

I know he will. Evan is always okay. He's capable and confident. I'm the one who isn't okay. Who isn't prepared to be without him for an entire year until it is my turn to age out of the group home.

Miss Pamela pulls me into her, and I lean into her strong, sturdy frame. "Shh. It's okay. It's all going to be okay. Don't you worry."

She rubs my hair and makes no move to end the interaction between us. She lets me cry for as long as I need. When the tears finally subside, I straighten and look at her pitifully, hoping she'll tell me what to do next.

"Okay, okay. That's enough crying and comforting. It's time to suck it up now." She lifts my chin and smiles to soften her words. "Use this as an opportunity to make new friends. Find out who you are on your own. You and Evan have been inseparable since you first came here. And he can be . . . a bit of a powerful personality. Rise to the challenge of standing on your own two feet."

I stare at my shoes, considering her words.

She bumps her arm into mine. "You're stronger than you give yourself credit for."

I watch her amble down the hall and disappear into her office. She's wrong. I've never been strong. Especially on my own.

I walk to the kitchen, wanting something to drink and the noise of people. Evan has been my only friend, my only companion, for six years. I've only needed to be without him for small periods of time when he was in therapy classes or one-on-one schooling. I have to do what Miss Pamela said and make friends with someone. I don't have a choice. I can't be alone.

I sit on the front porch, watching groups of people pass me. Whisper. Laugh. It feels like my first day all over again, despite the fact that this has been my home for the last six years. I've been here almost as long as I was with my father.

Megan and Hattie appear before me as if by magic, which would confirm my suspicions that they're a couple of witches. I'm only half-joking. I've heard weird chanting coming from Hattie's room more than once.

"All alone now, huh?" Megan says. She sneers, and I wince. Her skin is shiny, littered with angry red mountains that look threatening when she makes those types of facial expressions. Puberty hit Megan and Hattie in opposite ways. Hattie is all well-placed curves, flushed cheeks, and long hair. Megan is . . . not that. I wonder if Izzy would have fallen somewhere between them.

"She's still too good to talk to us," says Hattie when I don't respond.

"I thought the question was rhetorical," I say with a bored sigh.

Megan leans forward, bringing her pimples into my personal space. "You don't have your boyfriend here to defend you anymore. You might want to watch your fucking back."

"And you might want to *wash* your face. And your teeth, for that matter." I make a face and scoot backward. "Brush your teeth if you're going to be talking so close to other people's noses."

She draws her arm back like she's going to hit me.

"Ladies." Miss Pamela's booming voice comes from behind me. "Comforting Scarlett on the departure of her friend?"

"Yes, Miss Pamela," they say in unison, and I almost laugh.

"Get out of here, you damned vultures," Miss Pamela says dismissively, shooing them away.

Megan eyes me as they start down the walking path. I hear the groan of wood under Miss Pamela's feet as she goes back into the house.

I let out a breath and bite my trembling lip. Try to control my breathing. Evan has taught me to show only the emotions I want to show and to hide the rest. I'm not as good at it as he is. I never see him break. I can hold it together for the most part, but I always break eventually. I just have to hope it only happens when I'm not around the person I'm trying to deceive.

I focus on my breath. Think about things that calm my mind. What color I'll paint the walls in our apartment once I age out and move in with Evan. Maybe I can convince him to get a cat. I'd name it Marcus.

Rosa comes from around the side of the house and hops up the stairs gracefully. She is a year younger than me and arrived two years after me. I always thought we'd make good friends, but Evan wasn't interested in having someone else hang around. She's a petite and meek girl and spends most of her time alone out back, drawing and writing in a notebook she keeps pressed to her chest.

I decide I'll go out back tomorrow and try to start up a conversation.

Night has come too soon. In the last six years, I've only slept through the night when Evan was beside me. I very well might go insane this next year.

But darkness falls like it always does, and now I lie in bed, feeling like an elephant is sitting on my chest. Loneliness chokes me. My breaths come in quicker and shorter until I think I may mercifully pass out.

Eventually, my breathing slows, and the tears stop. I still feel like I want to cry, but I'm dried up. How pathetic I am. How weak.

A memory of my dad seeps into my mind, random and unwelcome. I do my best to keep thoughts of him at bay, but he sneaks up on me during long nights when sleep won't come. I remember being woken up by a scream in the basement. I was only nine or ten, just a while before the police took him away.

I crept from my room, down the hall, and toward the basement door. I was never allowed to go down there. Especially while he was working at night. But I was afraid, and I wanted my dad.

But before I could open the door and call down to him, he blew through the door, looking more upset than I've ever seen him. He was surprised to see me standing there in the kitchen, just a few feet from the door. But the surprise faded from his face, and it was replaced with what I understand now to be anguish. He fell to his knees and sobbed.

When I stepped forward and put my hand on his shoulder, he pulled me into him and cried so hard he could barely breathe. I was too afraid to ask him what was wrong, and he never told me. But the next day, he made me pack up my things, and he dropped me off at some house I'd never been to. He kissed my forehead and told me he loved me, and a woman I didn't know helped me out of his truck.

I sat on the woman's porch and cried until she made me come inside. A few days later, my dad picked me up. I heard him telling the lady that he couldn't do it. He couldn't be without me. I was happy because I couldn't be without him either, and I didn't know why he was even trying to be.

But I think I understand now. That he was trying to let me go because he knew he was a monster. Back then, I saw it as love that he couldn't let me go. But now I see it for what it really was. Selfishness.

I must've fallen asleep because I wake up with a start. I open my eyes, but I can't see anything. Can't breathe. I reach out and grab bare arms. Dig my nails in. Then yelp in pain when dull, hard blows hit my stomach and ribs. Sharp, spidery pain spreads across my torso. I flail, whip my head to the side, and I'm able to suck in a breath of air. A pillow. It's a pillow pressed to my face. A searing sensation hits me in the stomach, and for a terrifying moment, I think I'm being stabbed.

But no. It's pinching. They're pinching my skin, and for some reason, the childishness of it makes me laugh through the awful pain. Because as childish as it is, it hurts. A lot.

The attack finally ends, and I jolt up, throwing the pillow aside to see a flash of frizzy brown hair and a spindly elbow disappear behind my door. I didn't have to see any part of her to know who it was. I may not have any friends, but Megan and Hattie are my only enemies.

CHAPTER TWENTY-TWO

Scarlett — Now

Dan forced me out the door to go for a run when we got home. He said I was all wound up, and he wasn't wrong. I feel a bit better after three miles and a cool shower. Dan is on the couch watching TV when I come downstairs, and I snuggle up to him with my still-damp hair. He shifts and puts his arm around me, pulling me into his side.

"Feel better?" he asks.

"Much."

He picks up the remote and goes to a show we've been watching together. "Should we get a fire going?" he says.

I tell him yes, and he gets up to start the fire, bringing my favorite fuzzy blanket with him when he returns. The normalcy of the evening is so out of place, considering all that has happened. All that *is* happening. Could my birthday really have only been the day before yesterday? It doesn't seem possible.

Dan's grip on my hand opens, and I extend my fingers to press our hands together, palm to palm. I've always loved the way his hands dwarf mine. I love the feel of old burns turned to callus from years of cooking over hot stoves. Mostly, I love the way they always find mine. It's hard to imagine never being able to hold his hand again. The thought sits like a rock in my chest.

Difficult doesn't even begin to describe how hard it was to walk away from Evan. I was attached to him, heart and soul. But over the years, after finally having extended time out from under his influence, I started to realize our love was mixed with obsession and dependence, and I really don't know if we ever truly loved each other.

I used to think that love was not being able to live without someone. That's what the songs and the romance novels say. But, I think, sometimes love is more subtle than that. Sometimes it is a quiet contentment with another person. Not so much a raging storm but a stoic resolve. Love is not the chaos and heightened emotions that it is so often compared with.

Love is Dan. The man I know will be home at the end of the day. Who I know will be happy to see me. Who I know I can unburden the day's stresses and receive his, making each other's loads a little lighter.

A soft snore informs me that Dan has fallen asleep. I reach for the remote and pause our show, nudging his shoulder. He groans in question, unaware that he's drifted off. "Head up to bed, babe. I'll be up in a bit."

He leans over and kisses me before shuffling upstairs. My heart is heavy, and I want to lie next to Dan, but my mind can't settle. Morning means I have two more days before Evan's ultimatum is up. Not to mention, he is with my best friend right this moment. I grab my phone and pull up the app that shows all my camera feeds. The one I set up in Marin's house is dark but live.

She wouldn't be asleep yet. Marin is a night owl like me. I pull up the fitness tracker app that I have connected to her watch. Marin's heart rate is high. I text her phone, hoping for a reply but figuring I won't get one. I turn the volume up on the camera just in time to hear her scream.

I move for my shoes and car keys in an instant. I hear her call out for Evan. He's messing with her. But to what extent? I'm in my car and halfway down the block when I hear Evan. I park at the stop sign and watch the camera light up again.

I can hear them both talking. Evan explains that the breaker must have tripped. But I know it was him wanting to scare her. Scare me. Evan's face fills the camera screen. *Fuck.*

He wags his finger at me, kisses the lens, and then the feed is shut off. I get a reply from Marin telling me her power just randomly went out.

Are you ok?

Yeah. Thankfully Evan hadn't left yet.

Is he leaving?

I'm grateful for text right now so she can't hear the hopefulness in the question.

Yes): he has a work thing in Louisville tomorrow.

Is that true? Or just a lie he told Marin?

There's only one way to find out.

I drive out of town and park at the gas station by the entrance to the highway. I should have put a tracker on his car, but knowing Evan, he'd find it and mislead me anyway.

I text Marin back.

Oh no that sucks. Does he at least get to head out in the morning?

Three dots dance below her name. Then stop. Come on, Marin. Two minutes pass before she finally replies.

Nope. He just left. Boo.

Perfect. Now I just have to wait and see whether he gets on going northbound or south. Or at all. Ten minutes pass, and I think I see his car approaching. I send out a silent prayer that he doesn't need gas. It's late, and there is only one other car parked at the gas station, which I'm assuming is the attendant.

He turns onto the highway. Southbound. The route to Louisville. I sag in relief, and an overwhelming sense of déjà vu washes over me. This moment is all too familiar.

CHAPTER TWENTY-THREE

Scarlett — Then

Rosa sits in the same spot out back. I walk toward her, trying not to wince at the pain in my ribs. "What are you drawing?" I ask from a short distance. She jumps and looks around like she doesn't know who's talking to her. I point at her sketch pad.

"The house," she says, and I barely hear it.

"Can I see?"

She angles the paper toward me, and I move closer and sit beside her. "It's beautiful," I say. And it is. It's very realistic, coming to life with the colors she's working in.

"I drew this one too. Of Miss Pamela." She flips back a page and hands me the drawing pad. It is incredible how clearly she's captured her. It could almost be a photograph. She somehow shows her sternness and good nature in the pencil strokes.

"I bet she'd love to have this," I say. "You should show it to her."

"You think?" She looks down, and I know she's feeling self-conscious.

"I do. She would love it."

Rosa smiles and nods. "I'll give it to her at lunch."

We make small talk for a while, and then I stop talking to watch her draw. When it's time for lunch, I encourage her to go to Miss Pamela's office to show her the drawing. I tell her I'll meet her in the dining hall. I just have to run to my room to change. I've sweated through my shirt, and I feel icky.

By the time I make it to the dining hall, I'm feeling the most optimistic I have felt since Evan moved out yesterday morning. I never really had a chance to make friends with Evan around, and now I have someone new to talk to. Maybe Miss Pamela was right.

But my optimism is extinguished just as soon as it struck up. I walk into the room with a plate of food to find Rosa sitting at the back table. But she isn't alone. Megan and Hattie sit on either side of her. They're all smiling. Rosa looks up, and our eyes meet, but she quickly looks away, and I feel my insides twist.

I take my plate of food to my room and stay there the rest of the day.

The next morning, I sit on the edge of my bed, wiping sleep from my eyes. I slept hard, and my neck aches from the position I stayed in all night. I stand up and wince. My ribs are still sore, and I wonder when the pain will fade. There are loud voices in the hall. I listen through the door as they get louder, and I jump when a high-pitched scream echoes through the house.

Heart pounding, I fling open the door and run toward the crowd of people at the end of the hall. I hit a wall of backs just as I see Miss Pamela come out of her room, curlers still in her hair. People are packed in tight, and I have to shove my way to the front.

Hattie lies in a pool of blood, her legs splayed unnaturally. I look up at the wood railing on top of the stairs. It's a long fall. Megan is on her knees next to Hattie's body. And it *is* a body. That much is obvious.

Megan's screams sound animalistic. Miss Pamela pushes kids away, yelling something, but I can't hear her. Megan looks up. Our eyes lock, and a bubble of fear balloons in my chest. But something else too. Excitement, maybe. Megan turns feral when she sees me. She screams something that sounds like words, but they're too hard to make out.

She starts after me but slips in Hattie's blood and screams louder. Two men grab her and pull her away. Miss Pamela watches the scene, wide-eyed. She looks at me, and for a moment, everything goes quiet, and my mind blocks out the chaos. But then she looks away. Moves into action.

"You're a fucking psycho! You're a monster!" Megan shouts as she's pulled outside.

My ears ring with the echoes of her screams when the door closes behind her. Miss Pamela shoos everyone to their rooms with instructions to remain there until the end-of-lock-down bell rings. I walk back to my room and pretend not to hear the whispers from the other kids.

I open my door to retreat back to my room and jump when Miss Pamela grabs the edge of the door from right behind me. I step inside my room and feel myself shrinking as she stares at me for a long moment. "Tell me you had nothing to do with this," she says.

"I had nothing to do with this." I don't look away, though her glare makes me want to. After a minute, or maybe just a few seconds, she shuts the door. I can't tell if she believed me or not.

CHAPTER TWENTY-FOUR

Scarlett — Then

"You all packed up?" asks Miss Pamela from behind me.

I look over my shoulder just as I finish zipping up my suitcase. "Yes. I can't believe it's really time to leave."

Her hand rests like a weighted glove on my shoulder. "If you needed to stay for a few nights, I could make that happen."

I look up at her warm brown eyes and drooping skin that hangs from her cheeks like it's just as tired as she is. "I'm going to live with Evan. Why would I need to stay?"

She shakes her head. "I just mean, if you changed your mind about wanting to stay with Evan. You could stay here a few nights while we get another place arranged for you."

My hand goes to hers. Her skin feels like paper over bones. She's become frailer over the years. The stress of caring for rotten children slowly draining her life force. "I haven't changed my mind. It's where I want to be."

Sometimes it felt like this day would never come. And if it hadn't been for Evan teaching me how to get approved for release, it might not have. I could have been like one of the other sad, broken children turned into a sad, broken adult and moved from this place to an actual psychiatric facility.

Miss Pamela nods and looks around my empty room that is no longer really mine. The air is thick with unsaid words. I wait for them to come out because I know it's only a matter of seconds. She's never been able to hold her tongue for long.

"I don't think Evan is any good for you, Scarlett. You're not a bad person. You just can't seem to get away from them." She bites her lips, and I wait for her to get it all out. "I think it'd be a terrible thing for you to be with Evan. Like you just swapped your daddy out for him."

I flinch at her words. It's been a long time since anyone has mentioned my father. Even Evan caught on that he was a sore subject and stopped bringing him up. I used to think he was a good dad. A bad person but a good father. The older I got, the more I realized how messed up his idea of parenting was. The more I realized that I am the way I am because of him. Because of his blood in my veins and the way he raised me.

Evan says not to feel guilty about it. That it just is. But the guilt has eaten its way into my bones. It also just is.

"Evan isn't my dad. And I'm not eleven years old anymore either. I'll be fine."

She deflates in my peripheral. "Just know you can call me whenever you need to. If you ever do change your mind, I'll be there to help you. Okay?"

"Miss Pamela—"

"Okay?" Her eyes are intense, and I understand she needs me to affirm that I know I have a way out if I ever need one.

"Okay." I nod once and jump at the sound of a car horn from outside the front door.

Miss Pamela stands in front of me, looking sullen. She reaches out and tucks my hair behind my ear. I get a flash of red, and it stirs butterflies in my stomach. Miss Pamela let me put red streaks in my hair as an early birthday present, and I'm nervous to show Evan. I hope he likes it.

I stand awkwardly, not wanting to be rude to Miss Pamela but anxious to see Evan. Finally, she sighs and puts on a forced smile. "Happy birthday, Scarlett." She hands me a small black phone. "Put it in your things. Keep it turned off. My cell number is saved. It's prepaid and has sixty minutes loaded onto it. Just keep it hidden."

My first instinct is to roll my eyes. To tell her she's being ridiculous. And most of me does feel that way. But I find myself reaching for it, stuffing it into the center of my backpack between articles of clothing. I smile, tell myself I'm reassuring her. She's getting too old to worry like this.

"I'll stop by and visit," I say as I begin walking to the door.

"You better."

Evan leaps from the car when I step onto the porch. He grabs my bag and swings it onto his own shoulder as he takes my hand. The phone tucked away feels like a bomb. My stomach is tight, but I force it to relax. Focus my thoughts on the moment. On starting the rest of my life.

My smile grows, and I lean over to kiss Evan on the cheek. His excitement mirrors mine, and it helps to push any lingering feelings of uncertainty away. I love him. I trust him. He knows every part of me. The ugly, the weak. And he still loves me.

His job kept him busy this past year, and he wasn't able to visit nearly as often as either of us thought he would. I started to worry that he'd lost interest in me. Found another girl and left me behind. But that didn't happen. He's here, and we're finally together again.

I hop into the car and watch the big blue house and the big worried woman slowly disappear in the side mirror. I'll be back to visit. It isn't goodbye forever. No need to feel sad.

"Your hair," he says. "I love the red. It looks pretty on you."

I try not to look relieved. "Thank you."

When we turn onto the highway, I finally tune in to the atmosphere in the car. Evan is buzzing with excitement. It's contagious, and I sit taller in my seat. "I can't wait to see the apartment."

"That will come a little later. I have a surprise. For your birthday." He squeezes my hand, and I fight back the stupid grin, my cheeks pinched with the effort.

I try asking questions to figure out the surprise, but Evan is a vault. I sigh dramatically, sliding down in the seat. "The suspense is killing me!"

He laughs and steers the car to an exit. I bolt up and look around. "Where are we?"

He doesn't answer but doesn't have to. The signs say Lakeshore Drive. The beach. That's where he's taking me. Because on one occasion I mentioned that I'd only ever been to the beach once, and I loved it. I asked if one day we could live near the beach. Evan said Chicago isn't really the place for beachfront property. I didn't say that I'd meant one day leaving Chicago.

We park, and Evan runs to my door to open it for me. He pulls me along the parking lot and to the sand, where water crashes up just a few feet from us. I wish I had a swimsuit. Did Evan bring us something to swim in? He must have if he'd planned this surprise for me. I look over at him to ask but catch the top of his head as he bends down.

I begin to crouch down, too. To sit beside him on the sand. But stop when he looks up at me and pulls something from his pocket. What is he doing?

He grips my hand. I open my mouth, but he speaks first.

"Scarlett," he says, and he looks nervous, which is so out of character that it makes me nervous too. "I have loved you since we were kids. I can't imagine life without you. Will you marry me?"

My eyes finally focus on the gold diamond ring pinched between his fingers. I am speechless. My mouth still hangs open dumbly. Then, I look at his face. The face of the boy who sat next to me that very first day in the group home. The sun catches on his cheekbones, casting shadows on the rest of his face.

"Yes," I say. And I smile as his lips turn up and reveal a beautiful line of white teeth.

I glimpse a brief moment of surprise on his face, the only trace of self-doubt I've ever seen him experience. But it's gone in a flash, and he is spinning me, kissing me.

"Let's do it today," he says. "Right now. I don't want to wait."

Breathless, I answer, "Let's do it." Because I can't imagine spending another day not being his in every way that is possible. Because my heart is bursting from my chest in excitement and love and longing.

We spend the late afternoon waiting for our turn in the courthouse, gripping sweaty hands together, smiles never falling. We talk about the life we'll have like we did beneath the oak tree as kids. Traveling to Croatia and Singapore. Spending weekends at the farmer's market and at downtown coffee shops. Our evenings we'll spend at swanky whiskey bars. We won't have children. We decided that long ago. We have no business raising children.

When it is finally our turn inside the courtroom, I can't make my lungs work. Evan stands across from me in dark blue jeans and a black T-shirt. I love him so much it makes me dizzy and sends sharp sensations from my chest to the tips of my fingers.

Evan's eyes go glassy, and I can see myself in the reflection.

"I do," he says.

"And do you, Scarlett Wright, take Evan Brewer to be your lawfully wedded husband. To have and to hold from this day forward, for better, for worse, for richer, for poorer, in sickness and in health, to love and to cherish, until death do you part?"

"I do."

CHAPTER TWENTY-FIVE

Scarlett — Then

Saturdays are my favorite. As I'm sure they are for most people. Evan is always home on Saturday, where it is never a guarantee any other day. His work makes him travel all around the state. And he's been working for a promotion that will mean out-of-state travel. It's only a matter of time before he gets it. Evan always gets what he wants. So I cherish each Saturday before those are gone too.

I'm always home on the weekends. My job in public relations for corporate businesses is predictable in every way. The hours, the day-to-day. I enjoy the structure and routine of it. Maybe it's the chaos of my earlier life that has me craving constant familiarity. I tell Evan I hate my job. I wasn't sure why I'd said it when he asked me a few weeks after I started. I told him it bored me. But the pay was good, and so I'd probably stay there a while.

Evan's lessons of deception and manipulation have never stopped. We make a game of it. Going to bars and meeting other people, we pretend to be someone else entirely. It's fun. It allows me to use my creativity. But fooling people who don't know us from Adam isn't really a challenge. I wanted to see if I could fool the one person who seemed to know what I was thinking before I did. That's all it is, really. Fun. A challenge.

Evan has been quieter this morning. We walked to a coffee shop we haven't been to in a while for breakfast. The smell of baked bread mixes with gasoline and garbage. The hum of people passing and traffic on the street makes it hard to hear the people sitting next to me.

"Let's go back home," Evan says after he's finished his bagel. I nod and follow him onto the sidewalk, tossing two twenties on the table as I go. My stomach twists, turning my coffee sour in my gut. Something is wrong. Something is bothering him, and my mind spins wild possibilities of what it could be the entire walk home.

In the elevator up to our floor, he laces his fingers with mine, and my shoulders relax. He lets us into our apartment and sits on the couch. I follow him, sitting on the other end so I can see him well.

"I've been thinking a lot lately . . . about that trip into town when we were young. Your first one."

My eyebrows pull down as I recall the memory and try to breathe through the familiar heaviness in my chest. "What about it?" I ask dumbly.

"The man in the alley."

I wince but nod.

"I think about it all the time. And I don't know if he lived or died — wasn't important enough to write about in the newspaper — but I feel like I've been chasing that feeling. Do you know what I mean?"

I nod because it feels like what I'm supposed to do. I've thought about it a lot too. But not in a fond way, the way Evan seems to.

"I want to do it again," he says.

My saliva gets stuck in my throat. I clear it. "Set a homeless man on fire?"

"Yes — no. Not a homeless man. Not fire."

He wants to hurt someone again. Or kill them. The subject isn't out of left field. I am the daughter of an infamous serial killer. We've talked about death and killing plenty. We've done the things we've done.

Even so, his admission leaves me breathless. It's not like I haven't thought about it. When Iris, my manager, sends me passive-aggressive emails about expense sheets, I fantasize about pushing her into traffic. But I've never allowed myself to actually consider it a possibility. And now, here it is.

"I—"

"I know it's a big thing to just spring on you like this. But the urge is getting stronger. And I don't want to do it alone. We're partners. In all things."

Is he being honest? For the first time, I wonder if he has killed alone since he left Miss Pamela's.

"I don't know," I finally manage to say.

Evan nods. "Of course. Think about it. You don't have to give me an answer right now."

The central air kicks on, and I jump. Evan notices. My anxiety has improved a lot over the years. Or at least I've gotten better at hiding my tells. Evan moves across the couch and wraps his arms around me. I rest my head on his shoulder.

"I didn't mean to get you worked up." He smooths my hair, and I let myself relax. "This isn't something you need to stress about. Or feel guilty about. We're all mammals. Some mammals are hunters."

"Mammals hunt for food. Not for fun."

Evan pulls away gently, hands sliding to my thighs. "That's not true. Cats torture their prey for fun. Dolphins, lions, honey badgers. They all kill for the fun of it. To eat too. But also for fun. The self-hating do-gooders online are the ones that lie when trying to make people hate their own species, saying that humans are the only ones who kill for fun. It's bullshit."

I don't know what to say to that. I don't have the information to back up my claim because he's right. I read it on a post on social media once, and it stuck in my brain. I didn't even think to fact-check it.

Evan sighs and gets to his feet. "I love you, Scarlett. Whether you do this with me or not. But I know you. You know me. This is who we are, and the more we try to fight it, the worse our life will be. I don't want to live a lie."

I suck my lip between my teeth and nod. "I'll think about it. Okay?" I hate the sound of my voice. Dripping in weakness and self-doubt.

"Of course." He leans down and kisses me on the forehead. "I'm going to pop down to the gym. Do you want to join me or no?"

"I actually planned on a run today."

"Okay. I'll see you back here in a few hours. We can check out that new place in the loop you were talking about for dinner."

I nod. Smile. He turns and walks to the bedroom to change.

On my run, I think about the possibility of agreeing to Evan's insane request. A request I don't even fully understand. Does he want to hurt someone? Surely he intends to kill them. And then what? Will it end there? With one? Or is this the start of something I won't be able to stop?

When I reach the end of the path, I turn and run back toward the apartment. On the way back, I consider the possibility of telling Evan no. He will do it anyway. If he hasn't already. Would he leave me? Feel like I don't understand him the way he thought I did? Or like he doesn't know me the way he thought he did?

I feel sick by the time I press the twenty-third button on the elevator wall to go home. As I step out, my phone buzzes against my thigh. I slip it out while trying to fish my key from my back zipper pocket. I tap on a text from Evan. A video. I follow the link, reading the title of the video: *Animals who kill for sport (surplus killing)*.

CHAPTER TWENTY-SIX

Scarlett — Now

I don't know why I feel pulled to Chicago. It's a few hours away, and it's late, but Evan being out of town for even a little while means my loved ones are safe at home. This gives me the rare opportunity to be on the offense instead of defense. So I merge onto the northbound highway.

Seeing the apartment building I once lived in is jarring. It feels like another lifetime. *Was* another lifetime. I park in the parking garage and stroll into the lobby with my head held high and my shoulders back. The man behind the manager's desk is not one I remember seeing when I lived here. Seven years is a long time, and an apartment desk clerk is not usually a tenured job, so it makes sense. Though, I wish it was someone from before. Someone who might remember me.

Oh well.

"Hi, Lance," I say, reading his name tag. "I live in apartment 23B, and I've lost my key. My husband won't be home until next week to have a new one made. Would you — oh, hold on one sec." I pull my cell phone from my pocket and put it to my ear. "Hi, baby. No, not yet. I'm talking to Lance at the front desk now. I'll be safe inside in less than five minutes, don't you worry. I will. Okay. Okay. I love you too. Bye-bye."

I turn back to the desk. "He's all worked up and worried. He said to tell you he appreciates your helping me and to bring you down a nice tip before the end of your shift."

If I know Evan, he never took me off the lease of our apartment. It would be admitting I was really gone and never coming back, and I don't think his ego would allow it.

The poor man looks a little flustered. "One moment. 23B, you said?"

I nod, trying to ignore the nerves and the doubts. *He wouldn't have taken me off.*

He taps at the keyboard of his computer. "What did you say your name was?"

"Scarlett Brewer."

Please don't ask me for an ID. The only ID I have is for Scarlett Dwyer.

"Right. Okay. Let me grab the master keys."

I try not to look too relieved. "Thank you again for your help. You're a lifesaver."

I follow him to the elevator and continue to talk his ear off, so he doesn't have space to ask me questions or think about how he's never seen me here before. Maybe he's new. Because Evan hasn't had a wife here for seven years, and that's something someone working at the front desk should probably know.

He unlocks the door and smiles as he pushes it open.

"Oh, wait right there! Let me grab you some cash for being so helpful." I run to the kitchen drawer where we always kept our spare cash. There are two singles and a hundred-dollar bill. It's his lucky day. I hand him the hundred, and he stuffs it into his pocket.

"Thank you, ma'am."

"Thank *you*."

He walks away, and I shut the door.

I'm home. But not. I don't know how I feel. Only that it is surreal. Especially because not a single thing has changed since the day I left. Right down to my hairbrush left on the kitchen counter.

Our pictures still hang on the walls, and all my things are still where I left them. My old cell phone is plugged into the charger on the coffee table. When I step inside the bathroom, my makeup and face wash sit on the vanity. My toothbrush is still in the small black cup next to Evan's.

It's like the apartment has been frozen in time. Memorialized. I can see signs of Evan existing around the things I left behind. A different brand of shower gel than he used back then. A few dishes in the sink. But all my things have gone virtually untouched. Like I never left. It's unnerving.

The oddness of discovering Evan has kept all my things in place has distracted me for too long. There are cameras all over the apartment, and I've just been strolling around in plain sight. Evan will know I'm here now. Will he call the police?

I take my liquid eyeliner from my purse and begin coloring in the lenses of all the cameras I know about. Even though he'll know I'm here, I still don't like the idea of being watched.

I'm not entirely sure what I'm doing here or what I'm looking for as I start pulling out drawers and sifting through boxes in the closet. He threatened to turn me in. To make me take the fall for everything. So, he must have evidence of some sort. If I can find it and destroy it, it would mean I am safe from the threat of prison, at least.

The search feels futile, but I keep looking anyway. Maybe it's more of a retaliation for encroaching on my life. Invading his privacy because he has invaded mine. But I know I won't find anything. Evan is too smart to leave something that important in the apartment.

I'm almost ready to leave, sullen in my random, purposeless raid, when I catch sight of the crawl space door. If he's kept my hairbrush on the counter, surely he has kept the things I had in storage. I open the small door and crouch down to lean inside and pull the string for the light. Stacks of red boxes line the wall to my left. Gifts I'd given Evan over the years.

I push those aside and crawl deeper into the space. When I get to the back, I open a blue, plastic tote. And there is another red box. One that Evan never knew about and, from the dust that covers the lid, still has no knowledge of. I pull out the box and open the lid. There sits a stack of unopened envelopes addressed to Scarlett Wright, sent from Stateville Correctional Center, Inmate 78902, Luther Wright.

My father wrote me letters for years. I never opened a single one. At first, it was only because I knew it would make me miss him even more. And I was mad at him. He couldn't stop killing, even though it meant he'd one day get caught and he'd lose me. I hated that his love for me was not bigger than his dark urges.

It seems I like to repeat patterns.

Tucking the box of letters beneath my arm, I back out of the crawl space and turn the light off. I carry it out of the apartment, leaving everything I used to own behind once more.

I take the stairs down to the back entrance so I don't have to see the front desk guy. When I get to my car, I sit in the driver's seat, staring at the box. I wonder how many more he wrote that were never sent out after I called the prison and asked them to stop sending them to me.

I didn't want to deny his letters, but I was disappearing, and the thought of Evan receiving my letters was not something I could stomach. They were easy enough to hide from him. Mail was given to occupants of the Stark Home in private. I hid them under my mattress since Evan was only ever in my room during the night when they were tucked safely beneath us.

When I left the Stark House, my mail was forwarded to our apartment. But that was easy too. Retrieving the mail from our communal mail room was always my job. I was home far more than Evan was. So, I just continued to hide them.

If Evan knew about the letters, he would have forced me to read them so that he could read them too. He had been obsessed with my father in the way only a psychopath can be, and I wasn't going to let him influence my decision not to read them.

Though I'd let him convince me to visit him. Just the one time.

CHAPTER TWENTY-SEVEN

Scarlett — Then

"I don't want to do this."

Evan squeezes my hand and shifts to face me. "It's going to be okay. I'll be right there with you."

He doesn't understand that is part of the problem. But only part. I haven't seen my father since the day he was arrested. I have had zero contact with him after learning the truth about how I came to be. About how he raped my mother and then killed her after I was born. Every letter he ever wrote me still sits unopened and tucked away in a red box in my crawl space.

"You said he was a good dad. Why wouldn't you want to talk to him?"

Because it confuses me. To love a monster. To know that a man can slide a knife across someone's throat and watch the life leave their eyes and then tuck their daughter into bed and read her a bedtime story.

"It's time. Come on." Evan climbs from the car, and the bite of the cold air makes me shiver. On numb legs, I exit the warmth of the car and follow Evan up the sidewalk to the prison.

Illinois abolished the death penalty in 2011, so my dad will live out the rest of his life here. I think that's why we stayed here. Why Evan stays here. But I can't imagine living here with no end in sight. Death would be preferable.

Anticipation churns in my stomach. What will he say when he sees me? What has he been saying to me in his letters? Begging for my forgiveness? Or cursing me for abandoning him when he needed me most?

"You're panic spiraling," Evan says. "Stop. You're okay." He takes my hand and brings it to his lips.

We sit in a small space with steel dividers between other visitors and stare through a bulletproof glass, waiting for my father to sit on the other side.

Luther Wright. Notorious Illinois serial killer. The Chicago Harvester. Prisoner 78902. Dad.

He sits down, and my body forgets how to inhale. I hardly recognize him. His brown hair has been shaved down to his scalp. His once full face looks older with hollows at his eyes and cheeks. Wrinkles around his mouth.

My brain finally kicks in, and I suck in a breath.

"Hi, baby," he says, and his voice is the same.

"Hi, Daddy." It comes out a whisper, but he hears me. Smiles, though he still looks sad. His eyes go glassy, and I can't breathe again.

"How are you? Are you okay?" He leans closer to the glass, and I can't help but lean in too. Like a moth to a flame.

"I'm okay. Good." I nod, still unable to get my voice louder than a whisper. He puts his hand to the glass, and I mirror him. My heart aches with the urge to touch him. I'm nine years old again, and all I want is to hug my dad. Just once more.

Evan shifts beside me, and it breaks the spell. I pull away, letting my hand drop to my lap. Dad looks at him, seeming to realize his presence for the first time. He stares at him for a long minute, and I can't read his expression. "Who are you?" Dad asks Evan.

Evan clears his throat, scoots forward in his seat. "Nice to meet you, sir. I'm Evan Brewer. I'm Scarlett's husband." Evan has the voice he uses when he's trying to impress someone, and I wonder if it's because he is my father or because he's the notorious Chicago Harvester.

Dad's eyes slide from Evan to me. I try to smile, but my lips won't move. No one speaks. He just keeps staring at me, and I squirm in my hard, plastic chair. It feels like he's looking into my soul, and I want him to stop.

After a long, uncomfortable minute, he nods once. "It's my fault."

When I don't say anything, Evan looks between us, left out of the conversation. "What?" he says. "What's his fault?"

"I'm sorry, baby girl. I tried to stop. I couldn't—" He looks like he might cry, and I stand up. "It's my fault." The words fall from his mouth faster. He knows he is running out of time. My heart is lodged in my throat, and I need to leave. Need Evan to leave. "It's my fault, but it's your responsibility to change it. Do you hear me, Scarlett? It's on you. Don't you hide behind me. Or him."

His voice goes angry in reference to Evan. I grab Evan's hand and pull, but he resists. "We're done here," I say. We shouldn't have come. I knew it was a bad idea, and I let Evan talk me into it anyway.

Evan's attention is all on my father. Like he is his test subject and he's performing in an interesting way. He doesn't move to leave, and I can feel his energy shifting beside me. Getting nervous. Angry. This visit meant a lot to him, and it isn't going as planned.

"Scarlett. Just look at me. Please. Just look at me, baby," says my dad.

I can hardly see his blurry figure, but I can't help but listen. He is my dad, after all. I blink hard until I can see him clearly.

"You and I are not the same."

I can tell he doesn't mean this harshly. He means it in a good way. He is trying to tell me that he is bad and I am not, but he hasn't known me in more than ten years. My father has no idea who I am. What his influence and DNA have done to me. What the years without him have done. I yank hard on Evan's arm and leave the room. When I'm outside, I shut my eyes tightly. Trying to commit my father's face to memory. Knowing that was the last time I'll ever see him.

CHAPTER TWENTY-EIGHT

Scarlett — Now

When I climb back into my car, I start it but leave it in park. I push my seat back to have more room. The red box is heavy on my lap, like it holds more than folded pieces of paper. And I guess it does. Though guilt, regret, abandonment, anger, and love shouldn't have a physical weight to them.

I set the lid of the box in the passenger seat and dig to the bottom of the box. Some envelopes are thicker than others. I want to read them in order, but the outsides are not dated. With a deep breath that I keep in my lungs, I tear open a letter.

It's one page, front and back. And on the very top is the date. August 18th, 2002. Just over a year after he was arrested. I set the letter down and open another, place it below the last because it's from 2003. When I've opened them all and have them stacked from oldest to most recent, I hold them all in my hands to feel the weight of all his unanswered words over the years. They're even heavier than they were in the box, unopened.

I set the pile in my lap and begin to read.

June 30, 2001

Dear Scar,

I'm sorry. There is so much more to say. So much more you deserve to hear but more than anything, you need to know how sorry I am. And that I love you more than life itself. I won't ask for you to forgive me. I don't deserve it so I don't want you to do it. Okay? Don't you ever forgive me for what I did. Just know that I am sorry and I love you.

Love, Dad

I take a shaky breath. Fight the urge to shred the paper because part of me knows I'd regret it. He says he loved me more than life itself, but that isn't true. It can't be. Because he loved the darkness inside him much more. The high he got from carving out pieces of people and plopping them into jars. He knew it was wrong. He knew it would end with him in prison one day, and he knew what that would mean for me, and he still couldn't stop.

I shove the paper to the bottom of the pile and read the next one. And the next. And the next.

He didn't write every day, but he wrote a lot. He never missed a birthday or a holiday. He'd ask me questions about my life and who I was becoming. He'd tell me about his days, as mundane as they sometimes were. When it became apparent that I was not going to write back, he began theorizing about my life. Where I was and what I was doing. None of it was right.

Then I get to a letter he wrote after the first and only time I ever came to see him in prison. With Evan.

January 12, 2015

Dear Scar,

You came to see me today. I was so surprised to hear you'd arranged a visitation. I was nervous to see you. I spent the whole hour before pacing my cell. You looked beautiful. Exactly how I'd pictured you. I want to thank you for giving that to me though I know you didn't want to. I'll cherish the memory of seeing you for the rest of my days. Though it will be hard not to picture you as the girl you were when I left you. I wanted to say that first.

Now I know you never write me back and so I can assume you probably aren't reading these letters either. But they always deliver. They're never returned so I know they're getting to you at the very least. So maybe one day you will read this and so I need to say it if there is even a chance these words will get to you. I have no right to be fatherly to you, but I am your father.

You need to stay far away from that boy you came here with. I know he said you were married and that is another of my failures that will weigh on me until I stop breathing. Now I don't know what exactly he's done. What exactly you have done, but I could see enough. I could see how he was looking at me like I was the most interesting man in the world and not a disgusting monster.

I could see you too. Looking as guilty as you would when you'd sneak a cookie you weren't supposed to have. Hoping I wouldn't see the chocolate in your teeth. But I could see, baby. I could always see it and I saw it now.

That boy is like me, and I've heard the psychology theories on girls looking for their fathers in their partners, but you need to listen to me. Get away from him.

I told you before you left. You and I are not the same. It isn't you. I know your heart and I know it's good. It's always been good. I knew it the first moment I ever saw you.

All I ever wanted was a child. Someone to love me unconditionally. Someone I could be good for. I went into that adoption agency for the wrong reasons. I know that. I was looking for someone to save me, and instead, I found a beautiful little girl that I was cursing for the rest of her life. I promise I didn't know that at the time.

All I knew was your parents had died in a fire. The firefighters pulled you from your crib and you spent a week in the hospital. They made sure you didn't breathe in too much smoke. They tried finding family but there were none to be found. You'd just been put up for adoption that afternoon. It seemed like fate.

I know I never talked about your adoption. Or how you came to be at all. I wanted you to be mine. I didn't want you to question it or carry any kind of sadness about your real parents' fate. But I assume you know about it by now. You would have looked into it. Been told by the social workers. And I'm sorry it wasn't me who told you. It should have been me.

I stop reading. My heart slams against my rib cage. Yes, Dad. It should have been you. When I was a girl. When you could comfort me. Not in a letter that I wouldn't read until my thirties. Sobs work their way up to my mouth, coming from the depths of my stomach.

How could I have never known I was adopted? That my father was not really my father? How did it not come up with the social workers? Or in the required therapy at the Stark Home? And then there is my file that Evan sneaked into Miss Pamela's office to read. He told me my father abducted my mother. Impregnated her and then killed her after I was born.

The truth about my adoption would have been in that file. Evan lied to me. I feel sick. All this time, I believed I had some dark thing inside me that made me who I was. Like a trait I could change no more than my eye color. I believed Evan when he said I could not change who I was. I have done terrible things in the name of embracing who I am, and it has all been a lie.

Because I do not share the DNA of Chicago's most notorious serial killer. Whatever was wrong with him could not have been passed down to me. And so it was me who did all the awful things I've done. Not the part of my father that I allowed myself to hide behind. Just me. And Evan.

CHAPTER TWENTY-NINE

Scarlett — Now

It's late when I get back to Hoover. I guess it would be more accurate to say it's early. Three o'clock in the morning. Too late to try to go back to bed. Not that I'd be able to sleep with all the thoughts and lies and anger and disgust swirling around inside me.

I try to let myself inside the house as quietly as I can, but the alarm is set and lets out a warning beep when I open the door. I rush to the number pad and type in the code to prevent the thing from waking up the entire neighborhood.

Floorboards from overhead creak, and I wince, knowing Dan is awake. I shove the box of letters from my dad into the coat closet. Deep breaths. He can't see me all worked up. I have to calm down. He comes down the stairs just as I sit down on the couch.

He rubs his eyes with his fist and squints at me. "What are you doing?" he asks.

"Can't sleep. I went for a jog and just got back."

He shakes his head. "You're a crazy person. Do you need anything?"

"No, I'm good. Go on back to bed, babe. You have work in the morning."

"You sure you're okay? I can stay up with you." He crosses the room and crouches down in front of me, squeezing my knee.

I smile. "I'm sure. I'm okay, just restless. I'm fine. Promise."

He nods. "Okay. Try to come back to bed in a few. You still have a few hours before we have to be up." He gets up and kisses my head before heading back upstairs.

All I do is lie to him. All I could ever do is lie to him. You're not supposed to lie to the people you love. Especially not to this extent. It isn't fair. To know every piece of him while hiding so much of myself. The false history I've fed him over the years. None of it is fair.

And now, there are lies I've told because of the lies I was told. I never told him I was adopted. Because I didn't know. I never told him about my father's letters. He doesn't know anything about the things that make me who I am, and that is all my fault.

Who would I have been if I knew that my dad adopted me when I was a baby? What choices would I have made if I didn't believe the darkness in my father was passed down to me?

Evan knew it would have changed things. Even as young as we were when he snuck into the office to read my file, he knew what to say to manipulate me. He knew I was more likely to go along with his sick games if I believed I was rotten inside. Otherwise, he would have told me the truth.

When the sun comes up, I text Marin and cancel our brunch. I tell her I'm feeling a little under the weather. She texts back a few minutes later, asking if I want her to drop anything off for me at the house. I tell her no.

Dan comes back downstairs, showered and ready for his day. He pours his thermos of coffee like he does every morning. The routine that has been as stable as anything in my life. I never took it for granted. I always knew it'd one day get taken from me like everything else.

"Have a good day. Text me. I love you." Dan kisses me, and I hold on to him.

"I love you," I say into his chest.

He leaves, and I have to fight back tears. What a fucking mess I've made. What a mess *Evan* has made. As soon as Dan's truck pulls away, I grab the box of my dad's letters and move them into the bathroom ceiling compartment. Then I text Marin again and ask if she and Evan have plans to see each other again soon.

He actually called this morning and said he'd be back this afternoon.

But you'll be at work. Does he have a key?

He knows where the spare is.

Marin . . .

Scarlett . . . It's fine. Relax.

But, no. I will not relax. He'll be back in a few hours. And I'm running out of time. He's going to hang around to make sure I know that.

I go down to the basement, where I have my home gym setup. I take out my frustration on the punching bag for an hour before heading upstairs for a shower. Then, I head out.

Marin has talked about renovating the attic at least a dozen times. There is a really cute window that looks over the backyard, and she wants to be able to drink coffee near it on the weekends. But first, she needs to have the massive tree next to the window cut down or at least trimmed.

It's a good climbing tree. If Marin had wanted children, I would have tried to convince her to keep it. I liked to climb trees when I was younger. Before my world turned upside down and the police hauled away my father.

If Marin knew I'd climbed this tree, gaining access to her house through her cute attic window at least a handful of times, she might have me locked up. At the very least, she'd recommend antipsychotics.

I have an obsession with knowing all possible ways in and out of any place I'm in. I don't like feeling trapped. And I have a lot of free time.

Evan's car is parked out front. No doubt, he wanted me to see it. To know he was here. I stretch out from the branch nearest the window and push on the glass to open it. Using my upper body, I hoist myself up into the window frame and carefully step into the attic.

I can hear the television on downstairs, though just faintly. I listen hard for any other sound, trying to place Evan in the house. Walking along the edges of the attic and bending to the curve of the roof, I make my way to the stairs that lead down. Marin had them put in two years ago, replacing the pull-down ladder, which is as far as she's ever gotten in converting the space into anything.

I stand silently atop the stairs and listen again. The toilet flushes, and I have him located. I move quickly down the rest of the steps and slink around the corner into the kitchen as the bathroom sink turns on. A half-empty coffee mug sits on the counter. An empty one in the sink.

The bathroom door opens, and I pull my shoulders back, tilt my chin to be parallel with the ground. He doesn't see me at first. When he does, he jumps. Just a little. But enough to notice. Then he smiles.

"Hello, dear."

"Hi, Evan."

"Have you made your decision?"

"You lied to me."

His brows pull together. "What are you talking about?"

"My file. When you snuck into Miss Pamela's office to read it. When you told me about my mother. You lied to me." My heart picks up speed, and I can't keep the rage out of my voice.

Evan will think my show of emotion is weak. He'll think I can't help but lose control. I grab a knife from the block on the counter and fling it at him. He sidesteps it just before it buries into his chest.

"Woah. Okay, now. Let's calm down and talk about this like adults."

"Fuck you." I kick the chair in front of me at him, and as he flinches away from it, I swipe another knife and hurl it his way. This one nicks his arm.

He grins at me as he rubs the small cut on his outer shoulder. "Your aim needs work."

"Maybe," I say, and I pull my gun from my waistband, knowing I'm a much better shot than knife-thrower.

"Marin is going to have a lot of questions about why her boyfriend was shot by her best friend inside her house," he says quickly.

"She's going to have a lot of questions about a lot of things." I flip the safety off and chamber a bullet.

Evan lunges for me, but I see it coming and smash the heel of my hand into his nose before sliding out of his grasp.

"Jesus, Scarlett." He pinches his nose and tilts his head back.

"Why did you lie to me?" I'm full-on screaming now, tears streaming down my face and bile rising in my throat. "Why didn't you tell me I was adopted?"

His hand slowly falls back to his side. Blood drips from his nose, over his lips. "I wanted you to believe you were like him. And like me."

"Why?"

"Because I wanted you to be. I loved you."

I shake my head. The gun shakes in my hands. "You don't lie to people you love."

"You and I both know that isn't true."

"You only wanted to be with me because of who my dad was. You wanted to make sure I stayed with you."

He shakes his head. "I loved you long before you told me who your dad was. I *killed* for you before I knew. I was interested in your father, but I loved you regardless. Don't for one second think that isn't true."

"All the things I did . . ." I can't catch my breath. So many faces flash in my mind like a slideshow of my sickness.

I'm shaking and beginning to hyperventilate. Evan jumps at the chance to snatch the gun from my hands, but I don't even try to stop him because I'm certain I'm dying.

"What have I done?" I ask him. His eyes are concerned. Cautious and curious. He sweeps me into his arms, and my legs give out. He lowers us both to the ground, and he rocks me as I sob and choke on my tears.

Evan makes shushing sounds in my ear, running his hand over my hair. "I'm sorry, Scarlett. I'm so sorry."

He's not. I begin to pull away from him, getting myself under control.

"I'm sorry," he says again. "I didn't think you'd ever find out. I didn't think it'd hurt you this badly if you did."

"Stop lying to me!" I scream, and he flinches. "You're not sorry. You only care about yourself, and that isn't love. You don't fucking love me. You never did. But I did. I loved you, Evan. And every ounce of that love is gone now. I hate you."

The whites of his eyes redden, and a tear slips out. He gets to his feet, so I do too.

"If you need to blame me for the shit you've done, you go right ahead. That's why you're so upset, right? You think you wouldn't have done any of it if it wasn't for my lie. But there was no dark, terrible gene in you. You did it all yourself. And you can lie to yourself, but you can't lie to me. You act all holier than thou, but I know the truth. I know you enjoyed it. So *fuck* you too."

I suck in a breath like I've been punched in the gut. Evan stands with his shoulders squared like he's ready for a fight.

But I am not. Not anymore. Not right now. I turn my back to him and walk to the door.

On my way down the driveway, I pull my pocketknife out and crouch down next to Evan's car. I stab it into the tire, and it gives a satisfying *pop* before slowly lowering down. I go to the next tire and repeat the process. Then the next. Then the last. I hold up my middle finger as I walk in the direction of where I parked my car, knowing he is watching.

CHAPTER THIRTY

Scarlett — Now

I don't want to go home, but I don't know where else to go. My heart is still firing at a rapid rate, and my teeth feel like they might crack under the pressure of my clenched jaw.

He lied to me all these years, and I'm annoyed at myself for being surprised. For thinking there was a line he wouldn't cross. And his reaction to my anger . . . so cavalier. So self-righteous. Which shouldn't have surprised me either.

I slap at the steering wheel and shout into the silence. With shaking hands, I drive to the spot I told Evan about only three days ago. God, how has it only been three days?

I drop my head to my chest, and my shoulders begin to shudder under the sobs I try so hard to suppress. But they get the best of me, and I can't hold them back. Shame and guilt rack my insides. My cheeks burn like I've been caught picking my nose in public. Exposed. Gross.

Only that's not at all what I did. If only it were that innocent. But, no. I was exposed as the monster I really am. Not because of my father and the darkness I believed he passed down to me. In hindsight, I don't know why I ever thought that made it okay. Why did I believe my heinous acts could be excused because of who my father is?

I made every decision. I could have decided differently at any moment. So many moments. But I never did. I never chose differently. And that makes me a monster. It makes me a murderer.

CHAPTER THIRTY-ONE

Scarlett — Then

He groans as he starts to come to. I can't see my hand in front of my face. The cabin is so dark it feels unnatural. He'll be disoriented. Confused. He was just taking a piss in an alley outside a nightclub. Now, he's waking up with a headache in complete darkness.

The women scream almost immediately. They're more intuitive and realize they're in danger much quicker. A trait I believe is evolutionary. Built into our DNA over the centuries of being prey to the men around us.

This is the first man we've picked. I thought it would be easier. I thought maybe I wouldn't feel as guilty as I did with the women I listened to beg for their lives as Evan played his cat-and-mouse games, getting off on their fear. But I was wrong. It isn't easier. Least of all physically.

The man calls out, asking if anyone is here. I stay silent, tucked away in a hidden closet without a knob on the outside. My night-vision goggles lie on the floor beside me. There is an open slot I can see through if I stand on the built-in step. In case I want to watch. But I never do.

Evan whistles softly from the other side of the room. The man shouts. Demanding to know who the *fuck* is there. Evan only laughs in response. This enrages the man, and now I can hear walls and furniture being hit and knocked over. He has every disadvantage. He doesn't know where he is. He can't see. His head is surely in agony. He doesn't know his adversary can see him perfectly through his own night-vision goggles or that he wields a butcher knife.

I hear another shuffle, and the man lets out a shriek of pain, and I know Evan has sliced him for the first time. It will be shallow. Not life-threatening. Evan never performs the kill. He prefers to torture and to save the killing for me.

I push my fingers into my ears to block out the sound of the man crying. It's somehow worse than the women crying, and I don't know why. Two light knocks on the outside of my hiding spot have me standing up straight, controlling my breath. My signal.

I grab the goggles from the floor and position them over my eyes before pushing the door open, careful not to make a sound. My feet are bare, and I feel the warm blood under my toes, decide not to look down.

Evan sits in the chair in the corner of the room. The man lies on the floor next to the bed that is bolted to the ground. He is shaking, crying hard, gripping his side where one of Evan's cuts went a bit deeper than the others. I grab the knife from Evan's outstretched hand and move with purpose. I don't like to draw it out. Better to put him out of his misery.

In one quick motion, I pull his head back with a firm grip on his hair and slide the knife across his throat. He doesn't even have time to react. He bucks beneath my knees. I'd whisper something comforting into his ear if Evan wouldn't hear. But he's too close, and the cabin is too quiet. I start to stand when I'm stopped by the man's hand gripping mine. I freeze and look down. His face is turned to look at me, and his eyes stare straight into mine. Like he can see me, though I know he can't. It's too dark for him to see me. Right?

His grip loosens as the blood drains from his neck. I don't look away until the light in his eyes disappears completely, and all that is left is a dead, distant stare.

The bile is sour in my mouth as I swallow it down, burning my throat twice. On the way up and on the way down. I take off my goggles before flipping on the lights. There is a lot of work to be done.

I wanted to choose a man this time. This happened to him because of me, and my chest is tight with that knowledge. First, I remove his clothes. Then, I slice into his leg, sawing through his tendons that look like the skin of the salmon we had for dinner two nights ago. I fight back another of my stomach's attempts to turn inside out. His thighs are thick. Never missed a leg day.

Evan watches me from his chair across the room, a cigarette propped between his lips like a lover after sex. This is how it goes. He gets them here to the remote cabin Evan bought after I agreed to his request, and he watches as I take their life. He smokes as I begin cutting the body down to pieces. Sweat spreads over my skin, mixing with the man's blood. Cutting up a body is hard work, but I get better with each one. More efficient. The tools Evan bought me for our anniversary help a lot.

After his cigarette, he goes outside to prepare a spot for the body. He never leaves before I finish the dismemberment. When he's gone, I'm meant to shower. But before, I have to do something else first. And quickly so I'm not caught.

I yank out a few strands of the man's hair, making sure I pull from the root. I'm glad his hair is on the longer side. I take the Q-tip from my pocket and dip it into his blood, which is still wet on the plastic beneath his severed parts.

There is a plastic bag I stashed beneath the sink in the bathroom earlier today while I waited for Evan to return with our next victim. I put the hair and the Q-tip inside and then take it to my hidden closet to shove beneath the carpet beside my built-in step. It joins the other plastic bags filled with the hair and blood of every person we've brought to this cabin over the years.

I hurry back to the bathroom and start the water in the shower. But curiosity won't stop nagging me. I still don't know exactly what he does with the bodies. I assume he buries them. Maybe he burns them. Maybe there is water out there in the woods and he sinks their remains to the bottom. I didn't want to know before, but now, the not knowing scratches at my brain.

Leaving the water running, I go to the front door and peer outside, waiting for my eyes to adjust to the darkness. When they do, I can see the expanse of land between the cabin and the treeline. What if Evan is on his way back and he sees me out here? Will he suspect my act of rebellion?

No. I don't think he would.

Before I can think better of it, I run for the trees in the direction I once saw him go when I considered going with him to help. If he's burying them, maybe he goes to a different spot. I don't know.

But I only take a few steps into the woods before I know I've gone the right way. A dim light glows in the distance, and I can hear the sound of a shovel striking dirt. Does he bury his clothes and belongings with him? Or does he keep them? Trophies he doesn't share with me.

I'm about to head back to the cabin for my shower when the light starts moving toward me. I take a step backward. Can he see me? Should I run? He might get to the clearing before I can run the distance to get back inside.

My pulse races. I have to decide. But I've taken too long. I step outside the treeline, onto the grass, and sprint a few yards along the woods before launching myself back into the trees.

Evan will take the pieces of the man and bag them up before heading back into the woods. Then, he'll come back and clean up before making me a drink to enjoy while he showers. That is how it always goes. He'll hear the water I left running and assume I'm in the shower like I always am when he comes back to remove the body. When he comes back out, I'll go inside.

I watch Evan cross the open space and disappear inside. I pray he doesn't break the routine. That he doesn't all of a sudden decide he needs to tell me something or decide he can't wait to have me. That he doesn't open the unlocked bathroom door to find it full of steam but otherwise empty.

The seconds tick by, turning to minutes. I put my fingers to my mouth, absentmindedly about to chew on my nails. I freeze and let my hands fall to my sides. I haven't washed up. The man's blood is on my hands. Figuratively and literally.

Evan finally reappears with a large black trash bag slung over his shoulder like a perverted version of Santa Claus. I stay still until I see the light being hung on a distant tree. Then, I run as hard as I can until I'm inside the cabin again.

The hot water is already running out, so I have to wash off quickly. I'm breathing hard from the run and the excitement of yet another small, secret rebellion against Evan. I'm not sure why I do it. Or why it excites me. But each time I tell an undetected lie, hide evidence of our crimes, or observe him when he is unaware, I get a high that cannot be duplicated.

As I rinse the man's blood from my skin, I decide that this is the last time I will kill for him. He will have to do it himself if he wants to continue. Maybe I'll suggest we switch roles next time. I will find the person. Lure them. Then smoke and relax while he does the dirty work.

After my shower, I brush out my hair and wait for Evan to finish showering. I sip my drink, a dirty martini, as I sit at my makeup vanity. I've slipped on a new lace number I bought for tonight. The red lipstick I paint on my mouth matches the streaks of red I still wear in my hair.

The bathroom door opens, and I see Evan in the mirror behind me. My stomach flutters like it always does when I see him. I push thoughts of blood and body parts out of my mind and force myself to be here, in the present.

He's right behind me now, and he bends to kiss my neck. Goose bumps travel up my arms. I watch his reflection as his fingers slide up the nape of my neck, into my hair. He grips the strands and pulls my head to the side, getting more access to my neck, and I have to clench my thighs together.

His hand reaches around to cup my breast. His teeth graze my neck, and I close my eyes. Then, he is spinning my chair to face him. I open my eyes, and they lock with his. His stare is intense and hungry, and I want him so bad it actually hurts. He slowly gets onto his knees and pushes mine apart. He takes his time as he grabs one of my feet, massaging it as he places my leg over his shoulder, then the other.

I lose my breath as he lowers his mouth between my thighs. The teasing is relentless. His penchant for torture is not exclusive to homicide. I use my legs on his shoulders to arch up, needing more. He answers with his hands, with his fingers inside of me, pumping steadily as his tongue moves in slow circles. I'm panting, gripping the sides of the chair, so close to the edge, but then he stops.

He pulls me to my feet, spins me around gently, and pushes me onto the bed, face down. I pull my knees up beneath me and gasp, in pain and in pleasure, when his open hand connects with my ass. He's rubbing me again, and I move against his hand as we find our rhythm. Without breaking tempo, he slides into me, and I suck in a breath.

My moans make him move faster, harder. Another slap to my ass has me screaming curse words. He grips my sides, hard enough to hurt, and it sends me over the edge. I feel him begin to throb inside me at the same time, and I get a rush of euphoria.

We collapse onto the bed, and I try to catch my breath. Before I can, Evan is on top of me again, pulling off my lingerie. I jolt at his touch, still sensitive from moments ago, but he only grins devilishly and continues, never satisfied after a fresh kill.

CHAPTER THIRTY-TWO

Scarlett — Now

I must have fallen asleep in my car. My neck is stiff, and I feel disoriented. The time on the dash says it's 3.47 p.m., which can't be right. That would mean I slept nearly seven hours inside my car. I know I didn't sleep last night, but that's just insane.

I find my phone on the floor by my feet, and it verifies that it really is 3.47 p.m. Jesus. I roll my windows down and sit up straight, trying to wake myself up fully before driving home. Dan will be home by now and probably wondering where I am. I'm surprised not to have any texts or missed calls from him.

I put my hand on the shifter but pause when my phone vibrates. That must be Dan. I pick it up to call him, but the text is not from him. It's from another random unsaved number, and it's a picture that hasn't loaded. I tap on it to download the image, but nothing happens. This spot is a dead zone. I have to get closer to town.

I drive as quickly as I can, knowing Darryl will still be on patrol until five o'clock. Glancing at my phone every few feet,

I finally see the loading bar move and pull over to the side of the road. The picture opens, and it is Dan. He is sitting in our living room on our blue armchair.

The picture can only be from Evan. He is in my home. Alone with Dan. I tap on my camera app and wait for it to load. And there he is. Right there in my living room, talking to Dan. My tires spin in the gravel as I peel out. Darryl will have to follow me home if he tries to stop me.

CHAPTER THIRTY-THREE

Scarlett — Now

I grab my extra gun from beneath my driver's seat and run to my front door. I fling it open to find Evan and Dan sitting in the living room, chatting like old pals. They both look startled by my frantic arrival, but I know Evan's reaction is an act.

"What are you doing here?" I ask, eyes like lasers pointed at Evan.

"I was sitting at the car repair shop, waiting for my tires to be replaced. Some vandal sliced all four of my tires. I got bored and decided to check out downtown, and I ran into Dan. He invited me over for a drink. Hope that's okay."

I can tell Dan is confused by my bewilderment. I don't care to play it off anymore. I'm tired of the games.

"Scarlett, what's wrong?" Dan asks. His mouth pulls down at the edges, sensing something is not okay.

"It's my fault," Evan says before I can answer. Dan looks at him, confusion mounting. "The tension you're sensing is because Scarlett and I haven't been completely honest with you, Dan."

"What are you talking about?" Dan stands up. My heart pounds in my ears. I can't breathe. Can't speak.

But Evan can. And he does. "I've actually known Scarlett a long time. We used to be in a relationship. Though, I guess we technically still are. Right, my love?"

Evan looks at me the whole time he speaks, looking earnest and apologetic and everything he is not. I can't move my eyes away from him, too afraid to see Dan.

"You're full of shit," Dan says. "Look, man. I don't know what's wrong with you, but you need to leave." He takes a step toward him, his arm gesturing toward the door.

"Are you going to tell him, Scarlett? Or would you like me to continue?" Evan says, standing his ground.

"Get the fuck out of our house," says Dan.

I am still frozen. I could lie. Dan doesn't believe him. He wouldn't. Not over me. But we are not in a situation where lying can benefit me. Evan will not just walk out. He's revealing his hand. He's all in. Dan is in danger.

"Okay, if you insist," says Evan. His hand goes to his back pocket, and I flinch, thinking he's going to draw a gun. My hand goes to mine. But when his hand extends in front of him, it's a photo. Not a gun, but a weapon all the same.

I can see the picture from where I stand. Our wedding collage that Evan used to keep in his car. Or still keeps in his car. Dan is about to yell at him again, but his eyes catch on the photo, and recognition steals his voice. He sees me. Sees Evan. Us kissing in the courthouse. Our out-of-focus, smiling faces behind ringed left hands.

"You were married?" Dan asks, his voice a whisper.

"Still are, technically," says Evan.

Dan finally turns to look at me. I force myself to meet his eyes. It's the least I owe him. "That's why you wouldn't marry me. You're already married."

I open my mouth, but he cuts me off.

"Why didn't you tell me?" He spins to face Evan. "Why have you been seeing Marin?" His finger points to him and then to me. Accusing. "You both acted like you didn't know each other at dinner."

He shakes his head, and I want to throw up. Want to scream. To rip Evan's skin from his smug fucking face.

"I always knew you had secrets. I mean, obviously. I figured you'd tell them to me eventually. Maybe a little at a time—"

"Dan—"

"No. I trusted you. Even when you wouldn't talk about your past. Even when some of the details you did share didn't add up. Even as you hid shit in red boxes when you thought I was asleep. I still trusted you, and that's on me. I guess even in my wildest imagination, I never thought this is what you were hiding."

I open my mouth, but there are no words. Nothing I can say to make this better. Dan watches me, sadness in his eyes. "Who are you?" he asks, anger and pain laced in his words.

He walks for the front door, and everything in me wants to stop him, but another part wants me to tell him to run because I don't know if emotional is the only kind of pain Evan plans on inflicting today.

CHAPTER THIRTY-FOUR

Scarlett — Now

The door shuts behind Dan. It doesn't slam. Just clicks shut, and somehow, that is worse.

"Still hiding things in red boxes, are we?" Evan says, and my blood freezes. I hadn't quite caught that small admission by Dan. He saw me tucking my secrets away in my boxes, and I am not nearly as observant as I thought I was. And now Evan knows that I have something to hide.

Without forethought, I lunge at him. He isn't expecting it, so I'm able to get my hands gripped into his shirt before he can stop me.

I bring my knee up hard into his groin, and he folds in half. I throw my knee toward his nose, but I don't make contact. Instead, my feet leave the floor, and I'm staring at the ceiling. Evan grabs my wrists and pushes his weight onto me. I try to wiggle out from under him, but he's got me pinned.

He leans forward, his face close to mine. "Now, that was uncalled for," he says, his voice still coated in pain from the one hit I was able to get in.

"Fuck you." With all my might, I snap my head forward. The hit hurts me as much as it hurts him. I didn't use the right part of my head. But he lets go to grab his nose.

I fling myself up, grabbing his hair and yanking him to my right so I can get free. He shouts. Pain. Anger. I'm making him mad, but I don't care anymore. I get to my feet and steady myself. He recovers quickly and stands across from me, eyes alight with that familiar fire of the chase.

My stomach flips. But I am not an unsuspecting girl. I know who he is. What he is. How he moves. And I can hold my own.

He lunges for me, and I smash my palm into his nose, sidestepping his grip. He yells out his frustration but doesn't bother to staunch his bleeding nose. I take a step back, and he automatically moves forward.

In one quick movement, I pull my knife from my waistband and throw it at his chest. It flips end over end. Evan moves just in time, and it sticks into my wall. The knife seems to have pushed him over the line. His expression is no longer one of a fun challenge. He's done with this.

He leaps at me again, and the movement is faster than before. My ears ring before I realize what's happened. The pain from his punch doesn't even have time to register before my world goes dark.

My jaw aches like nothing I've felt before. I'm lying on the living room floor. I can't have been out for long. The light through the window still looks the same. There are sounds of movement above me, and it spurs me to get up. My vision swims, and saliva pools in my mouth, but I push through it and crawl forward on my knees until I get to the kitchen counter. I use the ledge to pull myself to standing as I breathe through my nose and try not to tense my aching jaw.

Evan is upstairs, and he is clearly searching for what I have been hiding from Dan. I slide open the drawer under the coffee maker and press on the false back, making a compartment slide forward to reveal a 9 mm. As quietly as I can,

I make my way up the stairs. I step over the second-from-top stair that creaks and tiptoe toward the sound.

My heart beats harder the closer I get. And it falls to my feet when I realize he's in my room. In the bathroom. He's already figured out where to look, and he could already have my biggest secret in his hands.

I step closer and turn the corner, gun first. He's on his knees on the sink, lowering a red box to his lap. Which one is it? My letters from my father? Or the one that will send my whole world crumbling, even more than it already is?

"Stop. Or I will shoot you."

He freezes, hands still gripping the red cardboard.

"Leave it there and get down. Now."

I can just make out the corners of his mouth turning up. He knows what he's found is worth a lot to me.

My finger squeezes the trigger, and Evan jumps as the bullet smacks into the mirror on the wall and it shatters.

"I will shoot you. Don't for a second think that I won't."

He sets the box on an empty space on the bathroom vanity and slowly slides himself off it, watching me, or rather the gun in my hand, the whole time.

"Police are sure to be on their way now that you've fired."

"Probably," I say. I step back, giving him room and keeping myself out of reach. "Leave." I'm not really nervous about the police showing up. One gunshot can easily be mistaken as something else. If I were to shoot off a few more rounds, then I'd be worried.

"How do I know you're not just going to shoot me in the back?"

"I can just as easily shoot you in the face."

He takes a step toward the door. I take another step back. He's moving slowly. Too fucking slowly. I can't lose my nerve. Because shooting him in the back is exactly what I intend to do. I have to. But I can't look him in the face when I do it, and I know that makes me a coward. I don't care.

But he knows my cowardice.

He turns as he passes me, keeping our eyes locked as he descends the stairs backward. My hands shake. *Turn around! Goddammit!*

My trigger finger burns. I need to pull it. Stop thinking and shoot. End all of this before it can get any worse. Before someone I love gets hurt or killed. Before he has another attempt to look inside my box of secrets.

He gets to the bottom of the steps, and I know my chance is slipping away. He dashes to the side, out of sight, and my arms fall. Hot tears spill down my face. I want to hit myself. Slap my face, punch my leg, punish myself for being such a weak fucking idiot. Why can't I kill him? What is wrong with me?

CHAPTER THIRTY-FIVE

Evan — Now

I need to know what she's hiding in that box. I should have tied her up after I knocked her out. I thought she'd be out longer than that. Thought I'd find something sooner, having the search narrowed down to two rooms: her bedroom and her bathroom. *Thank you, Danny Boy.*

She was desperate to keep whatever secret she's been hiding under that lid. I'm starting to realize she's been keeping far more secrets than I ever could have imagined.

Seeing her house, her room, and her life without me was hard. It didn't look like her. Not the Scarlett I knew with red streaks in her hair, who wanted everything in our apartment modern and monochrome. Her blue living room, red bedroom (though that one makes more sense), and yellow bathroom. It was all too much color for the girl I knew.

How is she so different from that person?

And what the *fuck* is she hiding in that box?

Answers. I need them. I need some goddamn answers, and I'm going to get them. I haven't worked this hard for so many years to not solve the mystery of my life. Maybe that has been what I've been after all this time. Not so much to have Scarlett back but to know why I lost her in the first place. I pride myself on reading people and situations. I'm gifted at controlling my environment, and Scarlett running away and starting a new life without me means that my whole life has been a lie. And if that's true . . . what does that mean?

I almost miss mandatory therapy. I could use another brain to help me sort all this out. Scarlett is obviously still hiding something, so I can't trust her to be forthcoming about why she left. I can accept that I allowed Scarlett to mislead me, but I cannot accept that I got it all wrong from the beginning. She loved me. Maybe she still does, but what does that matter now? She enjoyed the killing we did together. Maybe not the way I did, but she did enjoy it.

Everything is out now. Dan knows the truth about his little lover. At least part of the truth. And I have a new goal. I don't need an answer to my ultimatum. I need to know what Scarlett has been hiding in her red boxes. Whatever it is will be the answer for everything. I know it.

CHAPTER THIRTY-SIX

Scarlett — Then

I've developed an unhealthy obsession with watching the news. It is never not on, whether I am at home, at work, or at a hair appointment. It's always on. I stream it on my phone and listen with headphones when I'm not in the comfort of my own living room. The people we've killed are mentioned from time to time, and that is what I'm always listening for.

Soon after they go missing, they get a lot of airtime. After a while, they are only mentioned in passing, and you can see the world forgetting about them little by little. I don't forget about them, though. And I know their families don't. A few of them didn't have much in the way of family, but there has to be someone out there missing them.

The family of the man we killed is having a service for him, though they don't have his body. His mother tells the overdressed news anchor that she can feel he is no longer here. "A mother knows," she says, and I wonder if that's true. She's right. But how can she be certain? How can she push away that insistent hope that she will find him?

The television goes dark, and I spin on the couch to see Evan, remote extended outward. "Stop watching that crap."

"Someone needs to," I say. I reach for the remote, but he pulls it away.

"No. No one needs to. It's not going to tell you anything you don't already know."

"It might. The police are investigating him going missing. It will tell us which direction they're going. What if they find something that gives us away and we have to run?"

He sighs like I'm stupid, and I fight the urge to hit him. He doesn't often make me feel small, but when he does, it hits hard. "If they find something that points to us, they'll be knocking down our door long before you'll see it on the news."

I shake my head and throw myself back onto the couch. I can't argue with him. Partly because I see his point of view and partly because I don't want to.

"I have to go to work. I'll call you when I get lunch. Try to stop obsessing, okay?" He leans down and kisses the top of my head. I'm dressed for work, and I get up like I'm going to finish getting ready. He leaves before I do because he has further to drive. A few minutes after he leaves, I call into HR and take a sick day.

The man we killed was named Collin Hayes. His service is being held four hours south, and I have to drive fast if I want to make it on time. Collin's mother is catching a lot of flak for holding a service as he's been missing four months, and many people think he should still be assumed alive. But I admire her resolve. She doesn't care what people are saying. She feels her son is gone, and she wants to lay him to rest. His spirit, if not his body.

There are a lot of people at the service. Collin was a popular man. Or more people are flocking here because of the news. But I think it's the former because the majority of people look devastated, and you're just not that sad over someone you don't know.

Their grief acts like a chemical reaction, compounding my guilt tenfold. I want to talk to his mom. He was a grown man, but they were close. She knew something was wrong the very morning after we killed him. She said so in an interview. She didn't know he'd actually been killed, but I knew the timeline.

It's because I chose him that this one feels different, heavier, than the others. It is my fault alone that this man was taken from his family. I chose him at a bar. Knowing nothing else about him, I decided to take his life. And now all these people will never be the same. His mother may say she knows without a doubt he is gone, but she will never have that closure.

Because of me.

I force myself to witness their pain. Not to close my eyes or shy away from the grief that I've caused. Evan doesn't understand this feeling. He feels no remorse for the lives we take. He never seems to think of it again. But I wear it like a second skin.

In the moment of the kill, my heart races, and the adrenaline makes me feel alive. It is a feeling I can't get anywhere else. It's the lead-up and afterward that makes me sick with myself. But it is never enough to make me stop. To make me stop Evan. Despite the self-hatred, I always do it again.

I leave when his mother tosses dirt on his empty casket.

CHAPTER THIRTY-SEVEN

Scarlett — Now

My life has gone up in smoke, and I sat there and watched it burn. I hurt a person I love and who least deserved to be hurt. My stomach is sick with guilt and regret. What have I done?

A better person would call Marin and tell her the truth, but I can't bring myself to look at my phone. She should be safe for the time being. From Evan, at least. Not from the person she calls her best friend. Evan will want to let the pain he's caused fester before causing more. The question is for how long?

I sit on the edge of my bed, my box of secrets on my lap and my trail of destruction on my mind. I had no business staying here and making a life I knew deep down I couldn't keep. My chest tightens, and I slide off the bed, hitting my knees against the hardwood beneath my colorful rug. Why am I such a despicable human?

I pant on my hands and knees, trying to slow my breathing, but there is no use. It's gotten away from me. The room spins and swirls, and my chest tightens until it feels like I'm going to pop.

It's a panic attack. Not my first. But knowing what it is and that I'm not really dying doesn't do much in helping it to stop.

Focus. I need to focus on something. Anything.

The rug beneath my fingers. I think I might pass out. It's soft. I special-ordered it online when I got my new credit card. There are different-sized squares printed on it. Squares within squares. I count them.

Slowly, gradually, my pulse slows. My breathing deepens. I roll onto my side and draw in long, deep breaths. Tears fall across the bridge of my nose. Evan was too close to finding everything out. All of this would have been for nothing.

I get to my feet and retrieve the box.

Evan cannot see what is inside. I can't allow it. It has to be destroyed. I take the box down to the kitchen and put it in the empty stainless-steel sink. Frantically, I search the cabinet drawers for matches. A lighter. I could have sworn I had matches in here somewhere. Where the hell are they? I slam the drawer shut and squat down to the floor as a sob escapes my throat.

This is too much. I am not strong enough to lose everything I've ever known a third time. All I want is a normal, boring life.

The self-pity leaves a bitter taste in my mouth. How is it possible for life to feel so unfair and yet perfectly just all at once? Because if I'm really honest with myself, I know that I deserve so much worse. But like a selfish three-year-old, I want what I want.

I push out a frustrated breath and stand up. Then, I slap my hand across my cheek. Hard. I slam my fist into the granite countertop. Stare at the box in the sink.

I have to do it.

Jogging across the room to where my paper planner sits, I rip the top sheet off. I won't be having plans anytime soon, anyway. At the stove, I twist the paper into a torch and light it with the flame from the burner.

I move back to the sink and hold it over the box, willing myself to drop it and let it all burn. My hand trembles, and I can barely see through the tears that blur my vision.

Do it! Just fucking do it. There is no other choice!

I shout at the stupid box and throw the flaming paper onto the ground, stomping out the flame.

I can't do it. I can't destroy the most important thing to me. I'm just not strong enough. Selfless enough.

Pounding at my front door startles me. Could it be Evan? Dan? Marin? I walk cautiously toward the sound and lift onto my toes to see through the peephole. It's Darlene from across the street. She looks panicked. I swing the door open, and she starts shouting right away.

"You haven't been answering your phone," she says.

"What's going on?"

"You need to go downtown. Now!" She pulls at my arm, and I pull back.

"Darlene, what is going on? I need my keys. Hold on."

I leave the door open and run to the counter to grab my purse, which holds my phone and keys, waiting for Darlene to get out the reason she is so worked up. The possibilities send my nervous system into overdrive.

"It's Dan's restaurant," she finally says. "There's a fire. A bad one. Marin tried calling you and called me when you wouldn't answer. Go, now."

CHAPTER THIRTY-EIGHT

Scarlett — Now

I drive toward the smoke that billows over rooftops, a frightening shade of black. The closer I get, the more afraid I am, and I can't stop my hands from shaking. I try to grip the steering wheel. Maybe I should have accepted Darlene's offer to drive me. I turn the corner toward the restaurant and have to slam on the brakes. Emergency vehicles and random cars are blocking the road.

I throw my car into park and sprint toward the flames that dance and whip in the summer wind. Marin is at the front of the pack of people who stand watching the building nervously. A small part of me panics seeing my best friend. Does she know? Does she hate me? But there is no time for that now. No space for anything but finding Dan.

"Oh my God, there you are! Where the hell have you been?" Marin says when she sees me.

I don't answer. Only look around for Dan. This is his business. His lifelong dream. Where is he?

Marin grabs my shoulder. The contact throws me, and it makes me look at her again. Her face is afraid. Terrified. Sad. "Dan is inside."

I don't hear what else she says as I run toward the burning building. An arm wraps around my waist and yanks me backward, the force knocking the wind from me. I push at the hands that confine me, trying my hardest to tear toward the door that was once glass but is now shattered from the heat or from the firemen, I don't know.

"Scarlett, stop. You can't go in there. Rob is in there, and he's going to find him. Let them do their job."

I hear the words, but I don't. I'm still trying to push my way forward. "Scarlett! Stop, dammit!"

I stop, looking bewildered at the face of the person restraining me. Rick. He's training to join the volunteer firefighters.

"You think you're gonna be able to do something the fire department can't? You're just gonna be another person to save in there and distract them from getting Dan out. Stand here and wait."

His words finally penetrate my cloud of panic. He's right. What would I even do once inside? I'd just end up getting myself killed. Or someone else.

I collapse to my knees and press my palms into the gravel road. Pray to God that Dan walks through that door alive, even though I have no right to ask God for anything.

Something explodes, shooting more glass toward me and the crowd of people behind me. The ground shakes, and I wonder for a moment if it is God's answer to my prayer, telling me to go to hell. Rick is moving now, telling everyone to back up, telling me to back up, but I cannot move. I stare at the smoke and flames inside the building, searching for human-like shapes in the smoke.

And I think I see one. But maybe I am seeing what I want to see. I shuffle forward on my hands and knees. The smoke burns my eyes, and I squint. Two figures emerge. Dan's face is covered in dark ash, and my body goes weak with relief. His arm is slung over Rob's shoulder, and they shuffle hurriedly away from the burning building.

I climb to my feet just as another explosion from inside forces me back to the ground. This one is bigger than the last. I look up and see that Rick, Rob, and Dan are also on the ground. I crawl forward until my hand grips Dan's shirt.

He looks up at me, his eyes afraid and vacant until something in him recognizes me. His hand covers mine. He slides his thumb over my knuckles once. Twice. Then I watch as betrayal and pain paint his expression, and he gently but firmly removes my hand from his shirt.

Rob and Rick help Dan to his feet and walk him to an ambulance waiting a few feet away. Rick tells me I can go with him. He waves for me to climb into the back, but I stay rooted to the ground as Dan tells him no. Rick looks between us for just a second before slamming the door and slapping the side of the vehicle twice.

CHAPTER THIRTY-NINE

Scarlett — Now

The emergency room waiting area is empty except for a man with a bleeding hand in the corner. St. Michael's Hospital serves our county and two others. I don't know the man. He looks drunk and morose, but I have no mental space to wonder about him past that. I rush to the woman at the front desk and explain that Dan Thomas was brought in from a fire and that I'd like to go back to see him.

"Relation?" she asks in an overly chipper tone for the situation.

"Girlfriend."

She grimaces and makes an odd noise. "Sorry, hon. Family only."

"I am family. We live together. We've been together for six years."

"Not by law. I'm sorry, sweetie. It's the rules."

I grit my teeth. Resist the urge to reach over the desk and yank her bottle-dyed red hair from her scalp. Just as I'm about to continue my argument, the sliding doors behind me whoosh open, and someone calls my name.

"Have you seen him? Is he okay?" asks Theresa, Dan's sister.

"No. They won't let me back. Family only."

She moves past me and tells the woman she is Dan's sister. She hits the button and tells her he's in room eleven.

"Will you tell me how he is? Let him know I'm here?" I call after her.

She turns and stares at me for a second. "Why *are* you here?"

So Dan has told her. Which he has every right to do. "I love him, Theresa. The rest is complicated, but not the fact that I love him."

She turns without another word and disappears behind the large, wooden double doors. I sit in the nearest chair, the weight of my guilt pulling me down.

My stomach churns, and I think I could actually be sick. The blowback from my decisions is so much bigger than I ever imagined it would be. I only ever wanted to start over. To do the right thing. Initially, my decision was selfless. It just didn't stay that way. It never does.

I remember the first time Dan took me on an official date. I'd been staying at the inn while I fixed up one of the only houses for sale in the neighborhood. It was finally ready to move into, and Dan wanted to celebrate and reward me for the hard work, even though he'd done a lot of it himself.

I was slow to let Dan in. Which, looking back, is kind of funny. I stayed in Hoover because I met him and wanted to know him. If he hadn't been at the diner that day, I would have kept on driving for who knows how long.

But my emotional walls didn't deter him. He was persistent while still remaining respectful. I'd only ever been with Evan, who pushed my boundaries and made me believe it was for my own benefit. Dan was so different in every way, so it surprised me to be so interested in him.

I'm not sure how much time passes. Enough that I start to doze off in the hard, plastic chair. Movement beside me brings me back to consciousness. Theresa is sitting next to me, staring at her knees. "He's okay," she says. "They're starting the discharge papers now."

"Thank you." She didn't have to tell me anything, and I'm grateful for her gesture of kindness that I know I don't deserve.

She nods and stands up. She walks outside, and I let my head fall into my hands. My shoulders shake with emotion. *Thank you, God. Thank you for letting him be okay.*

I sit up and take a deep breath, trying to gather myself. What time is it? It's the first time I thought to check. I slide my phone from my back pocket, but instead of seeing the time, I'm distracted by the text. Another unsaved number.

It is a picture of Marin. Tied up. Black mascara tears streaming down her cheeks.

The box for Marin. Even trade. No tricks or she dies.

CHAPTER FORTY

Scarlett — Now

I am out of options. There is no scenario in which I win. In which someone I love doesn't get hurt. Or, more likely, die. So I pull into Marin's driveway, the box sitting in the passenger seat like an atomic bomb. Evan cannot see what is inside. And I cannot let Marin die. It's an impossible situation. Because Evan will kill her. Of that, I have no doubt. Trying to trick him or play any games will get my friend killed.

The front door opens, but there is no one standing there. It's my signal: *I see you. Come in.*

I follow his unspoken directions. Grabbing the box, I walk to the open door. Inside is dark and silent. Will he attack me? What he wants is within reach. He no longer has a reason to keep me alive. His desire for answers, for knowing, is far stronger than his desire for me ever was.

I should have just gone back with him when I had the chance. I was stupid to think I could keep running. But then, I don't know that going back would have solved anything. He'd still want the people I love dead. He'd still want to know why I left in the first place. Having me never would have been enough.

I close the door behind me. I hear a whimper. Female. Marin. It's coming from the other side of the house. Her bedroom, maybe.

"Put the box on the counter and go to her," Evan says from the darkness.

I step forward and do as he says.

"Don't try to be clever."

"I'm not. Just take it and go."

"Put your gun on the counter."

I hesitate.

"Now!"

I scramble for my holster and remove my pistol, placing it beside the box.

"Any others on you?"

"No."

"I don't believe you."

"It's the only one I have on me. Check me if you want."

He steps from the shadows. Dangerously beautiful. "Arms out, darling."

I raise my arms above my head and suck in a breath when he approaches me. He slides his hands over my arms, down my sides. He grips me tighter when he gets to my hips, and my eyes fall to his hands. I'm caught off guard by what I see.

"I never stopped wearing it. Only took it off once I found you. To give the tan line and callus a chance to lessen, though I doubt Marin would have noticed."

The gold band stirs up a mix of emotions. Nostalgia, longing.

His hands continue down my legs. Outside first. Then the inside.

Lust. Love.

He stands, and our eyes lock.

Regret. Hate.

"Good girl," he says, his voice low and deep. I can smell his cinnamon gum, and I get lost in déjà vu. All the times that were just like this. Seduction and sex with my husband while some helpless person sat tied up in the other room.

How depraved we have been.

"I have to ask," he says. "Which is the real Scarlett? The one from Chicago or the one here?"

"Can't both be real?"

He shakes his head. "You used to love the city. You loved simple colors and preferred modern style. Everything about your life here is different from who you were back then."

It's funny that, even now, the words are hard to get out because I know they will hurt him. "I hate the city. I hated the noise and the busyness. I hated that it never really felt dark, even late at night. I like colors and socializing. I like tight-knit friends who show up unexpectedly just to talk . . ." I trail off because his face is painted with pain so visceral I want to cry. I want to apologize and take the words back. But I don't.

"I'm sorry that I never knew you," he says in a tight voice. He clears his throat and looks at the box on the counter. "What could you possibly be trying this hard to keep from me?"

"I am begging you. Please stop this. Please, Evan." I know he hears the desperation in my voice. But he just shakes his head.

"It's too late now." He is standing so close. His hand moves to my face and cups the back of my head. His hand is large enough that he is able to rub his thumb along my jawline. My bottom lip. I close my eyes and try to breathe evenly. "I've missed you so fucking much," he whispers and rests his forehead on mine. "I'm sorry. For everything. I know it won't mean much by the end of all this, but I am. I just wanted you to know that."

He holds my face between his hands and kisses my forehead, pausing for a moment, and I think we both try to savor it. Then, he pulls away so quickly that I stumble. Before I can react, he has the box in his hands, and he's ripping off the lid.

This is it. It is all over. Everything I've done is for nothing. Evan always wins in the end.

CHAPTER FORTY-ONE

Evan — Now

I'm not sure what I expected to find inside. When I found it the first time, I noted that it wasn't particularly heavy. My mind went wild with the possibilities. I hear her beside me. See her fall to her knees in my peripheral. The urge to comfort her still surprises me. But my need to know what she is so desperate to keep from me overpowers everything.

Before I can take out the contents to see what they are, she's on my back. I hadn't heard her get up, too focused on finally knowing. I scream out in pain as her nails drag against the skin on my face and neck. I throw my elbow back hard and catch her in the ribs. The cracking sound triggers a niggling of guilt, but she'll be okay.

My reach far exceeds hers, and I stiff-arm her as she flails wildly, trying to grab the box despite her broken ribs. I push her back. Hard. She falls on her back just before her head snaps back and smacks the hardwood. I wince. Hold my breath until she moves again. Exhale relief.

She drags herself to lean against the wall. I point her gun at her. "Stay still, my love. That was a nasty fall."

"You pushed me. I didn't fall."

"Tomato, to-mah-toe."

I keep one eye on her, using one hand to hold the gun and the other to lift the top item out of the red box. Scarlett covers her mouth, muffling a sob.

The box is full of photos. The top one is of a girl. Maybe eight years old. Maybe a little younger. It's a bit far away, and I can't quite make her face out, but she stands on the porch of a white house. I look up at Scarlett, confused and unsure what the hell this is.

I shuffle through the box and grab another photo. "Who is this?" I ask, more to myself because I know she won't answer me.

I grab a handful. All the same little girl at different ages. Most of them are at the same white house. Some show another woman and a man with her. Then, one makes my heart stop.

Scarlett. Holding a baby. She knows this child. I look closer. Notice Scarlett's chest is bare. Her eyes are heavy with exhaustion and something else. A happiness — a pride I've never seen on her face.

The child is hers.

I look up at her, mouth open in awe and heartbreak. Her face is full of emotion, and in it, I find the missing link. The truth that is so obvious but so unbelievable my mind wouldn't accept it.

The child is *ours.*

CHAPTER FORTY-TWO

Scarlett — Then

Sweat drips down my lower back as I lean into the oven. It still isn't ready. I shut it and glance at the clock. Evan will be home any minute. I wanted to have dinner done and on the table when he got here. Not that he expects it, but it's a special occasion. It's our sixth wedding anniversary. And my birthday. He thinks I've made us dinner reservations downtown, but I wanted to try my hand at a real home-cooked meal.

I hear the door open and spin around, running to the hallway. "Don't come in here yet!"

"Are you wearing an apron?" Evan grins.

"Shh! Stay there. Just a minute."

I run back to the kitchen, his voice trailing me. "Where did you get an apron?"

"Passed down through my family for generations."

He laughs.

I plate the potatoes, which are done. And the asparagus. Which I hope tastes the same as at La Restaurante. The chicken is the last to be finished. The main dish.

"It smells delicious in here," Evan shouts from the hallway. "Which is weird since we have reservations downtown."

"Wait quietly, please!"

I stick the meat thermometer into the center again and exhale, lips parting into a smile when it reaches 180 degrees Fahrenheit. I use giant poker sticks to move the chicken onto the serving platter I bought and carry it to the table, along with the sides. I quickly shed my apron, throwing it onto the kitchen counter.

"Okay! You can come in now!" I say and grab two wine-glasses and a bottle of merlot.

"Wow, look at this," he says. His eyes lift to me. "Look at *you.*" He takes my hand and spins me. The hungry look in his eyes makes my stomach flip. "I don't know what I want to have first."

My cheeks burn. "Dessert comes after dinner, my love."

His lips form a pout. "I thought we made our own rules."

"We do."

Our eyes are locked, and my heart drums quickly under the thin fabric of my black dress. Evan closes the space between us, leaning down until his lips are on my neck. His hands trail down my sides and stop at my hips. He grips them hard, and I suck in a breath. My hands move automatically. My body responds to him in a way I have no control over.

I work the buttons of his shirt and rip it down, exposing his taut skin, stretched over muscle he works hard to maintain. His hands cup my ass, and he lifts me up. I wrap my legs around his waist, and he moves toward the table.

"Don't mess up my table setting," I warn.

He smiles against my mouth. "The floor it is."

His lips are moving down my stomach when I smell smoke. When Evan reaches the spot between my legs, I decide to ignore it. But we both shoot up when a piercing sound blasts through the apartment. The smoke detector.

Evan gets to his feet and runs to the kitchen. "Shit," he says as he disappears into a building cloud of smoke.

I scramble to my feet, racking my brain for what could have caught fire. All the food is out here on the table. But I forgot to turn off the oven. That shouldn't start a fire, though. The sound of the fire extinguisher makes me jump.

I run through the living room, opening windows and turning on the ceiling fans. Evan exits the kitchen, coughing into his elbow. "I'm sorry to say your apron did not make it."

My hands fly to my face. "The oven was so hot it caught fire on the counter?"

"You left a burner on low. It looks like part of the apron was draped onto the stovetop."

I must have left it on after cooking the asparagus. "God, I'm such an idiot."

Evan moves toward me just as the building alarm goes off. I groan, and Evan wraps me in a hug. We quickly re-dress and evacuate the building, looking for the building manager on the way down to tell him our apartment was the culprit and that everything is under control.

My whole face burns as Evan explains to the manager that we had a "little cooking accident" in our kitchen, but the fire has been extinguished. The manager says the fire department still has to come to ensure everything is okay before everyone can return to the building.

I bury my head in Evan's chest. "This is humiliating," I mumble into his shirt.

He pats my back. "Don't be embarrassed, babe. I'm only upset I didn't get to have dinner *or* dessert."

I slap his stomach half-heartedly because I am also upset about it.

"What do you say we find somewhere to eat while they handle all this? You look too pretty to spend all evening standing outside a smoky building."

"Okay," I say, defeated.

We have dinner and drinks at a rooftop bar. We're sitting near the glass edge, and I find myself looking down to tickle my fear of heights. Evan doesn't know I'm afraid of heights. I pretend I'm not. I've gotten good at pretending. Like pretending to drink alcohol the last few weeks. And pretending everything is normal and nothing has changed. Pretending I didn't see those two little lines that meant nothing would ever be the same again.

I expected to feel distraught when I found out another life was growing inside me. I'd never wanted children. Neither of us had. But I wasn't upset. Not even a little. It felt like a miracle. Like something that was always meant to be mine. It's hard to explain, even to myself.

"I want to talk to you about our plans this weekend," I say when the server takes our food order and walks away.

"Yeah? What about them?"

"I—" I had it planned out. The way I would broach the subject. It was meant to be softened with my home-cooked meal. And private between our own four walls. But I have to adapt. The conversation needs to be had. Evan is direct. He respects straight talk, so I just say it. "I don't want to do it. Not this weekend. Not anymore, at all."

His eyebrows arch toward his hairline.

"Where is this coming from?"

"Thoughts I've been having for a while." Not a lie. I've been thinking about this since I found out, three weeks ago now. I decided immediately that I wouldn't be telling Evan right away. And I also knew from the start that my child would not grow up the way I did. He or she would not grow up knowing about torture and murder as though it was normal.

"It feels like the only thing we look forward to anymore. The only time you put effort into planning something. I know you enjoy it. I do too. But I want to see what our life would be like without it. I don't want to be my father. Unable to control it to the point that we get caught. Are you still in control?"

"Of course I am. I'm in perfect control." His eyes are more expressive than they've ever been. He's been caught off guard, and that is rare for Evan. He isn't watching his response.

"Nine kills in six years. All around the same area. This year will be more than any other year before. I want to stop while we're ahead."

A small shake of his head and a tiny exhale. “Wow. Uhm — okay. You’re right. It’s more than I planned to do. And that alone means it’s too much. But to be done forever?”

“I need to know you can stop.”

“Forever?”

“Yes.”

A nod this time. “Okay, Scarlett. We’re done with it. No more.”

I look at him skeptically. It all feels too easy.

“Don’t look at me like that,” he says. “We’re done. I’ll put the cabin up for sale.”

“Do you promise?” My voice was strong until this point. Now, just a hint of desperation slips out.

Evan slides closer to me, taking my hands in his. “I promise, Scar.”

Part of me actually believes him.

CHAPTER FORTY-THREE

Scarlett — Now

Evan storms out of the house with the box in hand. I scramble after him, but he swings around, gun extended. "Stay put." He walks toward his car, and with one menacing look back, he disappears.

I sink to the ground, my breath coming in short and shallow. He's going to find her. My little girl. I can't breathe. Will he hurt her? Maybe I can get to her first. He doesn't know where she is yet.

A scream erupts from behind me. Marin. I crawl toward the bedroom, tripping when I attempt to get to my feet in a hurry. I get up again, running to her. Her eyes are wide, with black makeup smeared underneath. Her mouth is duct-taped, as are her hands and her feet.

I move to her, and she flinches. It makes me stop in my tracks. She's afraid of me. What did he tell her? I grit my teeth and step forward again. I don't have time for this. "This is going to hurt like a bitch. He got the tape in your hair. Ready?"

She nods, and I rip the sticky gray stripe to the left. Marin yelps but doesn't draw back. I finish removing the tape from her face before starting on her hands.

"What the fuck is going on, Scarlett?" she says, her mouth wet with saliva and tears. I should have started with her hands and feet. I don't know how to answer her questions.

"Evan is dangerous."

Marin scoffs. "No fucking shit." Her hands are free, and she helps me with her feet. When she's free, she stands and backs into a wall. "Who are you?"

"You know who I am—"

"Who the fuck *are* you?" she screams. Betrayal is clear on her face.

"What did he tell you?"

She shakes her head. "No. Uh-uh. You need to tell me the truth. All of it. Or I'm calling the police."

"Please don't do that, Marin. I'm begging you. He's going to hurt someone else I love, and I have to stop him. I can't do that if you call the police."

"Then start talking."

How do I even begin to defend myself? To get her to see that I am not the enemy? At least not until Evan is taken care of. I open my mouth, but the words won't come. I have no defense. I stayed in Hoover and befriended these people, knowing deep down that it would put them in danger.

"I lied to everyone," I say. "I lied, and I put you all in danger because I'm selfish. I was hiding from Evan, but it was only a matter of time before he found me. I'm so sorry." My breath leaves me when a cry attempts to escape my mouth.

She shakes her head. "Why didn't you tell me? When I showed up with him at dinner, you should have said something. Why would you let him stay with me when you knew?"

"I didn't know what he'd do if I said anything. I was trying to figure out how to keep everyone safe. You don't understand how dangerous he is, Marin."

She laughs humorlessly. "I think I have at least an idea."

She thinks she does, but she doesn't. I suddenly want to tell her everything. From the moment I met Evan 'til now. I want her, anyone, to understand the hold he had on me and why I did the things I did, even though I don't quite understand it myself.

I start to explain, but I'm interrupted by my phone ringing. I expect it to be Evan trying to get information on where to find our daughter. Marin looks at me like I've lost my head when I pull my phone from my pocket. "Are you seriously taking a phone call right now?" She's hysteric. With every reason to be.

"It could be him." But it isn't. It's Dan. He needs to go back to our house, where he might be safe behind the security system. I answer. But Dan's voice isn't the one on the other end.

"Hello, darling."

I put the phone on speaker, not wanting to keep Marin in the dark about anything else. "What have you done to Dan?"

"Nothing." His tone is that of a teenager. I can hear the exaggerated eye roll. "Nothing yet, anyway."

"Leave him alone! You have what you want. What are you even doing there?"

"I made you a promise, sweetheart. I told you I'd take it all away from you if you chose not to come home. What kind of man would I be if I left without having kept my word?"

"You've never kept a promise in your goddamn life," I spit.

"Ouch. Not true. And this is one I want to keep. I can't walk away and leave your lover unharmed for you to go back to. There are consequences to your actions, Scarlett. This is consequence number one."

I scream every terrible word I know through the phone, my hands shaking. But before I can have the full thought, my feet are moving. He said he hasn't done anything yet, and Dan's sister's house is just a few miles away. My hand is on the door handle when I hear Dan, and I freeze.

"Scarlett? Are you okay?"

I choke out a sob. "Yes. I'm okay. You need to get out of there if you can. Get back to our house and turn on the alarm system. Take your sister and her family—"

"Scarlett. Hey, shh. Listen to me. It's too late for that. Don't come here—" His words break off into a shout of pain, and I scream with him.

"No! Leave him alone! Please. Please, leave him alone."

"I'm okay, baby. Please don't come here. Do you hear me?" Dan's voice sounds further away. Breathy.

I hardly notice Marin taking my arm and leading me to the passenger seat. I didn't realize she'd followed me outside. She puts me into the car and runs to the driver's side, where she gets in and pulls away from her house.

"I'm coming to you. Please just hold on. What is he doing to you? Can you fight back?" I hold the phone to my ear, desperate. My insides are twisted up so hard I think I might burst.

"I need to tell you that I love you," Dan says.

"I know that. I know. I love you too. What's happening? Please tell me. Can you fight back?" He sucks in a breath, an inward hiss of pain, and I cry out for him. "Dan! Are you okay? What is he doing? What's happening?"

His words come again, rushed and frantic. "Listen. I love you, and I'm sorry we fought and I left. I forgive you, okay? Know that I love you and I forgive you and I'd still marry you in a heartbeat. You were the love of my life, and I don't regret a second of our life together."

Were. You *were* the love of my life. He's resigned himself to die.

"Don't you give up! I'm almost there!"

"I love you," he says again. He sounds weak. Tired.

"I love you. I love you so much, please don't die. Don't leave me."

"You take him out. You hear me? Fuck him up, Scarlett." It's a whisper, but his words are hard. Angry. The pain making him change his mind about asking me not to come. The line goes dead, and I can't breathe.

Marin slams on the brakes outside Dan's sister's house, and I catch myself against the dashboard. But before I go, I turn to Marin. "I need you to do something for me. I know you don't trust me, and you can reserve your right to hate me forever. But help me one last time."

She nods, that look of stubborn strength she wears so well on her face.

I give Marin her instructions, praying she remembers everything I've told her. "You still have a lot of explaining to do," she says. "Be careful. I love you."

I fight back tears and nod. "I love you. Don't forget to turn on the security system once you're inside. Call the police and have them come to you." I look at Marin one last time and fly out of the car, stuffing the phone in my pocket.

CHAPTER FORTY-FOUR

Scarlett — Then

Evan has sold the cabin. I almost asked if it was a good idea. If evidence or bodies would be found by new owners, but I know Evan wouldn't do it if it were possible to get caught. We have our first normal vacation planned for next week. We leave for Florida the morning after he gets home from a work trip.

I hop around the kitchen, blaring music and wiping counters while Evan packs. We're going to swim with dolphins while we're down there. And go on a boat through gator-infested lagoons.

"I'm jumping in the shower," Evan shouts over the music.

"'Kay!"

Singing along to the lyrics of a Taylor Swift song, I shake my hips as I make my way to the bedroom. Evan's suitcase is on the bed, ready to go. I'm not sure why, but a memory from Miss Pamela's surfaces. The notes Evan and I would leave each other. We haven't done that in so long. I skip over to the office and grab a sheet of printer paper, pulling the cap from a marker off with my teeth.

Have a safe trip. I love you. P.S. Nice Butt.

I press my lips to the paper, leaving a print of my lips below my message. Perfect. Evan will be out soon — I have to hurry so I won't be caught. The water is still running when I get back to the bedroom. The suitcase zipper is loud, and I wince when I pull it down and around to the side. I lift the corner to slide the note in and push it against the side of the suitcase so the clothes hide it, in case he realizes he forgot something and opens it before he leaves.

My hand brushes against something long and hard. I pull it out. It is a piece of stained wood with a silver ring and key attached to the end. The key to the cabin. But Evan sold the cabin. Maybe he's sending the key to the new owner? I put it back where I found it, and driven by pure instinct, I grab the note I wrote.

The water turns off, and I zip the suitcase closed, praying he doesn't hear it through the door. My fingers tingle as I turn to leave the room. The sticky sound of the bathroom door opening sends fear shooting through my veins.

I hold the note to my stomach and throw a glance over my shoulder. Evan is rubbing a towel over his head. I wait, drop my shoulders, and put on a flirty smile. When he moves the towel and sees me, he smiles. "Get out of here, pervert." He balls up the towel and tosses it at me.

I jump sideways, still standing with my back to him, and laugh. "You better pick that up!" I wink and walk casually back into the kitchen, singing out bits of the song still playing as I go.

He'll be out here in a minute. I turn on the tap and run the note under the water in the kitchen sink, then scrunch it into a wet ball of mush. I shove it into the garbage can and try to cover it with bits of food packaging and a banana peel.

I'm back at the sink, rinsing my hands, when I feel Evan's grip on my shoulders. "Oh, that's nice. Maybe I should book a massage while you're gone."

"You should." He kisses my shoulder before turning to the fridge and grabbing a water.

"Then I will." I turn off the tap and spin around to face him. "I wish you didn't have to go on a trip."

"I know. I wish I didn't either. But I'll be home in a few days, and then we'll have a whole week to get sun poisoning and possibly get eaten by sharks together."

"Far more likely it'll be a gator on that boat trip."

"Ahh. You're right."

I walk him to the door and hug him tightly.

"I love you, Evan. I couldn't live without you."

He pulls away, just enough that he can tilt my chin up to look at him. "You won't ever have to."

He kisses me hard, and I want to pull him back inside. Strip off our clothes and lie with my heart beating against his. There is a terrible feeling in my gut, and all I want is to be comforted by the one person in the world that I love. Evan likes to compare us to animals. I've never found it a very accurate comparison. But the instinct telling me not to trust Evan right now feels animalistic.

I watch him disappear behind the elevator doors, blowing him a kiss just as they shut. Then I grab my own car keys and follow him out.

He always stops to fill his tank at the gas station right before the on-ramp to the highway. I drive there and park along the curb down the street, watching him watch the gas meter tick up. He's irritatingly handsome. You can't help feeling jealous or slighted in some way just at the sight of him. He is proof that life is not fair, and no one likes to look at that. Because of that, his personality is even more important. He's always been so charming. It makes people feel guilty for disliking him.

He returns the gas pump to its cradle and slides into the car. I pull onto the highway a few seconds after him and have to force myself to keep breathing. Part of me is nervous he'll see me behind him. But I don't think he's cautious enough to look around. If he's truly going on a work trip, he has no reason to be paranoid and paying attention to cars behind him. Though, he could always just notice me by accident. I let my foot off the gas just a bit.

Forty minutes into this drive, and I'm starting to feel silly. I have no reason to think he's up to something. He probably just had the cabin key to give to the new owner. But do I know for sure he really sold it? He told me he did, but I never saw the paperwork. He said he put the money from the sale into one of our investment accounts that I wouldn't even know how to check.

I'm being paranoid. Is paranoia a symptom of pregnancy? I've been doing all I can to push the knowledge of the growing human inside of me out of my mind. I haven't told Evan. I don't know how to. Maybe I haven't told him because I know what he will say. What I should have done the moment I saw the lines on the test stick.

Evan and I have no business bringing another life into this world when we have taken so many. Even now. I am currently following my husband, not on suspicion of adultery like most situations like this, but on suspicion that he is on his way to kill someone. Still, I never even entertained the thought of ending this pregnancy. But that is exactly what Evan would expect me to do.

The exit to get to the cabin is coming up. I grip the steering wheel tightly as we approach. Evan's blinker flashes, and my insides sink. He could be dropping the key off on his way to his work trip. It's a real possibility. I hang back, driving slowly so I don't end up behind him on the exit.

The cabin is secluded, for obvious reasons. But I don't need to get that close. I can park behind the old church in town and wait for his car to reappear and get back onto the highway, proof that I am going crazy.

The old church was abandoned after a fire. The exterior is still in decent shape, but the inside is charred and broken.

I park behind it, giving me a view of the intersection Evan should come back through. My AC is blasting, and goose bumps cover my bare arms and legs. I tap the button to turn it down and sit back and wait.

Dread fills my chest with each passing minute that I don't see his car pulling up to the stop sign. Should I drive up to the cabin and confront him? Confront him about what, exactly? What if he met up with the new owner and got sucked into a conversation? I'll look insane just pulling up unexpectedly. And then Evan will know I didn't trust him. And that would break his heart.

But then there he is. Passing through the stop sign and heading toward the highway. I exhale and let the tension melt from my shoulders. What's wrong with me? Evan made me a promise. And he may be a monster by most people's definition, but he wouldn't lie to me. He wouldn't break a promise.

We are the same, him and me.

I'm going to tell him about the pregnancy on our vacation. We can do this. We can be parents. Plenty of terrible people have children, but we can be better. We've stopped our terrible hobby. It can all be left in the past.

It's time I close this chapter for good. I pull out of the parking lot but find myself turning right, toward the cabin, instead of toward the highway. Maybe I need closure. To say goodbye to this dark part of me. Hopefully, the new owner is tucked away inside. I only need a minute.

If someone wasn't there, I'd have the urge to toss a match onto the wood floor and watch it turn to ash. It could join the church in flames and maybe be washed of all the evil done here.

The cabin sits at the end of a long, wooded road. No other houses or buildings of any sort are on the road. Two hundred acres of seclusion. The town is a few miles and a few turns, consisting of a couple of old farmers and a few town drunks.

So when the cabin comes into view, along with an empty gravel driveway, I'm confused.

This road is the only way in or out by vehicle. Is the new owner here without a car? Maybe it's a couple and one has gone into town for supplies. I get out of the car and jog along the treeline before cutting across the lawn. The west-facing wall has two windows. One sees into the living area and the other into the bedroom, but the curtains are drawn over both. I circle the cabin, trying to find a view inside, but every window is shut. The way we always keep it. And the key Evan has is the only one that exists.

Something doesn't feel right about this. I should have followed Evan back out. Followed him to Indianapolis just to quiet my suspicions. But there is another way. I jog back to my car and park in my previous spot behind the church, then start the long trek back to the cabin on foot.

If Evan is telling me the truth, I will be sitting outside this cabin all night, bored and getting bitten by mosquitoes. But if he's lying . . .

This is how we've always done it. We come to the cabin and set up. Evan goes out and brings someone home. I kill them.

A wave of nausea hits me, and I fold over myself, ready to release my stomach contents into the grass. But it passes. "Easy there," I whisper, rubbing my stomach in a circular motion. I'm still not showing. I can't wait to see what I will look like with a rounded stomach.

I sit in the grass, leaning my back against the cabin on the west-facing side, where I won't be able to be seen from the drive up or the driveway. By the time I hear gravel crunching under tires, I'm half-asleep, and my left leg is numb. My heart pounds in the pit of my stomach, and I hope against hope that the car is not Evan's.

I hear footsteps. Two sets. A female giggles. Relief floods through me. It's not Evan. They were always brought in unconscious. It's the new owner. I had to have missed them leaving somehow. Or maybe Evan dropped the key off and left it under the mat for them. I laugh silently and wait for them to get into the cabin so I can run back to my car and go home.

"Right this way."

Evan's voice.

The clack of heels on the wood porch moves from the steps to the door. Unsteady. She giggles again. What is happening? Evan wouldn't cheat on me. He's capable of murder. Torture. A litany of terrible things, but not this.

He's changing the way he does it. Without me involved, he is testing out other methods. Bringing her in alive instead of having her wake up already tied down.

My thoughts are confirmed when I hear her scream. Her heels hammer into the ground, and then there is a loud thud on the other side of the wall I'm leaning against. I jump away from it but then move back quickly when I see she has knocked the curtain aside.

Heavy footsteps come toward the window, then away. I can hear her struggling. Kicking things over. Crying. Yelling. My chest is tight. My legs ache to move. To intervene and help her. I stand and peek through the window. Evan is on top of her, his hands around her throat. A hot tear slides down my face as two parts of my brain battle.

Run inside. Run away.

Run inside. Help her.

Run away. He lied. He hasn't stopped. Has probably never even planned to stop. He's evolving. Perfecting his methods. Run.

My indecision is costly. The woman's legs stop kicking, no longer fighting for her life as it slips away.

Run.

CHAPTER FORTY-FIVE

Scarlett — Now

The house is dark. Evan's car isn't here, but it must be close by. Probably guarding his new tires. The front door is unlocked. Dan told me not to come, but he also said to take him out. To fuck him up. And I have every intention to, though he has the upper hand. I'm walking into a trap, but he won't kill me. He wants me to suffer the losses he's inflicting on me. If Dan is truly dead, killing me would be a kindness.

Theresa, Dan's sister, is the first one I see, sprawled across the bottom of the stairs. I press my fingers to her neck, careful to keep my eyes and ears attentive. There is no pulse that I can feel, and I fight back a sob. Evan ended her life, but her death is on my hands.

I pull out my phone and text Marin.

Call 911. Have ambulance sent.

I have to move quickly. I have to be out of here before the police come, but I can't delay Theresa or Dan or anyone else Evan has hurt getting help. I didn't feel a pulse on Theresa, but it could be faint. She could still be alive.

I move around the corner of the entryway, but a noise stops me. A sniffle. I step backward, and my eyes fall to the closet door. My heart pounds in my ears. I pull open the door, and I'm met with big brown eyes, reddened from crying. Sam. Theresa's son. I hold my finger to my lips and angle my body to hide that of his mother's beside us.

"Come here. Stay really quiet. I'm going to take you outside, and you're going to run across the street to the Morrisons, okay? Help is on the way, and you'll be safe there." He nods, and his little lip quivers.

I'll kill Evan if I get the chance again. Any doubt or hesitation I once had is gone. I just pray it isn't too late.

I pick Sam up, and he buries his face in my neck. He's shaking, and my heart breaks for him. I pray Theresa makes it. That the ambulance is close. I have to hurry. I have to find Dan.

I open the front door and quietly send Sam across the street. I wait as he slaps his small hand against the door. Mrs. Morrison stays up late reading in her living room. She'll let him in. As soon as the door opens and I know he is safe, I shut myself back inside the house.

Brent pops into my mind. Theresa's husband. I don't know if he's home or not. The lower level of the house is to the left of the entryway. The living room and the kitchen. The upstairs is just ahead of me. I need to check downstairs first.

Something on the floor through the doorway to the kitchen catches my eye. A shoe. I run toward it and find Dan tied up to a wooden chair, his head slumped onto his chest. Blood stains the front of his shirt, and the tops of his jeans and his clothing are slashed in numerous long slices. I cup his face with my hands and lift his head. His eyes flutter open, and I cry out in relief.

"Help is on the way," I say. His eyes widen in alarm, focused behind me. Before I can look, I hear a *thwap*, and everything goes dark.

CHAPTER FORTY-SIX

Scarlett — Then

My hands shake the whole way home. I can't stop the tears from coming, and my thoughts fly around me like the winged keys in Harry Potter, elusive and assaulting all at once.

My finger jams at the controls on my door until the windows move. I roll them all down, letting the highway air whip around me. The wind mixed with passing cars makes a deafening hum, and I allow it to drown out the noise in my head. Just for a minute.

Because all I have is a minute. I roll the windows up and force my breaths to be slow and full. Evan taught me that you can induce the type of feeling you want to portray by just manipulating your breathing. If you act panicked, for instance. Breathe quick and shallow, contort your face to look sad or worried or angry, and your heart will begin to race. Your nervous system will be triggered, and you'll actually start to feel that emotion. Your body doesn't know the difference between real panic and pretend.

It's the same for all emotions. Slow your breathing, sit up straighter, make your face neutral, and your heart will slow its wild beating. Your thoughts will become less chaotic. And that is what I do. Because this is no time to panic.

I park the car in our typical spot around the back of the apartments and let myself in through the back door, taking the elevator up. I don't want to kick up my heart rate right now. It'd be too easy to fall into hysteria. Once inside, I sit on the edge of the couch and look around our apartment, our home, and my vision blurs. I blink the tears away. Not now. Not yet.

I have to leave. There is no other option. I will not subject my child to the same life I had. My baby will not wind up in a home without a protector because Evan and I are in prison for our terrible crimes. This is the life I was given, and I refuse to pass it down to another generation.

Evan reminds me often enough that we cannot help who we are. I can't help that I came from my father and an act of evil. I can't help that evil seeped into my bones as they formed in the womb. I'd accepted this life of horrors. The sick way my heart pounded faster as someone else's slowed to a stop. The way it made me feel powerful and worthy of the love that Evan gave me. The way it made me feel connected to the people I loved most. Evan. My father. We are all the same. I wasn't strong enough to try to be someone else. To even attempt to fight the darkness that runs through my veins.

But I cannot let that be my child's life too.

Because as much as I believe that this terribleness inside of me has been passed down, like my eye color or my attached earlobes, what if he's wrong? What if I can give my child a chance to have a good life? One without all the terrible things we have done.

Evan will never stop. He's made that clear. And I know him better than to think he would allow our child to be given up for adoption. He doesn't want children, but he wouldn't want someone else to have what is ours. He'd either want me to have an abortion, or we'd keep it.

I won't do either. I can't.

And so, to give my child a chance at life, I have to give up mine. It's a sacrifice I am willing to make.

I walk through the apartment, unsure what to pack. If anything. I'll need as much time as possible. And if anything is missing, it will tip Evan off that I've left. I plug my phone into the charger on the side table next to the couch and stuff the cash from my purse into my jeans pocket.

There is one more thing I must take with me. I reach into the crawl space and shiver when a cobweb tickles my arm. Evan identifies himself as a minimalist. He doesn't own much, and he doesn't store anything. The crawl space in our bedroom is filled with my things alone. And stuffed into a corner, inside another box, is a red box containing the worst kind of secrets.

Once I've pulled it free from its dusty hiding place, I open the lid and look at the evidence of our crimes. Nine locks of hair. Nine bloody Q-tips. Evan would flip if he ever knew about them. And all this time, they have sat in our room, beating like Edgar Allan Poe's Tell-Tale Heart. I close the box and carry it beneath my arm as I go downstairs to have the front desk order me a cab.

My first stop is thirty minutes away. I climb out of the cab and ask the man to wait for me with the promise of more money. The blue house looks to me how I imagine I must look to it. Mostly the same, just a little older. The paint is peeling in a spot near the door, and one of the railings is leaning a bit to one side. The steps creak under my weight as I move to the front door. Visitors are supposed to be scheduled, only arriving every other Friday. But it's an emergency, and I don't think the same rules apply to Miss Pamela as they do to the children she cares for.

I'm struck with nostalgia when I walk into the front hallway. The smell of wood, laundry detergent, and a hot meal. The sounds of children talking, laughing, arguing. I move toward Miss Pamela's office before I can get too swept up in it.

She sits behind her desk. And while I have grown over these years apart, she has shrunk. She is not the solid mass of a woman that I remember. But when she sees me, she smiles, and I recognize her again. I sit across from her like I have so many times.

"Scarlett Wright. I'd been hoping to see you again."

I don't correct her on my last name. "I'm sorry I didn't come before—"

She puts a hand up. "You're here now. And I suspect I know why." She bends over the side of her chair and pulls out a drawer. She hands me a big manila envelope. "Oh. Wait." It takes a few seconds longer than it should for her to hoist herself up and out of her chair. She grabs a book and sets it on the desk. It's an encyclopedia. Sordello — Textbooks. She flips through the pages, and I notice white envelopes tucked into the pages with names written on them. She pulls one out, *Scarlett W.* written across it.

I take it when she holds it out across the table.

"What is this?" I say.

"Open it."

I do. I pull out several pieces of paper. Cards. A state ID. Social security card. Passport. The picture is the same as the one on my current documents. The name is almost the same. Scarlett Dwyer. I know what is in the large manila envelope she handed me first. For the past five years, I've been sending Miss Pamela money to keep for me. I pulled out small amounts of cash with nearly every transaction I made when Evan was not with me. Cashback is a beautiful thing.

I never truly believed I'd need the cash. Eventually, Evan and I would grow old and no longer be able to continue killing. Or we'd be caught and hauled off to prison, and the money would go to Miss Pamela or to the new owner of the home if she were to pass.

I may be a coward, but I am not an idiot. I know who Evan is. And I am the same. But you don't marry a serial killer and not prepare for a way out. Even if you truly believe you will never use it.

The documents, however, are a surprise. I wouldn't even know how to get them. "How did you get these?" I ask.

She shrugs. "Being in this line of business, you make a few contacts. I don't have them made for every child, just the ones I think might need them one day. I update them as the years go on. Pray they'll never need them."

There is a knot in my throat. I nod and wish that I could tell her she is an angel. She reaches across the desk and puts her hand over mine. It's cold and dry, and her skin feels like paper. But it is comforting all the same. "Go on now," she says.

I stand and watch as she eases herself back into her chair. Her features scrunch like the movement is painful, and I wonder what hurts.

"Stop looking at me like that."

I smile thinly, caught showing what I'm sure she thinks is pity. "You're sick." It isn't a question. Because though she is old, she isn't old enough to be this frail.

She nods, confirming what I know. "For now."

"What is it?"

"Nothing I can't handle. God is on my side. I'm not being taken out just yet." Her grin is mischievous. Confident. It comforts me as I'm certain she meant it to. If God takes sides, he'd be on Miss Pamela's.

"Take care of yourself," I say. "Thank you. For everything."

Miss Pamela nods with something like love in her eyes before her image blurs behind my tears. "You get out of here. Be smart. Be careful."

"I will."

I open her office door and step into the hallway.

"Oh, and Scarlett?"

I stop and look behind me. Her eyes are stern but not angry. "Be kind too."

I close her office door behind me, and as I look to my left, I watch a boy come out of what used to be Evan's room. He doesn't look like Evan, but it strikes my heart all the same. I already miss him.

All I need to do is have the cab take me back home. It would be like nothing changed. I could keep my life and the man I love, and . . . everything would stay the same. I shake my head like I can shake Evan's hold on my heart. I can't back out. It's not just about me anymore.

CHAPTER FORTY-SEVEN

Scarlett — Then

After Miss Pamela's, I have the cab drive me to a seedy-looking motel. I need to save as much money as possible because I don't know how or when I'll be able to make more. And for the first time, the thought occurs to me that my job will not know I won't be coming in. On the bright side, I'm not due back for two weeks because of the vacation Evan and I were supposed to go on. I'll be long gone by then.

Evan's lessons and games have set me up nicely. When we were younger, he always knew when I was lying and what I was feeling, even once I got better at deceiving others. But I practiced, and eventually, he couldn't always read me so well. I don't think he ever knew that.

I'd let him think he caught me in lies and feelings. Showing frustration or anger and pretending to be trying to hide it. Giving only small tells so he didn't catch on. I lied about things I liked and disliked too. Telling him I love the city and would die of boredom if we moved to the country. In reality, the city overwhelms me. I crave a slower pace.

I pretended to be much more introverted than I really am. That one was harder. Turning down invites to hang out with work friends. Asking to leave parties early. I want friends. Get-togethers. But I wanted the power of deceiving Evan even more.

After a long night at the motel, I walk to a used car lot and buy the cheapest thing that looks like it won't explode. My eyes are heavy as I take to the road. I couldn't sleep. Evan will have tried to call and text me by now, and I wonder what he is thinking about me not answering. He'll think something is wrong. Will he come home early? It's not like he actually has work to do.

I drive for hours in no particular direction and find a small house tucked back from the road with a *For Rent* sign sticking out of the grass. It's getting late, and I don't have a phone, so I drive from the house, careful to remember the turns, until I come to a spot where I can park until morning.

I come across a church, and I'm instantly reminded of the burned church down the road from our murder cabin. The one I parked at to discover my husband is lying to me and that he's a killer with no ability to stop. I pull into the parking lot and shut off the lights. I'll sleep in my car for the night and find somewhere to buy a prepaid cell phone in the morning.

I awake to a tap on the window. The world moves slowly around me as I try to pull my seat up. When I finally manage, I look out the window with sleep-blurred vision, expecting to see a police officer. Instead, it is a man in a suit. I roll down the window.

"Hello, I saw you sleeping in there — well, hoped you were sleeping — and I wanted to make sure you were okay."

"I am," I say. "Okay, I mean. I'm okay."

"Can I get you something to drink? Or eat?"

I start to shake my head and reach for the gear shifter when I realize the car is no longer running. I left it running because even with the sun gone, the night was humid, and I couldn't sleep without the AC running. But the car is silent now. I turn the key to the off position and try to start it again. But it is silent. Not even an attempt to turn over.

I turn back to the man. "Yes, please. Thank you."

I climb out of the car, glaring back at it like the traitor it is. It's what I get for getting the cheapest car on the lot. The man is walking toward the church. He is tall and thin, his suit slightly too big for him. He holds the front door open for me. Sweat drips down my lower back, and I shiver. Can evil people really burst into flames by walking into a church? I guess I'll find out.

I step through the threshold and, to my relief, do not catch fire. The building is old but in a way that shows its history and beauty. The red brick exterior stretches upward, making it look slender and regal. The inside is beautiful, with the morning light coming through the stained-glass windows.

"I'm Dennis Cline, by the way. I'm the pastor here at Grace Church. The kitchen is just back here."

"Megan. Thanks again for your help." I don't know why I tell him a different name. My new paperwork uses my real first name. But I feel stupid taking it back, so I leave it alone.

I haven't gotten a good look at the man's face, but his hair is blond, lighter in some spots that I suspect might be gray. He flips on a light, and the kitchen is cast in a fluorescent glow. He opens the fridge and hands me a bottle of water. I thank him and sit at the small round table a few feet away.

"We have Pop-Tarts, protein bars, aaaannnd . . . cereal," he says, looking through the cabinet.

"A protein bar would be great, thank you."

He hands me three of them, and I smile, grateful. "I'll get out of your hair. I appreciate the food and the water."

"Please feel free to stay. We have service starting in an hour, but you're welcome to stay down here. If you'd like, I can take a look at your car after service. Seemed like it wasn't wanting to start."

I hesitate. He wouldn't help me if he knew who I am. What I've done. And it's wrong of me to accept his help knowing I am who his church fears most. But what choice do I have? I have no phone. And now, I don't have a working car. I still don't have a change of clothes.

"Okay," I say finally. "Thank you. Seriously. I can't thank you enough."

He smiles, lines forming around his eyes. "It's no problem. There is a shower around that corner" — he points behind me — "and a whole closet of things. Help yourself to anything you need."

The now familiar knot forms in my throat, and I nod, not wanting to be annoying with yet another thank you.

"I'll be upstairs if you need anything. If by chance you want to join the service, you just take the same stairs that we took down here and go right instead of left. You'll come out a door close to the entrance instead of the stage."

I nod again, sure I will not be attending the service. I haven't been since living at Miss Pamela's, and even then, the pastor came to the house. This is actually the first time I have ever stepped foot inside a real church, though it feels much the same as the dining hall did on those Sunday mornings. Back then, I swear I could feel God like a static charge in the air. I feel that here too.

Dennis leaves, and I eat my protein bars at the table, sipping the water between each bite. When I'm finished, I make my way around the corner to the shower and closet of "things." The closet holds everything one might have in their own bathroom closet. Shampoo, conditioner, soap, towels, washcloths, feminine hygiene products. And at the bottom is a box full of folded clothes. On top are unopened packages of socks and underwear. I grab a change of clothes and supplies for a shower.

The hot water is a relief. The burn feels good, even though I've been sweating for hours. I let the steam build, and when it's thick enough, making me feel a little obscured from the world, I cry.

I am so out of place in the world without Evan. I don't know who I am. Where I'm going. What I'm doing. I'm showering in the basement of a church. But somewhere in the deepest parts of my mind, there are other feelings. Ones

I am almost more afraid to acknowledge. I have enjoyed and reveled in my small defiances of Evan. This one is bigger. Scarier. But it makes it that much more exciting. Freeing. Neither I nor Evan ever thought me capable of running away and being on my own.

I shut off the water and let it drip from my body before toweling off. The clothes fit rather well for being picked out of a donation box. A plain black T-shirt and jean shorts. I slide my tennis shoes back on and fold my dirty clothes into a pile, placing them on the table. There are footsteps on the stairs. I don't know what I'm afraid of, only that I am, and I back up, bracing myself. Three people. Two men and a woman. The first man startles when he sees me.

"Oh, hi. Dennis said someone would be down here, and yet you still surprised me." He laughs, and it sounds natural, like he does it often. "I'm Jerry. This is Stacey and her husband, Amar."

I try on a small smile and nod. I try to speak, but it comes out a squeak. I clear my throat and try again. "I'm Megan. Nice to meet you."

"We're just grabbing coffee and water before the service," the woman says. Stacey. "We'd love it if you came up to watch."

"No pressure, though. If you're tired, there's a couch on the other side just past the shower. A TV too," says Amar.

"Thank you," I say.

They make their drinks and head back up the stairs. Stacey looks back, smiles, and waves. These people are friendlier than I'm used to. Maybe it's because I'm in a church and they're taught to care for the downtrodden.

I make my way to the couch and sit on the edge of the cushion. After a moment, I scoot back, trying to force myself to sit comfortably. No one is down here, sit like a human! But I am uncomfortable in my own skin and adjust again. I sigh and stand. Pace the room.

The walls are wood panel, and it reminds me of the house I lived in with my dad. He hadn't redecorated since the seventies. I hear the service upstairs begin, the music muffled through the ceiling. It reminds me of the church services that were held in the group home. The ones I attended even though Evan never would. Even though he said it was stupid.

My feet move toward the stairs without my having really made a decision to go. Dennis's voice, magnified by a microphone, speaks to his listeners in the same kind but conversational tone he had when speaking to me.

I follow his directions, leading me to the back of the church. Or would it be the front? I guess it depends on how you look at it. Just before I open the door to the big open room, my eyes travel down my body. My jean shorts and plain shirt. I feel underdressed. But I'm drawn forward by . . . what? Curiosity? Nostalgia? Desire for forgiveness? Or is it just another way to separate myself from Evan? A small act of resistance that only I will know about?

I push through the door and quietly make my way to an empty seat in the back. No one looks at me. The sermon continues, and I tune in to it like I did when I was young.

Evan thought the existence of God was impossible. It didn't make sense to him. I always failed to explain my beliefs, especially back then when my words felt weak and his were so strong and sure-footed.

But to me, it only makes sense that there *is* a God. How can you explain the impossible world we live in where everything in nature works together so perfectly to sustain life? If even the smallest change to the system would mean death to all life? When this impossible balance does not exist anywhere else that we have been able to discover? How can that happen without a God?

Dennis speaks about sin. Something I know all too well. He tells his audience about where the word "sin" comes from. An archery term that means "missing the mark." He says that is why we will always be sinners. Not because we are inherently bad, unable to be good, but because perfection does not exist outside of Jesus, and therefore, we will always "miss the mark." But that God calls us to be more like Jesus today than we were yesterday. That is all we are being asked to do. To try to be better every day.

That feels achievable. It isn't much to be better than I have been. I can do that.

After the service, people filter out through the doors, but I stay rooted in my seat. Movement in my peripheral catches my attention, and I look over to see Stacey.

"I'm glad you came up. Dennis said he needs to look at your car after the service. I'm having lunch at my house with just a few others from the worship band. Would you join us while Dennis gets your car running? Those protein bars can't have been that satisfying."

I want to say no. I wanted to hear the service, the message. I would be lying if I said I didn't find some comfort in God. But church people rub me wrong. They've all been nice. But their overt niceness makes me suspect ulterior motives. Like they're sugaring me up to join their ranks.

Stacey smiles and leans in to whisper, "It's just lunch. We're not trying to recruit you." It's like she can hear my thoughts.

I'm letting my thoughts show on my face. I adjust and smile back with a bashful embarrassment. "That sounds nice. I'd love to."

CHAPTER FORTY-EIGHT

Scarlett — Then

Stacey and Amar's home smells like vanilla and campfire. A large dog runs to greet us at the door. He wiggles his body side to side, and it looks like he's using all of his willpower not to leap onto us, which I appreciate because I'm certain he'd knock me over. I've never had a dog. I bend down to pet him, and he juts his nose into mine, licking my entire face and knocking me off balance. I tip over onto my butt and laugh at the dog's eagerness to be as close to my face as physically possible.

"Frank! Back up. How many times have we talked about personal space?" Amar says, reaching a hand down to help me up. I take it and get to my feet. The dog sits at Amar's feet, still wiggling side to side. "Sorry, he's a big meatball."

"That's okay," I say. I reach a hand down and pet his head, which Frank takes as an invitation to ram his body into mine again.

"Fraaaank," Amar says in a warning tone. Frank sits again, and I laugh.

"I like his name."

"He wanted to name our first child Frank. I negotiated down to the dog," Stacey calls from the kitchen.

I laugh again because a baby named Frank sounds even funnier to me than a dog named Frank.

"It's a great name," Amar says.

Amar moves around me to answer a knock at the door, and Stacey offers me a seat at their dining room table. Another couple and an additional woman take the seats around me. They make introductions and, to my surprise, don't mention anything about church or the service. They ask me questions but not probing ones.

Stacey brings out a feast for lunch. Roast beef, potatoes, vegetables, bread rolls, salad, cheesecake. It's like a five-course dinner, but you get all the courses at once. We all help ourselves, and I find the tension in my shoulders easing as I listen to their casual conversations about the new store they're putting in downtown, how much the Grant boy is charging to mow lawns this summer, and the garden Stacey wants to start next year.

When lunch is over, Stacey takes me back to the church to check on the status of my car. It's parked in the same spot, and Dennis isn't near it, so we venture inside. We find him downstairs watching TV. Stacey hugs me goodbye. I squeeze her thin shoulders and feel like I'm leaving a friend. It makes me feel desperate.

"I got the car running," Dennis says as he hands me the key.

"That's great. Thank you so much." I reach into my purse and pull out money. "I have money. Please let me pay you—"

He holds his hand up, a stop sign. "No, no. It was my pleasure. I used to work on cars as a kid, and it's been a long time since I was able to get under a hood. It was nice."

I nod, accepting his generosity.

"I don't want to intrude. But I was just wondering where you're headed," he says. His brow line pulls down, and he bites the inside of his cheek. He's trying to act casual, but he's nervous. And that makes me nervous.

"Uh . . . I — I was actually going to call about a house I saw a few miles from here for rent."

"The one on County 239?"

"I'm not sure the name of the road. I know the way there, though."

"The man renting that house isn't one I'd recommend doing business with." His eyes travel up and to the left. "I'd like to show you something. If you have the time."

I have nothing but time. So I nod, and he leads me up the stairs and out the door. The sun is intense, and I have to squint at the blinding light. I follow Dennis's feet along the gravel toward the back of the church. My heart beats harder, but I'm not sure why. I'm not afraid of this man. His eyes are kind, but even so, I have a knife in my waistband.

When my eyes finally adjust, I see that we're approaching a small building structure. A house. Dennis stops outside it and stares at it for a few seconds before turning to me. "This used to be where the pastor lived before we were permitted to live off the church grounds. It's been a while since anyone has lived there. It probably needs some work. But it has water and electricity. Paid for by the church."

I can only assume he is telling me this as an offer. But it seems too ridiculous for that to be what's happening. Why would he offer me a free place to live? What are the chances that I parked in the lot of this church and was offered so much?

When I don't respond, because I don't know how to, Dennis speaks again.

"You're welcome to stay here. Until you get on your feet. And I'd like to help you get there."

"I'm pregnant." The words bubble out of my mouth with no warning. I haven't said it out loud or told anyone before now. It feels like an admission. A chance for him to revoke his offer so I don't feel like I am tricking him into more than he agreed to.

He smiles. "Congratulations. That's wonderful."

The sting of tears behind my eyes makes me blink hard, but I smile too. Because it *is* wonderful. And it is the first time I've been able to believe that. Even if just for a second before all of my reality returns to mind and I remember that I am not fit to be a mother.

The house is small and stagnant. Stacey, Dennis, and Amar help me clean it, air it out, and fix it up a bit. Stacey brings things from thrift shops to decorate the walls. She brings me food even when I tell her not to.

I drive into town to get groceries and clothes, looking over my shoulder always. Stacey tries to convince me to make an appointment with an OB, but I refuse. They never pry and try to find out why I am in this situation. Which I'm grateful for. But they don't understand. I don't want there to be any record of me being pregnant. Nothing for Evan to find.

Stacey brings over a fetal heartbeat monitor one afternoon. "I figured if you can't go to the doctor, you should at least get to hear your baby's heartbeat at home."

Warmth and fear spread through me in equal measure. What if there is no heartbeat? What if my baby has left me without my knowing and all of this is for nothing?

Stacey moves the device around my belly, just recently starting to protrude. Every passing second without finding anything sends my pulse into a frenzy. But then I hear it. A quick thrumming that reminds me of a bird for some reason. I smile and cry into my hands.

She comes late one Sunday evening. The pain shooting across my round belly is so intense I can't see. The house phone sits beside me, and I call Stacey, who has been prepared with our plan. Call Dennis and Lorna, a friend from church who works as a doula.

I wait for them to get to me, writhing in pain, making sounds I've only heard come from animals.

We are all just animals, Scarlett.

The pain pushes thoughts of him away. It is so full and all-encompassing that there is no room for anything else but this. I hardly register when they burst through the door. Lorna leads me onto the bed. I don't remember getting off it. She talks, but I don't hear her. I start to push because that is what my body says to do.

The voices in the room are muffled sounds. I cannot make out a word. But I feel the excitement in the air. The nervous anticipation of a miracle. The beauty of the ugliness it requires to bring new life into the world. I scream and feel myself catch fire.

And then the pain is gone. She cries into the silent room, and I'm in awe of her. Euphoria makes me weep and laugh as she is placed on my chest. My beautiful girl. My beautiful Phoenix.

After Lorna tends to me and makes sure both the baby and I are okay, she and the others leave to give us time alone. I haven't talked about my plans once she arrived. And I don't want to think about them now. I just want to soak in the quiet moments with my baby. My daughter.

I touch each tiny finger and each tiny toe as she eats for the first time. Her small cries sound so fragile. Her hair is dark. Like Evan's. A sob builds in my chest, making me jerk when it erupts from me. Phoenix startles. I rub my fingers down her head, and she settles back into me.

What would Evan think of her? Would she change his heart the way she has changed mine? Was it unfair of me to take that possibility from him? No. No, his possible redemption will not come before her. Cannot. Nothing comes before her. No one.

Still.

I imagine him sitting at my bedside. A look of awe on his face. A faint smile on his lips. Love in his eyes. For her and for me. For us. And I let myself grieve that reality.

I bought a Polaroid camera a few weeks ago. I lean over now and take it from my nightstand drawer. Phoenix has fallen asleep in my arms. I position the camera to fit us both in the frame and snap a picture. She doesn't even flinch at the flash. I use my free hand to set the camera down on the bed and pull the photo from the printing slot, shaking it until we come into view. A tear slips down my cheek, and I kiss her head.

* * *

Phoenix is a week old. I can move around fairly comfortably, and I know in my gut that it is time. It's Sunday morning, and the sun hasn't yet risen. I have to hurry. I tuck my daughter into her car seat and swing her diaper bag over my shoulder. I leave the key to the house on the counter and do not lock the door behind me. I've already loaded a bag of my own things into my car, and I start the short drive.

Stacey and Amar's bathroom light is on. They're up early, as I knew they would be. I leave the car running, taking Phoenix and her bag from the back seat, and I walk up the steps to the front door. I set her before the door, squat down, and kiss her head.

"I love you more than anything. Have a beautiful life, my sweet girl."

I ring the doorbell and run.

CHAPTER FORTY-NINE

Scarlett — Now

I'm aware of my head throbbing before I'm even aware that I am awake. Alive. Seeing Dan made me lose my concentration. I knew he'd be waiting for me, and I still let my guard down. How could I be so stupid?

"Wakey, wakey, wifey." Evan's voice is smug. I can feel my face contort in anger, but I still can't open my eyes. "Oh, come on. We don't have all day."

I hear footsteps. Then Dan screams, and my eyes fly open. "Stop! You demented fuck." I spit at him, and he grins. My hands are bound behind my back and held up uncomfortably high, probably tied to the cabinet pull.

"There you are." Evan crouches down to be at eye level with me sitting on the ground, leaning against Theresa's kitchen counter. "Now, we only have a few minutes, so I'll get straight to the point. Tell me where she is, or I'll slit Danny Boy's throat."

I scream at him. The snarl sounds like it came from a wounded animal instead of my mouth, but then maybe we are one and the same.

"Yell all you want, but I only have a minute, and I'm not fucking around, Scarlett." He grabs him by the hair and yanks his head back to expose his throat.

Dan's eyes are wide and panicked when they find mine. The moment they connect, he calms. "It's okay, Scarlett. Don't tell him anything."

Does he know what it is that Evan wants to know? Did Evan tell him? He has to know. Otherwise, why would he be so okay with losing his life for the information?

"I'm sorry," I say, half a whisper, half a sob. I can't tell Evan where to find our daughter. I can't put anyone's life in front of hers.

"I know. It's okay."

"Oh, for fuck's sake. Fine. How about this instead? Tell me where she is, or I will kill the little boy hiding in the coat closet." He looks to Dan now.

I shake my head, and it explodes in pain. "He's safe. He's not here anymore."

"I know that, love. I'm not an idiot. I watched you send him across the street. I might have time to take care of him tonight, but if not . . ." He shrugs. "There's always the rest of his life. But I can guarantee he won't celebrate another birthday."

"Why are you doing this?" I yell. "Why do you want to know where she is? What are you going to do?"

"Well, take her home, of course."

I won't meet Dan's eyes now. Because sentencing a child to death to save my own is worse than letting Dan die for her, despite the fact that I love Dan. I know it's wrong, and I know Dan won't tell me this is okay. But I still cannot tell Evan what he wants to know.

"I'm sorry, Scarlett," Dan says. I look toward him. Toward the pain and regret laced in his words because I don't understand them. "She lives in a white house on the corner of 41st Avenue in Steele County."

My mouth falls open, and my chest tightens so much that I can barely pull in a breath.

"I'm so sorry," Dan says, looking at me. He turns to Evan, who is smiling his evil, self-satisfied grin. "Don't hurt my nephew. Leave him alone."

Evan nods once. "You have my word. Thank you, *Dan*." He angles his head at me with a look of annoyance. "At least *someone* here is helpful." He sheaths his knife in the inside of his jacket and takes a step back. "I can see there's some things that need to be discussed here, so I'll give you guys some privacy."

And then he's gone. Moving toward my defenseless little girl. "How did you know?" I ask. I can feel the panic climbing up my chest. My throat. I yank against the binding on my hands.

"I saw the pictures in your box. I'm so sorry. I invaded your privacy, but I just had to know. I heard you messing around there a few times when you thought I was asleep, so I looked one day while you were out. I knew she was your daughter right away. She looks like you."

I don't know what to say. He knew. For who knows how long. I am not nearly as stealthy as I thought I was. But that still leaves unanswered questions. "That doesn't explain how you know where she is. The pictures don't show her street name or the county."

I watch his face fall. Shame. "I followed you. You leave every year on the same day with random excuses." He shakes his head. "I'm sorry. And I'm sorry I told him. I couldn't let him hurt Sam."

"I know," I say. I yank against the ties on my hands again. Sharp pain and a tearing sensation tell me I've broken skin. Dan starts thrashing in his chair, pulling and hopping the wooden legs against the linoleum. He uses his feet and the limited range he has to turn his chair, back facing the cabinets. I watch as he kicks back, slamming the woods and likely his hands against the counters.

I'm crying, and I can't stop. I can't get free, and neither can Dan, and Evan is on his way to take my daughter. With an angry shout, Dan throws himself straight back, somehow managing to get a little air instead of just tipping back. I hear the sickening sound of his head smacking the ground but also the incredible sound of the wooden chair breaking.

His movements are slow, but he's still moving. "Are you okay?" I ask.

"Yeah," he says. And against all odds, he rolls away from the chair he was just tied to.

"Oh my God. You did it." I sob, mixed emotions overwhelming me. He crawls to me and starts working on freeing me. "I'm so sorry for everything," I say.

The faint sound of sirens stops us both. But only for a second. Dan's fingers work quicker. "Don't be sorry. This is on that psycho. Not you."

I shake my head despite the pain. "You have no idea. This is all my fault. I'm a terrible person. A disgusting person."

"You are the love of my life," he says and yanks hard on a piece of rope. I wince, but he keeps going. "You plan surprise birthday parties for your friends, show up to people's houses with chocolate, and listen to them cry for hours when they're hurting. You helped your neighbor do her landscaping when she was recovering from surgery. That's who you are."

It's who I tried to be. Who I wanted to be after all the horror I've done.

"You protected that little girl from that evil man, even though it meant you had to be without her too."

"Her name is Phoenix," I say. "My daughter's name is Phoenix."

"It's a beautiful name. A strong name." He pulls once more, and my hands come loose. The sirens are louder. Almost here. "Go. Hurry. You can still save her."

I lean over and kiss him on the lips. "Thank you. And I'm sorry. So sorry. Where are your keys?"

"Hanging on the wall next to the door. I love you. Go."

He is so pale, and it scares me. But help is close. He'll get the help he needs. I stare at him for a second, just taking him in. I will never see him again. Neither I nor Evan will be alive to see tomorrow.

CHAPTER FIFTY

Scarlett — Then

It's hard to stay on the road when I am breaking into two. But I have to keep going. Because no doubt, they will come to look for me. Try to help me. Because they don't see that I am beyond help. Phoenix is the one that needs to be cared for, and leaving her with parents that will love her and give her a good life is the only way I can make sure that happens.

I drive for an hour before pulling into an empty spot in a small downtown area. I don't remember seeing a sign telling me its name. Something about it is comforting. Cozy but active. It isn't the ghost-town feeling I got in Steele County that I just left. But it still has the small-town charm.

I look at my face in the rearview mirror and cringe. Using my fingers to rake through my hair and running a finger under my eyes to wipe away old makeup, I try to make myself look somewhat presentable. But my heart isn't in it, so I climb out of the car, looking just as disheveled.

The sign on the store promises the best coffee . . . in the world. It's a big promise, and in my self-pity, I know I'm looking to be let down. A bell rings above my head when I enter the air-conditioned bakery café. I jump and stare up at it.

"It ain't gonna hurt you, dear." A woman stands behind the counter, an eyebrow arched into her wrinkled forehead.

I step forward and look around for a menu.

"What are you looking for?" the woman asks.

"A menu?"

She shakes her head. "Nope. What are you looking to get?"

"Uh — a coffee." I look behind me. Gesture at the door. "Best coffee in the world . . ."

Her eyebrows knit together like I've said something confusing, making me second-guess my ability to read. But then she moves and pulls a mug from somewhere beneath the counter.

"Go and sit down. I'll bring it to ya."

I do as she says and find a spot in the back. I can't stop picturing the car seat sitting on the porch. Her face before I ran away. All my mistakes run through my mind one after the other. The ones I made and the ones made for me. I wonder about my dad and what he thinks about being stuck in a jail cell all day. I wonder what Evan is doing now. If he is looking for me. I wonder what Stacey and Amar are doing with Phoenix. What they think about me for leaving my child on their doorstep.

"Here ya go." The woman sets a steaming cup of coffee on the table and slides it in front of me. "I put whipped cream on top because it looks like you could use it."

I don't know what that means, and she walks away as if it needs no explanation. I take a sip, bracing for the burn on my tongue. But the whipped cream cooled it just enough to be drinkable. There are hints of vanilla and brown sugar. It's incredible and might very well be the best coffee I've ever had. I laugh softly at my desire and expectation to be let down by the promise on the sign outside.

"Excuse me."

I look up to find a man standing over me.

"I didn't mean to interrupt the joke between you and your coffee, but you're sitting at my table."

I look around, embarrassed. Did I not see his things claiming his spot? But there is nothing. "I'm sorry. I didn't realize someone was sitting here."

"Well, I just got here. This is just where I always sit."

I stare at him, unsure how to react. I grab my cup and lean forward to stand. He can have his seat.

"Oh no," he says, putting a hand up to stop me. "Please. Join me."

"Technically, you're joining me . . ." I sit back. "Inviting yourself to join me."

"Maybe inviting you to let me join you."

I open my mouth, then shut it, shaking my head. "This is a confusing situation."

"That's usually how I go about picking up women. Confuse them. Not that I'm trying to pick you up."

I arch an eyebrow.

"Not that I wouldn't try to pick you up. You're very pretty. But probably not available. Or from around here. Clearly, you're not. Where are you from?"

I stare at him with wide eyes. His neck starts to turn red in patches. Before I can respond, he starts up again.

"This went a lot differently in my head. A lot smoother. I'm sorry."

I can't help it — I laugh. And he smiles, laughing at himself. "Are you always this nervous?" I ask, finally able to get a word out.

"Uh — well, we don't get a lot of new faces here. I definitely don't get this nervous around Mae." He nods toward the other side of the building, and I assume he's referring to the older woman who made me the coffee.

"You should. She's a coffee-making extraordinaire."

"Ah, yes. Best coffee in the world. Is that what brought you here?"

"Kind of. I was just driving through but stopped when I saw the sign. I had to try it for myself."

"And what's the verdict? Best in the world?"

I take another sip. "I think it is. At the very least, it's the best I've ever had."

He nods. "I only asked to be polite. Hoover is fully aware of the treasure we harbor here."

The smile feels out of place on my lips. Like a betrayal to my daughter. I should not be smiling for any reason on the day I left her.

"What happened just now? Your face got really sad all of a sudden."

I shake my head. I'm doing it again. Letting my emotions show on my face when I don't mean to.

"Sorry. I'm pretty exhausted."

"Are you close to your destination?" he asks.

I don't know how to answer. I have no destination. I am drifting. But drifting isn't the right word. Drifting makes it sound passive. A calm, aimless traveling around. That's not what I'm doing. My travel is aimless but active. I am not drifting. I am running. With nowhere to hide.

"No," I say. "I'm not."

"There's a bed-and-breakfast on North College Avenue."

"Is there a college nearby?"

"No. Nor is the one-and-a-half-lane road an avenue. We don't know who named the roads around here." He shrugs.

I drink the last of my coffee and stand. "Thank you for the company. And the bed-and-breakfast recommendation."

He nods and stands too. "You'll probably need a coffee and some breakfast before you get back on the road tomorrow. I'll be here bright and early, so maybe I'll see you."

"Won't there be breakfast at my bed-and-breakfast?"

He shakes his head. "The Turners are wonderful people, but Mrs. Turner can't cook to save her life. I wouldn't risk it."

"Good to know," I say, smiling. I turn to walk to my car.

"Wait. I didn't get your name."

I turn around and really take in the man for the first time. He has a friendly, open face. Bright eyes. Soft brown hair and blue eyes. Closely shaven facial hair. He's tall and looks to be in good shape. His hands look tough. Calloused with a few old scars and a few newer-looking marks. Burn marks, maybe.

"Scarlett," I say. I don't know why I tell him the truth. I'm just tired. Of running. Of being sad. Of being alone. Of lying. Of life in general.

"I'm Dan. I hope I'll see you tomorrow morning, Scarlett. But if not, it was really nice to meet you."

CHAPTER FIFTY-ONE

Scarlett — Then

The sound of sizzling wakes me up. For a split second, I am sure someone has broken in. But then my eyes settle on the left side of my bed. His indent is still there. Dan stayed over last night. Something I haven't allowed to happen since I decided to stay in Hoover.

I can hear him downstairs, humming as he cooks, and I smile. We drank last night and I went too far with it. Allowed Dan to get closer. I didn't even wake up when he got out of bed. I have to be more careful. But the numbness the alcohol provided was just too hard to resist, knowing today would come. Phoenix's birthday.

My chest is tight, only allowing for short shallow breaths, but I try my best to keep breathing. Sometimes I wonder why I bother. Trying to keep breathing, that is. I don't deserve life after I've taken so many. I have no purpose.

But then I have nightmares that Evan has found my little girl. And I know I am still here because I can't allow that to happen. He would come for me first. He doesn't know she exists. Yet.

Dan comes through the bedroom door with a tray of food.

"Oh my gosh. Are you serious?" I ask, eyeing the mountain of eggs and pancakes.

He grins like a schoolboy. "I figured you could use something to soak up those mojitos."

He sets the tray over my lap and climbs back into bed with me.

"Thank you," I say. He leans over and kisses my head.

It feels strange. To be sharing a bed with someone other than Evan. To have someone else's lips pressed to my skin. Guilt bubbles in my core, but I try to stuff it down. Let it simmer with the rest of my guilt.

After breakfast, I pace the house. My body is restless and my mind even more so. Phoenix is one year old today. She should be crawling now. What foods does she prefer? Where are her ticklish spots? Has she said any words yet? 'Mama' as she smiles up at Stacey?

"Are you okay?" Dan asks. "Look, I know last night was a big deal. If you need time, I completely understand that. I can go."

I press my fingertips to his lips. "Everything is okay. There's just something I have to do today."

Without having clearly decided, the decision is made as soon as I say it. I move through my house, packing a bag.

"Can I ask what?" Dan calls from the living room.

"No. But I'll be back soon. In a day or two."

I stuff clothes and my toothbrush into my bag. I run into my bathroom and lock the door. The ceiling tile moves away easily, and I stretch to reach the box. I replace the tile, climb down from the sink, and carefully open the lid of the box.

A picture of Phoenix and me sits beside the Polaroid camera I used to take it. I put it in my bag and jog downstairs. Dan is near the door. Dressed with his shoes on.

"I'm glad you stayed over," I say. "I'll call you when I'm back home."

The lines in his forehead get a little shallower and he offers a weary smile. "Okay. Are you sure you're okay?"

"I'm sure. I'm sorry I'm being weird right now. I just . . . can't really explain."

He nods. "As long as you know you're being weird." He leans down and kisses me on the mouth. My heart races. The first time I've kissed him sober.

I watch him leave in his truck from the rearview mirror of my car. A Jeep Compass I bought a month ago. I got it before I planned to return to Steele County, but I'm glad now. They won't recognize this car.

The drive from Steele County to Hoover is one that replays in my mind almost daily, so remembering the way is not a problem. I just have to do it in reverse. My fingers drum on the steering wheel and I lean forward in my seat like it might make me go faster. The idea of seeing Phoenix is exciting and terrifying, all wrapped up together. What will seeing her do to me? Why am I such a glutton for emotional turmoil?

I pass through a larger town halfway to my destination and stop for gas. There is a Best Buy across the way, and I decide to check it out once my tank is full. I have my old Polaroid camera, but I don't anticipate being able to get close enough for it to work. I need a better camera.

A young salesman helps me find a decent camera with good zoom. He even tells me how to have pictures printed by taking the memory card to a Walgreens photo kiosk. I thank him and continue on my way with my new camera.

Nausea increases the closer I get to Stacey and Amar's home. When I turn onto their street my heart feels like it might crack a rib. What if they're all outside? This town is practically abandoned. They will look up at a passing vehicle. I decide to park in a gap in the woods at the end of the road.

I can walk along the back treeline and see the house from behind. The ground is uneven, and I use the hair tie from my wrist to make a tight bun in my hair. Ticks might scare me even more than Evan.

I can see the white siding of Stacey and Amar's house. My heart jumps to my throat. And then, a terrifying thought occurs to me. What if they didn't keep her? Could they have given her away? Surrendered her to the state? I'm running now. As much as one can run over leaves and sticks from decades past.

I'm right behind their house now. I back up and draw further into the woods so they won't see me. I know Stacey only works voluntarily for the church so she should be home. Unless she is at the store. Or unless she decided to start working again. I haven't been here in nearly a year.

I scan the backyard. There is a garden, and it is exploding with plants and flowers. It makes me smile, knowing she got the garden going that she wanted late last summer. The back door opens, and I jump like I've been caught. I sink lower to the ground and closer to the trunk of a large tree.

Stacey walks to the garden in a summer dress with her hair down. She crouches down and leans forward, pushing leaves out of her way. But then she looks back to the door she left open. Amar emerges from the house. I suppress a sob when I see the baby in his arms.

Her hair is still dark, pulled into tiny pigtails, and she wears pink shorts and a white shirt. Amar sets her in the grass next to Stacey. She leans forward and bats at the plants. Stacey pulls a leaf forward and tickles her face with it. I light up inside when she lets out a shrieking giggle.

She is happy. They are happy. I take out my new camera and zoom in. I can see her features now. How she has my nose and Evan's eyes. She will grow up and know that her parents did not give birth to her. Without Stacey's blonde hair and Amar's dark skin, she will know they are not her birth parents. I can only hope that they tell her nice things about me. Tell her that I loved her dearly. Maybe they will even be kind enough to tell her I died so that she doesn't feel the need to come look for me once she is old enough.

I hang around their house like a timid stray cat for days. Eager for just one more sighting of my little girl. She likes to be outside, luckily. She plays in the grass and rips out leaves from the garden when Stacey isn't looking. She laughs a lot. A happy baby.

It feels like the day I left her on their porch all over again when I decide it is time to return to Hoover. As I drive away, I already know I will be back. I can't stay away completely. I'm drawn to her in a way I can't fight, even if it would be easier to just let her go. I need to know her, but all I will ever get is stolen moments from afar.

When I finally will myself to leave, I seek out a tattoo parlor. I don't know where the urge has come from. It came on suddenly and forcefully. I find one with a 'walk-ins welcome' sign halfway home to Hoover. This will be my first tattoo. Evan always said it wasn't smart to have them. They're just an easy way to be identified.

The man makes quick work of my simple request, and in less than an hour, I'm getting back into my car with a small bandage on my wrist. Beneath the white gauze is the black outline of a phoenix.

CHAPTER FIFTY-TWO

Scarlett — Now

My worst fear has come to life. He knows we have a child. A daughter. He knows her face. Her existence. And now he knows where to find her. I have to hurry. My only hope is that, knowing the way, I can get there just before him and get them all to safety.

Trying to get there quickly without getting pulled over for speeding is an impossibly thin line. I find myself speeding several times before I realize and let off the gas pedal, just enough to bring myself back within the limit.

I do my best to focus on the road. On the here and now. Not what has happened. Not what will happen in the near future. Just right now. Just driving. I'm aware of the fragile footing I have in sanity. If I allow my mind to wander, I will lose that war and tumble into madness.

One hundred miles to Steele County. Eighty. Sixty. Fifteen. Exit in one mile.

Now. Now I allow my thoughts to look ahead. Only the next few steps. Get to Stacey and Amar's house. Look for signs of Evan. Get them out. Save them. Save *her*.

All thoughts and plans fall to the ground, along with my heart, when I approach the house and see Evan's black sports car. I should have done more than slash the tires. I should have set it on fire. Driven it off a cliff.

I grab my gun and sprint for the house. It's dark outside, but there are lights on in the living room and one on upstairs. Should I go through the front door? Do I have time to be stealthy? Or has that luxury come and gone?

I get my answer as I climb the stairs. The front door is ajar. I take a step forward. There is a crash in the living room and a scream. My heart does a flip as I run into the house, gun drawn.

"Where is she!" Evan shouts. "Come on out, sweetie. I'm not going to hurt you." Evan spins when I enter the room, pulling Stacey closer to him and jabbing the gun under her chin. "Oh, hello there, darling. So glad you could join us."

"Let her go." I don't look at Stacey. Can't bear the fear, the confusion that I know will shine in her tear-filled eyes.

"Why would I do something like that? I'd like to meet my daughter." He turns his attention to Stacey. "Tell her to come out," he says through gritted teeth.

"She isn't here! I told you that."

I take a breath. Meet Stacey's eyes. Is she really not here? Is she safe? But Stacey's eyes dart to the side. In my peripheral, I can see some sort of chest, and I understand that Phoenix is hiding inside it. I don't follow her eyes. Don't give Evan anything he can use. But she's too close. If she cries or makes any sound at all, he will hear her.

"Evan. Let her go and leave. I'll go with you. I swear I will. Let's just leave." I have the desperation in my voice, but I beg, willing to bathe in the shame if only my daughter will be safe.

"It's too late for that, I'm afraid. You hid our child from me. Why would you do that?"

"Well, I fucking wonder!" I'm getting heated. Emotional. Desperate. "It's all over, Evan. By now, the police know everything. They know the names of every person you brought to the cabin. They know where to look for their bodies. And they have DNA evidence."

"And how do they have all that?" Evan asks, gripping Stacey tighter against his chest.

"Because I sent it all to them." Well, Marin sent it to them for me. "So take this opportunity to get out of the country before they can stop you. Leave. Now."

He laughs. "I'll leave just as soon as I have my daughter."

"No. You will leave now!"

"Or what? Huh, Scarlett? What are you going to do about it? You can't stop me. You've had every opportunity to stop me, and you haven't. You're weak. Come on out, sweetie!" He scans the room, looking for hiding places, dragging Stacey with him, careful to stay tucked behind her.

"I'm not weak," I say. Though I don't believe it for a second, and Evan knows it.

He laughs. "Yeah, you are." He makes a sympathetic face. I want to smash out his perfect teeth. My heart beats wildly as he moves toward the chest. "You *run* and you *hide*, but you couldn't face me. Even back then. You had to be goaded. Pressured and walked through the kill. You never had the stomach for it. And you don't now. Even to save your child. You could do it if you had the balls. You know you could, and what you'd have to do, but you're too weak to do it."

But that isn't true. He only thinks it is because I allowed him to believe it. Convinced him to believe it. Because not all the lives I took were in Evan's presence. My foster mother. The way I sliced across her throat as she slept because she called me the spawn of Satan and refused me dinner that first night I spent in her home. Hattie when we lived in the Stark Home. To stop their torment and to send a message to Megan. Evan doesn't know that I have always been capable of taking a life. I just didn't do it for fun the way he always has.

Evan kicks the chest, and time stands still.

CHAPTER FIFTY-THREE

Evan — Now

A small whimper comes from the chest I've just kicked. The woman in my arms wails like an animal, and I know I've found her. My daughter. Scarlett's gun is still trained at me, so I hold the woman closer, blocking her shot as I lift the lid of the chest.

The girl is small, huddled in the corner of the box. She lifts her head and starts to cry when she sees me. "It's okay, sweetheart. I'm not going to hurt you."

I know how that must sound when I'm gripping the woman she knows as her mother around the neck and holding a gun to her back. But I try my best to hide the gun. I'm angry Scarlett got here as soon as she did. I wanted to have a chance to talk to my daughter without holding this woman hostage, but I can't let her go. Scarlett hasn't been able to kill me before, but I don't feel as confident in that now she feels the little girl is in danger.

She isn't, though. I wouldn't hurt the girl. The small angel that is half me and half Scarlett. I just want to talk to her. To touch her face. "Come on out," I say.

"Don't you touch her!" screams the woman in my arms. She bucks against me, and I yank on her neck. But she doesn't stop trying to get free. With only one hand on her, I'm starting to lose my hold. I catch sight of the girl again, and her eyes are wide with fear. Something about it hurts.

Plenty of people have looked at me just like this, and it is a look I recall before bed each night. It's this look that makes me crave the kill over and over again. But on her, on my daughter, it is heartbreaking.

I flash back to the times my father came into my room, his belt already removed and gripped tightly in his fist. The time my oldest brother held me under the water in our pool as a joke until I felt myself losing consciousness, only to come up and see my father watching from the doorway. The time the police came to take me away and my mother wouldn't look at me.

My daughter is afraid of me, and why shouldn't she be? Is this why Scarlett kept her from me all this time? Why she kept her even from herself?

The woman's head snaps back and cracks my nose. Everything disappears behind a bright white light of pain. I shout automatically but quickly remember the terrified child and stifle my cries along with the intense urge to snap the woman's neck.

I tighten my grip and shove the gun harder into her spine. "Stop. Or I will shoot you right in front of her," I whisper into her ear. She goes still.

I just want to talk to the girl. I just want to know her name.

CHAPTER FIFTY-FOUR

Scarlett — Now

She is so small, huddled in the corner like the little bird she has always reminded me of. Evan continues trying to coax her out, but she is frozen in fear. Stacey's face is painted in pure anguish and panic as she fights against him to get free. Evan whispers something in her ear that makes her freeze. She looks at me.

Protect her.

I don't hear the words, but I read them perfectly on her lips. I nod. Of course I will. I will always protect her. Before I know what is happening, Stacey pushes herself, and Evan, backward. They fall over, and the gun goes off. Phoenix screams. I run toward them. Their bodies scramble, and there is blood, but I can't tell who's been shot.

I grab Phoenix from the chest and push her toward the door. She cries out for her mom, but I don't stop. I grab my phone from my back pocket and call 911 as I set her down in the yard. "Stay outside. Talk to the police on the phone. They will come and get you, okay? Stay outside." I run my hand along her cheek and then run back inside.

They're both on their feet again. Evan has her secured once again, and now I can see that blood seeps from Stacey's stomach. He pulls her directly in front of him and forces them both a step forward. I point my gun.

"I want to talk to her!" Evan says. "Bring her back inside, now."

"I'm not going to do that," I say.

Evan jabs his gun into the side of Stacey's head, but her face stays composed. I try to get a clean shot on him, but he keeps her head perfectly in front of his. If I shoot anywhere else, he will shoot her again, and this time in the head.

Blood drips down Stacey's leg. She isn't going to make it. I know it, and from her face, I think she knows it too. Evan takes another step forward. "Get out of the way, Scarlett. I swear I will shoot her. Move." Spit forms in the corners of Evan's mouth, and as he steps forward again, I see that he is crying.

He is in a dangerous state. Even more dangerous than I have ever seen him before. I've never seen him lose control like this. I've never seen him cry, and I'm terrified of what it means. I look at Stacey again, and they take another step forward. My hands shake. I don't know what to do.

But then Stacey nods. And I understand what she's telling me. She knows she is not going to make it out of this, and she knows I cannot stop him with her in the way. I know it too.

I don't think. I shoot. Stacey drops to the floor, a bullet in her brain, and Evan steps back, surprised. I pull the trigger again, and he stumbles backward, the same shock still on his face. He grabs his chest, where blood is starting to spread, and drops to his knees. I hurry to him and rip the gun from his hands, though he didn't so much as point it in my direction.

"You did it," he says. His voice is wet, and my stomach turns.

"I did." I help him into a lying position. His hand finds mine. I don't pull away but instead lace my fingers with his. They still fit perfectly. "I am not weak. I was never weak.

Having the capacity to be evil and choosing not to be requires more strength than you've ever had." It's something I needed to say. Even if he doesn't hear it, I needed to tell him.

"What is her name?" he asks.

I almost don't tell him. But who am I to deny a dying man's last wish? "Phoenix," I say. His eyes shine with recognition, and his fingers move to the tattoo on my wrist. I put the gun to his temple and squeeze once more, jumping at the sound. His fingers twitch, and with his death throes, he squeezes my hand for the last time. My throat is tight with emotion that will spill over any minute now. But I don't have time for it. Not yet.

I use a blanket from the back of the couch to cover Stacey's body. I lean down and kiss her head. "I'm so sorry," I choke out with a sob.

I go over to Evan and sit next to him. It was always going to end this way. I hold the gun up to my head and close my eyes.

"Stop!" Phoenix screams, and it scares me so bad I almost pull the trigger from jumping.

"I told you to stay outside. Go outside!" I try to stop crying, but it's useless. The tears have started, and they won't be stopped.

"You're my mom," she says like she's figured something out. I stop breathing. How could she know that? Why would they tell her? "You're my belly mom. I lived in your belly, and you gave me to my mom and dad to take care of me."

"How do you know that?" It comes out in a whisper.

"My mommy shows me your picture. She tells me the story for my birthday."

What picture? What story? My mind is racing a million miles a minute. I struggle to get a breath in. She shouldn't be in here, in the same room as these dead bodies. Her dead family. The police are on their way. I have minutes. Maybe less. They'll arrest me. I have to do this now.

But . . .

She knows.

"Please don't do that," she says again, and her eyes are on the gun still in my hands. I move it behind my back. What do I do? I can't go to prison. I can't even begin to imagine the charges I will face. The police have everything they need to lock me away forever, and I cannot live my life behind bars. I cannot turn out just like my father.

But her eyes are pleading with mine, and I can't look away. I have abandoned her once, to keep her safe, but abandonment is still what I did. And now I've taken the only mother she's ever had. If Amar is dead too, she'll go into the system. Like I did.

But that will happen whether I put a bullet in my skull or not.

Blue lights flash outside, and I am out of time. Now or never. My sweaty hand grips the gun. I can wait until the police come in and take her out. Shoot myself before they get to me. Even point my gun and let them do it for me. But her face is haunting. And Evan's words start to ring in my head, already haunting me like I knew he would.

You run and you hide, but you couldn't face me.

I've never been able to face anything. Not my dad. Not my demons. Not Evan.

I slide the gun away and release a breath. I hear car doors. Before I'm ripped away from her, I run and fall to my knees at her feet. I hug her, and she hugs me back. I can feel her heart beating against my chest, and I remember all the times I listened to it beat through my belly with the Doppler.

"I love you. I've always loved you, and I'm so sorry."

A police officer shouts and says he's going to enter. I open the door before he kicks it in. He looks at me, then at Phoenix.

"Are you both all right?" he asks, but he doesn't wait for an answer. He pushes us toward the stairs, where another officer corrals us to a vehicle as he enters the house. I let them take her to be checked out at the ambulance and pull one of the officers aside.

"The man and the woman in the living room. I shot them. I killed them."

She looks at me, stunned, but then breaks out of it and pulls out her handcuffs. I don't resist. I let her cuff me and guide me to the back of a car. As she is putting me in, I hear a shout for medics. "There's a live one upstairs. Let's go!"

I cry with relief. Amar is alive. At least for now. She hasn't lost everyone.

CHAPTER FIFTY-FIVE

Phoenix — Sixteen Years Later

I scribble my name on the last paper and slide it across the mahogany desk to the lawyer. He gives me a polite, perfunctory smile before rising and shuffling out of the small office. I don't smile back because his paperwork could have waited until tomorrow, but he insisted he stop by before the funeral to get it "all squared away."

But that is what it is now. Squared away, I mean. I am officially the new owner of Stark Home for Children. Just as Miss Pamela requested in her will. I knew it was coming. She told me so. But it still felt like a surprise when the lawyer said it aloud at the will reading just one day after she passed.

Christian, my business partner and fiancé, pokes his head through the door. "Bus is here. Everyone is loading up."

"Thanks," I say, and he nods before attending to the kids. The bus will take us all to Miss Pamela's funeral. Today will be hard. But there is a silver lining. My mother will be there. The prison granted her special permission to attend the funeral. She will be dressed in normal clothes, free of the gray prison clothes and silver cuffs that usually adorn her when we see each other.

And I have news for her.

But that is for later. For now, I lock up the office and stand in the hallway. This place has been my home off and on for so many years. After that terrible night when the psychopath that was my birth father showed up at my house and changed my life forever. He died. My mom died. Not my birth mother, but the one who raised me up until that point.

They thought my dad would make it. They found him badly wounded but still alive upstairs in my parents' bedroom. But he didn't make the ambulance ride to the hospital. With my birth mom — Scarlett — in prison, I was officially alone in the world.

Scarlett made a call, and there was Miss Pamela. She fought hard in the courts to gain custody of me. And she won. Not that she had anyone to fight with besides the state. And so I grew up at the Stark Home. Not like my mother and father did. I was not a "patient." My bedroom was upstairs, away from the other kids. I attended public school. My life became as normal as it could have been in the situation.

I was allowed to visit my mother on the weekends. At first, she tried to convince me not to see her. She didn't want me to see her like that. But she and Miss Pamela talked for a while, and then she didn't say anything about not coming again.

My mother was allowed to attend my high school graduation, and she was so proud when I managed to do it two years early. I got my undergrad at UIC and went straight into law school. That's where I met Christian. He was studying law to be an advocate for children in the system. We were a match made in heaven since I grew up in a place that could use his passion and expertise. He began working for the Stark Home shortly after graduation. I got a job at a mid-level law firm, but my real aspiration for becoming a lawyer was personal.

The bus arrives at the funeral home, and upon entering, I see that my mother is already here. She sits alone, though her guards are a few feet away, in the front row of chairs, staring at the open casket. I walk over and try not to look at the body in the box beside me. Dead bodies are still terrifying to me, despite years of therapy.

My mother looks up when I approach and smiles sadly, a tear escaping down her cheek. She stands and hugs me. I watch the guards over her shoulder as I squeeze her in return. They don't seem to mind. My mother has been a model prisoner for the last sixteen years.

We sit, and I train my eyes on my knees. She laces her fingers with mine and sniffles. "She'd be so proud, you know? To see you taking over at the home."

"I know," I say. She told me how proud she was the night she fell asleep and didn't wake up. Cervical cancer. That's what took her in the end. I found out later that she had fought, and won, breast cancer a few decades ago. But like it often does, the cancer returned and refused to leave without her. But by then, she was tired and ready to go. She told me that too.

I can hear people in the lobby. We won't be alone for much longer. The children from her home, both present and past, will come to say goodbye. She made an impact on so many, many lives, and I look forward to shaking hands with each and every one of them. But first . . .

"Mom," I say.

She looks at me with the mix of joy and pain she always wears when I call her "Mom." She never forgave herself for what happened to my other mom, Stacey.

"I want to tell you before everyone gets here. In person. Face-to-face." I can tell I have her attention now. "I filed a motion for a retrial on your case."

She shakes her head. "What? No. We don't need to do that. I am where I deserve to be."

"You're not. And the motion was accepted. New evidence. The courts agree that you deserve a retrial. I'm getting you out."

THE END

ACKNOWLEDGMENTS

This book has been my favorite to write so far. It was an idea that sprung up halfway through writing my second book and it refused to be pushed to the back burner. I'm so glad to finally have it out in the world and out of my head.

First and foremost, thank you to anyone who has read this book or any of my others. I say this every time, but it really is a fantasy-level dream come true that I get to write stories and people read them. It's wild. I'll never get used to it. And thank you specifically to those of you readers that take the time to leave a review. Good or bad. Reviews are social proof and it is extremely hard to sell books without them. So THANK YOU!

I also want to thank my lovely book club: Venissa Ivasiecko, Kelli Thompson-Patrick, Eriana Ivasiecko, and honorary member Jake Vickery. Our book club sessions are truly one of the few social interactions I actually look forward to, and your love and support honestly means the world to me.

A special thank you to my friends and family who continue to support me and my books. I honestly never expected this level of support. It has been eye opening in the best way. Thank you for buying my books, for sharing social media

Made in United States
Cleveland, OH
18 February 2026

33560820R10152